From The Women's Press Ltd
34 Great Sutton Street, London EC1V 0DX

Barbara Machin was born in Oxfordshire in 1951. She went to Hull University to read English and then lectured in Further Education in Manchester. After joining Granada Television as a reporter she worked as an Associate Producer in the drama department and during that time had her first two television plays broadcast. She left when awarded an Arts Council Writing Residency for poetry in Ipswich and since then has worked extensively as a playwright.

Television work includes 'Pattern Of Life'; 'Casualty'; 'TEXC'; and episodes for the second series of 'South Of The Border'. Radio includes 'The Flying Colours' and 'Gabrielle And The Gargoyles'. She has worked with Youth Theatre writing plays for the stage and a libretto for a children's opera.

She is currently working on the next novel, more plays and a collection of poems.

Barbara Machin

South of the Border

The Women's Press

For Nina

And love and thanks to Becks, Jon and Matt, Dad, MC and all my dear family and Lask, Ed and India.

My gratitude to Sue Wilkins, Caroline Oulton, Phil Kelvin, Pauline Asper and Jen Green for the chances.

First published by The Women's Press Limited 1990
A member of the Namara Group
34, Great Sutton Street, London EC1V 0DX

This novel is based on the BBC TV Series *South of the Border* created by Susan Wilkins.
Copyright © Barbara Machin and Susan Wilkins.

British Library Cataloguing in Publication Data
Machin, Barbara
   South of the border.
   I. Title
   823'.914 [F]

   ISBN 0-7043-4227-8

Typeset by AKM Associates (UK) Ltd.,
Ajmal House, Hayes Road, Southall, Middlesex.
Printed and bound in Great Britain by
Cox & Wyman, Reading, Berks

One

Pearl headed for the square of sunlight above her. The narrow ferry steps funnelled hundreds of over-tanned holiday-makers up from the car decks. Blocked in the queue, she side-stepped a barrier and slipped through closed doors into an empty restaurant.

'Close-ed.' The Spanish waiter was polishing glasses in the dark, his white cloth like a cloud in the shadows. He didn't bother to look up. Pearl casually selected two wine glasses, removed crimped pink serviettes and dropped one in each pocket. The astonished barman looked up, his lank hair flopping across his face, and called out to her in a torrent of Spanish. Smiling vaguely, she blew him a kiss and slipped back on to the staircase.

Up on the promenade deck the afternoon was close and oppressive. A light wind whipped at the canvas awning and rattled the strings of coloured lights. White chairs and tables sprawled in crazy groups where passengers had left them. A uniformed waiter was busily putting them to order as if disciplining a badly behaved party.

Pearl placed the glasses on a table and produced a bottle of red wine from her rucksack. Finn would join her as soon as she had cleared the car documents at the purser's office. She eased the cork out of the bottle and felt the foreignness beginning to evaporate. Her head was full of colours: white buildings, dried brown landscapes, oranges, olive groves, women dragging in the fruit in nets, the hammering heat of driving.

It had been their first job abroad. Pearl poured the wine. Looking out on the harbour, she guiltily remembered her promise to phone the office before they boarded. Millie had looked harassed and tired as she'd briefed them. The solicitor's office had been awash with paperwork and the phone had rung as they left. She'd heard Millie's voice carefully explaining custody of children, calming the caller, using words to dispel fear. It had been well past midnight. Pearl imagined her sitting at her desk now, waiting for them to ring. Her client would be anxious and his son was in court the day after they got back. Uncomfortably she shrugged the thought away.

Their assignment had been tough. Millie's schedule had left them no leeway, and operating on the cheap had opened up some dangerous territory. They would never have been on the road so late that night if they hadn't been racing to get to Madrid without a stopover.

'The petrol gauge has always been knackered, you know that,' grumbled Finn as they had rolled to a stop on a dirt garage yard outside a small bar. 'You've got to keep track of the mileage – I've warned you before.'

'But it never seems quite so crucial down Deptford High Street, does it?' They'd glared at each other in the orange neon of the bar sign. 'OK' it flickered on and off uncertainly. Finn was unforgiving.

Striding across a yard littered with crashed cars, Pearl headed for the bar to find the owner. This is what she hated about foreign travel, she decided: this loss of balance, the confusion between the grateful smile and the come-on. A line so clearly visible in South London and so blurred here. She could be letting herself in for anything, just by being there. And smiling. Smiling was dangerous, but how else was she going to charm the guy into opening up his petrol station.

The bar had whooped and cheered as a tiny man with a woman's earring listened to her explanation. He nodded enthusiastically and led her through crowded tables towards the night. Reaching the door, he paused to talk to a slob in a tight nylon T-shirt. The man's mouth worked moistly as he ran his eyes from her bare arms to her thighs and grinned.

'*Las mujeres "negre" estan muy caliente!*'

Pearl saw the meaning in his puckered lips and felt her fist tighten. If she'd been a man she'd have knocked him to the floor.

Señor OK pulled her away, unaccountably agitated. He pawed

her bare arm and said something imcomprehensible through broken teeth. Pulling down her sleeves, Pearl walked briskly towards the car. She had no choice but to be positive.

Finn was tuning into some manic pirate station on the car radio. Wild chatter suddenly turned into punk flamenco and the man delightedly grabbed Pearl's hand and started to gyrate rhythmically.

'Switch it off, idiot.' Pearl was getting jumpy.

Finn stared at the man unsmiling. He was stroking the car, leaving greasy lines in the dust, his earring glinting.

'Let's get out of here,' she mouthed. 'You don't need Spanish for beginners to see he's a total creep.'

'Where do you suggest?' Pearl kicked the car with frustration. The little man buckled as if he'd been winded, and with a yelp threw a switch, unscrewed the petrol cap and started to fill the car. Pearl maintained a fixed smile as the petrol drummed into the empty tank. He chattered incessantly, his silvery shirt, badged with sweat, reeking of diesel, glowed on and off with the orange OK.

When he'd finished, he pointed at them and himself excitedly and started to scribble something on a card. Pearl hurriedly pushed money at him and turned to go. He shouted, grabbed her by the shoulder and tried to reach into her pocket. Pulling away violently, she threw herself into the car and they lurched back on to the highway. In the wing mirror she saw him marooned in the shadows, waving and shouting in the pump spotlight.

They drove on through the darkness, smarting. Finn's hand trembled visibly as she clicked the milometer back to zero. Pearl was shaking and furious. She'd been frightened; reduced to all the awkwardness of sixteen again. Her jacket smelt of diesel. She glanced at Finn, her face tight with concentration, frowning against the oncoming lights. They kept their silence. Pearl ached with indignation, the foreignness making the familiar unbearable.

The next morning, bleary eyed in the sunshine, Pearl had pushed her hand into her pocket and with amazement pulled out the petrol money and a greasy card. On the back of an advert for the garage was scrawled in spidery writing, 'Tottenham Hotspur OK'. The 'OK' was underlined.

She tried to smile. So the whole scene had been about their GB sticker and an emotional Spurs fanatic. Ironic really, when you considered the case they were on. Finn shrugged it off and ordered tea. As far as she was concerned the guy was still a creep.

Their contact had arrived at ten o'clock precisely, weaving his way through the tables, hair gel gleaming in the sun. Punctual, courteous and utterly untrustworthy, he was the perfect alibi. He wrote out his statement on Millie's forms, and, licking his finger tips, counted the money. He insincerely offered to buy them a drink. His English was impeccable.

Pearl started her second glass of wine, the tannin rusting her tongue. Long shadows had begun to seep through the harbour, making water and land the same. In broken English the metallic tannoy announced that the boat would sail shortly, and the car ramp clamped shut. Passengers were starting to jostle up on to deck for one last look at Santander. The hot wind tore at the deck chairs and there was a hint of rain. Someone was triumphantly reading out headlines from *The Mail*. They were practically back in England. Pearl stared around, anxious for Finn.

A noisy family settled around a table near her. The well-dressed wife dipped into a leather bag and opened a novel, but her eyes drifted as she read. The children chattered and for a moment her husband seemed transfixed by the turning pages. He looked pained and detached, staring angrily down at the water. Pearl watched him and wondered if he was having an affair, longing now to be with someone else. The thought lingered and became Fitz. Turning her back on the sea she shut down the memory automatically; slammed the door on him like a reflex.

The children's laughter shredded against the heavy drubbing of the ship's engines. They waved wildly. A little girl wearing pink sunglasses ran back to her father, clutching at his knees. 'She's waving at us – definitely – honest – she's going crazy.' Pearl hurried to the railings. There, amongst a gaggle of customs officials, was Finn, jumping up and down and waving her jacket above her head like a flag.

The metal steps rang out as they ran up to the first deck, leaving the excited chatter beneath them. Finn stopped to catch her breath and looked back at the steady blue flip of the light on the parked police car.

'How was I to know I'd need my passport to get back on the boat?' She sat down on a step and sighed as Pearl blocked her way, waiting for an explanation. 'Let's just forget it, right?'

'But what the hell were you doing?' She was thinking of Millie's face. 'Finn . . .?'

'I had to post a card. It was urgent.'

'But we're back in twenty-four hours – a postcard will take days, maybe weeks.'

Finn stood up awkwardly as if considering the thought and then bolted past her up the stairs.

Up on the observation deck an occasional flash of sheet lightning lit up the racing clouds. The harbour pulled away. Finn craned over the edge to watch. Pearl was at her side like a shadow, her thick tangled hair catching the wind.

'It's my auntie if you must know.' Finn's face whitened, her short dark hair accentuating the shadows round her eyes. She shrugged. 'It *had* to have a Spanish postmark, to prove I'd really been here, OK? She'll think it's a really big deal, me going abroad.'

'Does she know you're . . . a detective?'

'Not exactly.' Finn looked uncomfortable. 'You see I'd already told her I was something else.'

Pearl curiously examined her friend's boarding pass. Under 'Occupation' she had declared herself a solicitor.

'You could get into trouble,' said Pearl, sternly handing it back. Finn looked defensive. 'When they say nationality you're not meant to put Geordie.'

It was early evening by the time they sailed and the storm had gathered itself from the sea with torrential rain and gale force winds.

Two long hours later Finn clung on to the handrail and gazed despairingly at the heaving grey waves.

Pearl felt protective. They had had teamed up nearly a year ago and she still knew very little about her.

'Not a lot to tell.' Finn would always shrug away from questions. Nobody had emerged except this auntie whom she never saw. Pearl hugged herself against the cold and felt empty for them both.

'How much longer?'

'Six hours – at the very most.' Pearl tried to sound encouraging. 'I'm sure the worst's over – the wind's dropped a lot.'

'Try telling the sea that,' whispered Finn, the colour of lino. 'I've got to crash out. Where's the cabin?'

Dreading the question, Pearl had been staring at the plunging wake of the ferry. She rubbed her eyes and offered Finn her sun lounger. 'I got it refunded. I thought we'd have a slap-up meal instead.'

Finn looked dazed, her face papery. 'I think I'd like to die now.'

Piling more blankets over her, Pearl resumed her worries about Millie. Spray left her skin salty; she could taste it on her lips as the ship plunged forward. The ferry was obviously running late.

She started to count the hours round her watch. Finn looked up at her.

'Don't tell me you're worrying about being late for the office?'

'Not just that.' Pearl was having trouble remembering what day of the week it was. 'You haven't forgotten Rufus' record launch tomorrow, have you? We promised him. He's even got network radio coming for an interview. The record's released today and I told Mum we'd pick her up and take her there.'

'I don't believe this.' Finn slumped into the lounger and hugged her knees. 'I'm at death's door and you're getting into light entertainment.' She pulled herself up unsteadily as the boat ploughed sideways and yawed back with a sickening lurch. 'Are you sure it's still six hours?'

Pearl nodded. 'We'll never make it.' Calculating Southampton to London, she added on the rush hour gloomily.

'There's plenty of time. You planning on sinking?' Finn closed her eyes. 'It's been put back till six. Rufus left that message, about it being changed . . .'

'Which you didn't give me.' Suddenly sympathetic with relief

Pearl bent and massaged Finn's forehead. 'And I've just thought of something else.'

'What's that?' Finn's skin was tinged the palest green.

'We haven't adjusted our watches. So that means we've got an extra hour.'

Finn groaned and merged with the moss-coloured blanket. 'It's nothing like the movies, is it?'

'Never is.' Pearl stroked her partner's hair apologetically, then straightened up purposefully and strode away, shorts flapping, across the heavy deck. Finn watched her, stricken.

'You get some sleep.' Pearl shouted back. 'I'm going shopping.'

Two

Millie stared through her own name backwards in gold on the window. Below the solicitor's office the evening had become a mass of umbrellas. The rain beat on the window.

'Bloody summer, bloody weather. I could have done with a foreign trip myself.'

'You didn't schedule much time for sunbathing,' Krish watched Millie pacing restlessly, wavy dark hair framing her strong attractive face. He switched off the computer and let the the screen wash to black.

Millie drank flat Perrier from a polystyrene cup with bites nibbled around the rim. 'Pearl promised to phone. They're cutting it fine as usual.'

Krish raised an eyebrow and slammed his file shut. 'And this is the Big One of course.'

'Since when could you afford to be so superior?' Millie felt a sudden wave of irritation. 'In case you'd forgotten, this practice has to function as a commercial business.'

Krish put on his jacket, straightened his silk-backed waist-coat and adjusted his white cuffs. Millie smiled at this ritual and watched him comb his thick black hair, frowning into a small mirror perched on a filing cabinet. She noticed for the first time that it gave him a direct view into her office.

Millie saw him shaping to be good advocate. His timing was so acute that arguing with him had developed the precision of fencing. Krish patted aftershave on his olive skin. Millie caught a scent of something like sandalwood. She threw the papers in the bin, angry with him for reminding her of his idealism.

'If I'm willing to help fat cats pull their sons out of the shit, that's your business,' he said, buffing his shoe with a tea towel.

'It's your business too.' Millie re-engaged. 'You know very well this practice cannot run on legal aid, high ideals and irregular hours.'

'You don't have to convince me.' Feeling uncomfortable he switched on the miniature TV monitor on his desk. The news flickered images of a plane disaster.

'I do,' Millie was adamamant. Krish reluctantly turned the sound down. 'I happen to care what you think – damn you.'

'You're helping that man break the law.' Krish slumped back in his chair, not meeting her look. 'An MP's son goes to Spain to watch a football match with a pack of animals who tear the place apart and stab a policeman. And you officiate when his dad fixes him up with an alibi?'

'I met the boy, Krish. He didn't do anything. He's a total wimp. He ran away and hid in his bedroom. He got rounded up later when they got on the train. All we're doing is keeping him out of court.'

'And his powerful father out of the papers?' His voice was hesitant, backing down now. 'Hope you're going to charge him the top whack.'

'What do you think? His price will mop up some of the extremely loose ends we've got around here. Clients who don't pay at all?' She sighed. 'That's how we can afford them.'

Krish nodded. He was getting round to an apology, wondering how to frame it.

'Turn the sound up.' Millie was staring at the screen. 'Quickly.'

A good-looking man with untidy blond hair and a red tie askew was being interviewed against the noisy background of a factory. He was speaking urgently, almost shouting, pushing hair out of his face. The shot suddenly cut back to the studio.

' "Red" Foxton. Do you know him?' asked Krish.

'Sort of.' She was frowning, still staring at the screen. 'Do me a favour, will you? Could I borrow that? Just for a few days?'

Krish looked puzzled. Millie flicked through the channels. 'Laura's coming to stay for her birthday – it's bit of a tradition. She's got her own TV at her dad's. I'd like her to feel really at home.'

Krish gestured generously, interested in his boss's ability to move through the gears, changing from one passion to another.

'Perfect mum as well is it?' He smiled: he was saying sorry.

'Naturally . . .' Millie didn't even look up. The man with the red tie was back on the screen and she was following every word.

The following morning the rain continued to decolourise the city.

Phones set each other off under mountains of paper. Krish answered one and padding it against his shoulder spoke rapidly to the other. Millie reached for her coffee and watched his thick black hair lying damply on his collar. If she skipped lunch and got this case sorted and the paperwork shifted she could keep the next few days comparatively light, might even take some time off with Laura.

She looked up suddenly and saw Krish beckoning urgently and mouthing a name. She took the receiver from him.

Her client, James Roland, MP, came straight to the point: was there a problem? He wanted his mind put at rest.

Millie swallowed and took a calculated risk. 'No problem sir. It's all under control.' Krish drifted from his own call and looked alarmed. 'Fine. I'll see you in your office tomorrow morning.'

She replaced the receiver like a time bomb, talked evenly as she punched numbers. 'Just leave it to me Krish, every client has a different pain threshold. He's paying me to worry for him.'

Millie got through to Southampton ferryport and listened to a halting recorded message about bad weather forcing ferries to wait outside the harbour through the night. It took her an hour to get through to the enquiry service and a warm Spanish voice read out to her the arrival timetable and suggested she add four hours. Millie thanked her and promised herself never to cut corners again.

Krish was waving his phone at her again, smiling this time. She snatched it gratefully.

'Pearl? Just tell me what time you can get here.'

'Mum . . .?' Laura sounded anxious. 'You sound frantic . . . I was hoping this would be a good moment?' Catching the silence, she ploughed on. 'There's been a slight change of plan – nothing major, right?'

Laura always talked in a morse code of hyhens and questions but the phone made it sound blunt like a telegram. 'Maybe the weekend's OK?' She apologised, 'I know you're always busy but . . .'

'. . . I'm not usually busy at weekends actually,' said Millie, her heart tightening, trying to keep it light. 'Are you saying there's a problem with tomorrow?'

'Oh Mum . . .' Laura appeared to be changing the phone from one ear to the other. 'Look, I used to tell lies about this sort of thing – but we're past that now we aren't we?'

'Of course.' Millie was on autopilot, making her voice smile.

'Great. Right. Dad and Gill have offered to take me to Paris, a surprise for my birthday. Gill knows this pianist – he's going to play a concerto for me. In his flat. Montmartre. I've never even flown before.' I know, thought her mother. I know.

'Mum?'

Millie nodded. If that's what she wanted to do. 'I thought you weren't that keen on Gillian?'

'Mummy – we *live* in the same house,' Laura laughed. 'And it will be great – like two birthdays – I don't have to have my presents on the day.'

Of course. Gill had probably by now done more motherly things for Laura than she had done herself. How many childish untruths had protected her from the blindingly obvious? Still, it was a shock, like something physical rending. Millie was alarmed to find herself capable of tears.

'Look it's busy here love – phone you tonight? Oh – all right then, when you get back.'

She tidied her desk, if she could get the debt file logged and final warnings out, she could go through those briefs before there was any likelihood of the alibi papers arriving.

'How about a late breakfast?' Krish looked concerned.

Millie shook her head automatically. She'd forgotten to tell her to have a good time and was possessed with the thought that her daughter was coming of age without her.

He handed her her coat, still damply creased, and Millie put it on without thinking.

Stabbing on the answerphone, Krish took her arm protectively, as if the room were shipping water.

Three

'It's going to get nasty, Trev.' John Foxton, general secretary of the National Union of Automotive and Vehicle Engineers, ran his hands through his mop of blond hair.

'Couldn't we discuss this calmly over a drink?' Trevor Mitchell shut the shop stewards' office door against the factory din and lodged himself on a table. He lit one cigarette from another.

'Time for talking's run out.'

Foxton slumped into a chair covered with cigarette burns and poured coffee from a thermos. Sipping from a plastic cup he re-read the letter issued by management to the workforce that morning. Expressed as triumph for the old established Turnbull Motors, it announced the merger with Schneiders in Düsseldorf and the rationalisation plans for the factory. It would mean the termination of up to two thousand jobs. Redundancy or de-skilling the plant was to be the new reality. The vigorous lines of the managing director's signature concluded each letter with an algebraic flourish.

'Nigel Pearson,' Foxton read the name aloud with loathing. He had seen this move developing for months and had driven up from London as soon as he had received the call from the shop stewards that morning. The moment for action had arrived.

Foxton pulled out a file and started to check figures. 'This meeting's crunch time for the membership. When I've told them the facts – they've got to decide for themselves.'

'Come off it, John, that's over-dramatising and you know it.'

Foxton frowned. He took off his tie and folded it carefully in his case. Trevor looked older these days. His face was puffy, his hair thin and flat; he'd become overweight, lumpy in his clothes. But John still looked to him for an opinion he trusted. Trev had been a loyal union man all his life, and helped and advised him in the early days, knew everyone. It unsettled Foxton when he criticised him so openly.

Trevor was slightly red in the face. Small broken veins flecked his cheeks and his eyes were watery. 'You'd be mad to fight this, John. If the lads strike they're dead and you know it. This isn't the local plant you're fighting any more – this is rationalisation, Pearson and his bastard multinational. They'll hammer the union – find a way round you – like a tank through a daisy field.' Trevor banged the table. 'What's bloody more, this government's given them a written invitation to go ahead. It's a set-up. The kindest advice you can give those men is to go for a good settlement.'

Foxton watched his old friend pour whisky from a hip flask into his coffee. He didn't bother to argue. He was checking the words like an excitement inside him, holding them back for when he'd need them shortly, in front of all the car workers, leading them into the battle.

Trevor felt a bad headache coming on. Now he watched Foxton opening a locker door and angling the mirror, psyching himself up, and despite his anxiety he admired him. He took a slug; fear weighed like a stone in his chest. He wished he had the courage to tell him now. Warn him. If the strike went ahead they'd all be in danger.

In a small office above the yard where the men were gathering in a solid blue mass of overalls, a small birdlike man in a dark suit cleaned the window with his handkerchief.

'Allow me, sir?' Mepham, geometric and watchful in an Italian suit, hovered then shrank back as his superior turned with a withering look. His identikit good looks betrayed a moment's disturbance then shifted back into a square-faced smile. His slender fingers smoothed black hair.

'Perhaps you could find some refreshment, there's a good man.' Nigel Pearson arranged two chairs by the window. 'I only intend to occupy this office for as long as is necessary to ascertain the outcome of the meeting. But a drink would be agreeable.'

Pearson looked back down with a tic of displeasure as a ripple of cheers started for the stewards assembling on the platform. As managing director of the Nottingham plant for twenty years, he considered himself a veteran of industrial disputes. He had personally generalled the fierce and fiery days of head-on battles and mass walk-outs. They'd survived and with massive subsidy had expanded. Now it was time for change and firm leadership.

A cheer went up from the workforce and John Foxton emerged from a side door and pulled himself up on to the platform. Moved by their greetings, he waved and watched every face turn towards him like men and women waiting for rain. He raised an arm to hold their applause, and waiting for silence, felt the adrenalin kick. Foxton measured the moment of quiet before he began to speak, softly at first, his voice serious with concern, his hands slicing the air as if he was sharing it out.

Settling into a seat at the back of the platform, Trevor Mitchell dragged heavily on his cigarette. He glanced upwards to catch sight of Pearson's face above them rigid with contempt.

Nigel Pearson leant forward stiffly and pushed the window open to catch every word. Ministerial eyes were on him to lead the new multinational trend, and forging a new prototype contract with the workforce was essential. Redundancies were inevitable, but the memory would fade. His future now promised eminence, and a hot-headed nostalgic like Foxton was not going to stand in his way. Grey, elegant and impassive, Pearson looked down on his enemy addressing the workforce and tapped a cigarette on a silver case.

'And before you vote – think on this,' Foxton paused. 'We're not just fighting for jobs today – we're fighting for a principle. We're not just going to lie down and let management dismantle what the unions have built up over centuries.' He left a pause again and the cheer went up, slightly ragged this time. 'We're fighting for the principle that British carworkers are not going to become the unskilled labourers of Europe. Make no mistake about it – that's what your new bosses want.'

The roar was genuine now – angry. Foxton pulled them back for his final assault. He didn't need to consult his speech notes, he was flying. He waited to let them shout out, to catch the next wave which would bring them all to the brink. He pulled at the red tie and loosened the knot.

Trevor Mitchell, union treasurer, shifted uneasily on the platform, his heart hammering, his palms damp. The men suddenly went quiet, anxious for more fire, more reassurance. They were facing weeks maybe months without a wage. In the blur of faces some were scared. One man's voice came like a crack in the waiting.

'Can't live on slogans, John, can we?'

Foxton's voice was kind, like a parent, 'We've got a tough fight ahead of us. But I promise you this. Whichever way you decide, the union will back you every inch of the way. On that I give you my word.'

As the stewards counted the sea of hands Foxton smiled and glanced back to Trevor who was lighting a cigarette, his hands shaking. His friend's briefly nodded congratulations sewed a stitch of fear between them. Foxton didn't blame him. You needed strong nerves for this business.

Pearson finished his whisky and considered Mepham's reflection in the window. This brash young man's appointment had been made entirely on the basis of ambition. Mepham's immorality had been hired like acetylene to cut through obstacles.

'I think Foxton did rather well, don't you?'

'That's irrelevant sir,' said Mepham, aware that his test lay before him. Gripping the whisky bottle by the neck, he nodded respectfully and followed Pearson out of the office.

'Don't under-estimate the man, Vincent.' Pearson walked with military steps down the corridor. The use of the christian name was threatening.

'On the contrary.' Mepham cleared his throat. Holding a laundered handkerchief to his thin lips, he tensed his angular prefect's face. He made Pearson wait for him, slowing his steps and making him turn and look him in the eye.

'Foxton's leading NUAVE out – that's as predicted. So now we'll regroup and get Freddie Jones in. We'll make a single union no-strike agreement with his lot and then move ahead with the rationalisation exactly as planned.'

Thrusting his hands in his pockets, Mepham sauntered after his master. Pearson mulled what appeared to be an acid taste. 'Jones will have to accept those fifteen thousand redundancies himself, don't forget.'

'I'll be taking care of that.' Vincent afforded a smile. 'I've already had some informal meetings and sewn some seeds against Foxton. Jones is a touchy man and, frankly, getting on a bit.'

His voice became more assured. 'Jones will accept them because by the time he's installed those men won't be here. He'll simply clean up on a one hundred per cent membership of all the workers who are left. Believe me, that's a powerful incentive. Neat and tidy for all of us.'

'Foxton will fight of course.' Pearson parried automatically but was pleased. The plan had a clarity about it. As he'd agreed with the minister only the other night, these matters had been too vague, too messy for far too long.

'Freddie Jones will be coming in for a meeting next week.' Mepham decorously tapped lift buttons and punched home his point.

'Foxton *is* a problem sir. But it's being dealt with.'

'That sounds very promising,' said Pearson, holding the lift doors open for a moment. 'Keep me in touch with your progress — but not the details.'

Down in the yard the men were singing as a sleek car eased its way through the crowds. A camera crew positioned itself for a snatched interview.

Foxton spotted them and composed himself. He knew this game well enough. They'd goad him and insinuate and he'd respond with calculated rhetoric to match the pictures of his men massed and swaying behind him.

The car doors swung open and Foxton paused watchfully. 'We're not Luddites, we're honest men.' He repeated the next day's headline obligingly as the soundman edged into a better position. 'They want to make their engines in Dusseldorf and their chassis in Turin. This plant will be whittled down to a few hundred de-skilled assembly line workers. What do our new bosses care what happens to this town? It's the future we're negotiating.'

Foxton slumped into the back seat next to Trevor. He waved as they forged through the crowd, then crumpled.

'You'd better start moving some money around, Trev. Set up a strike fund. We'll need fifty grand a week minimum.'

Trevor took a slow slug from his flask. 'It may not come to that, surely?'

'It's a certainty.' Foxton was busy again, scribbling a list. 'Those guys want us out. Full stop.'

'You could talk to other unions, it would strengthen your hand?'

Foxton shook his head. 'Wouldn't work. Just another way of selling out. We'll go it alone.'

Trevor offered him the flask and he motioned it away wryly. 'No thanks – I have enough trouble sleeping as it is.' There was something discomforting on his mind, something to do with the man who had shouted out. He wanted to push it away, not give it space to trouble him.

They turned on to the motorway and the miles to London were more predictable, calming. Foxton was almost speaking to himself, rehearsing the days ahead.

'This is going to be a long haul, Trev. You'd better earmark a million and that's just for starters.'

The older man made one last attempt. 'We can't afford to strike John. You know that.'

'And we can't afford not to.'

Foxton felt alive for the first time in years.

Four

Millie locked her car and headed for the drifts of music behind high hedges. The rain had stopped and the low evening sun was steaming every lawn in Greenwich. Through the drooping trees she could see Kate's front door, and could catch the babble of party noise drifting from the back garden; the ebb and flow of couples. Hearing footsteps advancing, she turned quickly and ducking wet laurel branches almost ran for the wicker gate. Millie hesitated and decided to go home. She'd refused Kate's invitation because of Laura's birthday, so she wasn't expected anyway.

'Is that you, Mil?'

It was too late. Kate had spotted her and edged her way past a couple having a silent argument in the front door. She hugged Millie and looked into her face. 'I know that expression,' she said gently. Millie sighed. They had known each other from law school when her friend's passage as black woman lawyer had been precarious. They had shared most things that mattered since then.

'Where's Laura?' Kate quickly decoded the silence and focused her attention on Millie's bottle of Sauvignon. Kate felt a wave of affection for her best friend, apparently so emotionally ordered yet so easily disorientated by love. She linked her arm and walked her through the peony bushes sweet with scent and bowed with rain, into the back garden.

Someone was watching Millie. She seemed to feel a cool breeze across the garden. Kate chattered on she as she nudged the cork with her thumbs. Millie looked curiously over to the barbecue. A man in late sunlight walked a few paces forward into the shade, then stopped uncertainly and ran his hand through his untidy blond hair.

John Foxton. Millie held herself very still. It had been years and years. Impossible to forget after all that had happened. She had convinced herself that she had totally contained it, shut it away and made it safe. But as she looked at him now, that old tug between them was an disturbing as ever. Something had told her it would always be like that and in a crazy way she felt relieved that so much was true.

'I had no idea he would be able to make it. I thought he'd still be at the factory.' Kate was offering to steer her towards the conservatory. 'Dave must have invited him. It's not a problem, is it?' She tailed off, watching her friend anxiously.

'Not at all,' said Millie evenly, knowing full well that John Foxton was someone she had hoped never to see again.

He wavered on the edge of the barbecue and observed men accustomed to obscene prices in restaurants talking animatedly about the aphrodisiac qualities of eating of smoky chicken. He wasn't hungry.

'I've often wondered,' Millie said, offering him a glass of wine, what it would be like to meet you again.' He smiled the wry smile she had not forgotten, and turned his glass curiously in his hand, catching the light.

'And . . .?' Typically he pushed her with his own reticence.

She had led him across the lawn and answered his question privately. It was like slowing the heart, stepping right back into an abandoned happiness. It was like before the misery.

'It's a shock,' said Millie, meeting his look. 'But that's all.' She laughed and lied, and he feigned disappointment, she thought, quite convincingly.

'I've been reading all about you in the papers.' Millie felt marginally calmer. Foxton sipped his wine and watched her carefully. She looked a little older. Her expressive face was thinner, and tiny lines traced around her eyes whenever she smiled or frowned. Small flecks of grey had appeared in her dark hair.

'They say you won't negotiate,' Millie challenged him. He found it upsetting to hear her talking as if she didn't know him.

'Rubbish, Mil.' She heard him use her name casually, already wanting to tell her things, confide in her. 'They're playing the unions off against each other.' Foxton automatically loosened his tie.

Millie nodded. 'Over a thousand redundancies sounds bad.'

'It could be much worse, they're hiding the extent of it. They think they've got us cornered, but we know how to fight.' He heard himself making the speech, noticed a few heads turn, saw her look. 'It's been a long time, Mil.'

She decided to go back to the house, disarmed by the way he stared at her.

'How's Laura? She must be . . .' He checked himself, awkwardly colliding with memories. 'She must be quite grown up by now?'

He was visibly shaken as he walked with her into the conservatory. The wide vine leaves greened the light and Kate's exotic flowers filled tubs and pots. Millie touched delicate waxed orchid petals and heard her voice answering steadily as if she were in court.

'Laura's eighteen today. She lives with her father most of the time. Comes down for weekends with me – that sort of thing.' She waited for his shock. He owed her that.

'You and Ben aren't together any more?' He faltered, wanted to know everything. He was paying out the past through his fingers so quickly he felt it burn him.

'We divorced. It seemed the sensible thing to do really.' Her tone was deliberately dispassionate. She was drawing on a hurt she thought she had dispatched many years ago, a lifetime ago. But here it was as jagged as ever, drawing blood.

'I didn't know that.' He was curiously disjointed.

'No reason why you should.' Her reply was throwaway, a gambit to take them through to the safety of food and other people. She was already on the move, steering him towards French bread and wild-rice salads. Millie resolved to leave as quickly as possible.

Evening sunlight bleached the red neon signature of 'The Slab' nightclub, at the top of the redbrick warehouse. Pearl hurried her mum through the entrance and waited anxiously for the clanking lift trailing cables through the black shaft.

A blast of noise billowed down the stairs. Pearl didn't dare look back at Rose, it sounded as if the show might be finishing. In her fragile state she wasn't sure she could shoulder the responsibility for Rose missing Rufus' first interview on national radio. She also doubted she'd ever hear the end of it from her brother. Support between them was taken for granted. They didn't waste words on it but it was there, on the line. That's what had made it so easy with Finn. She worked the same way.

Pearl looked round cautiously. Finn was grey and had propped herself wearily against the wall.

'Where's the loo?' Her skin looked patchy with damp. 'Think I might just pop in and powder my nose.'

Pearl's smile met her mother's expression of horror.

'This is one terrible mistake, child. Rufus won't want me there. Besides it'll only encourage him. The boy can't sing. And he's big-headed enough as it is.'

'It's rapping, not singing, Mum. I think we've missed it anyway,' said Pearl, ruefully sliding back the cage door of the lift.

The interview was only just starting. The Sound Systems had been blaring to work up some atmosphere for the DJ's introduction. Pearl found herself smiling and clutching her mum's arm too hard. Rose was transfixed.

Resplendent in Bermuda shorts, black shades and reversed baseball cap, Rufus was centre stage. As he talked, Pearl suddenly realised he looked older. He was confidently giving out name checks to his backing crew in a carefully rehearsed set. Grinning broadly, he dubbed his mother Queen of Rap, and then turned gratefully to his sound engineer. Denzil, thin, angular and shiny as cedar, had been working frantically on the microphone and was gulping from a large bottle of lemonade. He smiled shyly, wiping his mouth.

Rufus bowed lavishly to their scattered applause and suddenly ducked down behind the amplifiers and produced a huge bunch of vividly coloured flowers. 'And finally, my main man.' He brought them to silence. 'My manager. The guy who makes it all happen.'

Denzil pushed into the huddle round the mixing panel and pulled Fitz reluctantly towards the spotlight. Rufus grabbed his hand and hugged him, making him face the audience. Fitz smiled and looked embarrassed. Held by the spotlight his handsome face was suddenly sketched with shadows, his jaw shaded by a closely shaved beard. His expressive eyes searched beyond the lights to where friends and press stood in clusters. Pearl caught her breath. Now their relationship was over she was going to have to get used to seeing him and not caring. Waving, Fitz blew a kiss, almost generally. Pearl turned her face away from the light.

'They said it was solid imagination, P. Played it nationwide on the radio.' An hour later Rufus was jigging, still fired with the excitement of the interview.

Pearl was pulling tissue paper off a bottle.

'Oh man.' Rufus caught the champagne cork as it ricocheted off the ceiling. 'Where did you get this? It's pink.'

'Duty free,' said Pearl, pouring.

'A whole cabin's worth,' added Finn drily.

Across the room Fitz was wrapped round a tall elegant girl moving vaguely to taped music. Her black lace blouse melted against the colour of her skin. Pearl sipped the bubbles and suddenly felt her good humour evaporate. Flat and angry she looked over to Finn sitting half asleep against the wall. Against her own advice she heard her casual question sharp with resentment.

'Who's that girl dancing with Fitz?'

Rufus was effusive, 'Oh that's Sally. She's really nice.' Finn opened her eyes and scowled at him.

'Time for me to split.' Pearl kissed Rose, pulling away from her questions, and nodding to Finn she headed towards the door.

'Wow.' Rufus stared. 'What was that all about?'

'You tell him, Denzil,' said Finn, getting to her feet.

The dance floor rolled like the deck of the ship, wide and empty. Swaying to the music, Fitz pressed his face against Sally's neck and closed his eyes. As Pearl skirted the dance floor, angrily talking to herself, trying out her recriminations, the doors swung open and a crowd of kids came in shouting noisy congratulations to Rufus.

Pearl felt her heart hammering and turned back to face the

dance floor. Denzil had been watching her anxiously and raising an eyebrow, he nudged Finn.

Fitz moved without listening to the music and pushed against Sally's warm skin to stop himself from watching Pearl. His partner nibbled his ear appreciatively and mistaking his anxiety for passion, slid her hands slowly down over his buttocks. Fitz pulled away, his discomfort increasing as he tried to stage-manage their movements.

When he opened his eyes and saw Pearl standing a few feet away he stopped moving and smiled cautiously.

'How you doin', Princess?' Sally disengaged and turned defensively to face Pearl, darting an indignant look at Fitz. He gracefully ushered her towards the bar, and parting her straightened black hair whispered into her ear. She gave a strained laugh and glanced back at Pearl. She kissed his cheek, holding his head down towards her.

Pearl stood her ground in the centre of the empty floor and Fitz walked back towards her, clearing his throat self consciously, his hand to his mouth.

'Care to dance?' He held out his hand.

'Outside, Fitz.' Pearl was unsmiling. 'Let's try and keep it dignified.'

The stair well was badly lit and the concrete steps echoed. Fitz attentively held the door open for Pearl and felt it slam against his hand as he followed her.

She watched carefully as he waited for her to speak. He smiled vaguely. Fitz, ambitious, charming and undependable; an independent record producer operating out of a tiny studio complex at the back of his record store. Fitz, married man, father of two, her former employer, her former lover. The finality of her own summary fell on her like a grieving. His dark skin looked blacker in the shadowy light, and as he touched his fingers to his forehead, Pearl noticed grey hairs. Her anger felt locked up and useless.

'What's up, P?'

Pearl sat down on the top stair with her back to him. 'You'd make a lousy detective.'

Fitz thought about the quip and dismissed it. There was something despairing in her voice, not what he had expected.

'Talk to me, Princess. You'll feel better.' He sat down beside her, catching her mood, not daring to put his arm around her.

Pearl shut her eyes and smelt cinnamon from his hair oil. He took her hand and she stood up, shrugging him off. 'We've done all the talking, Fitz.' He jumped to his feet as she started to walk down the stairs.

'So what's this all about?' His voice echoed. Pearl didn't answer and her steps fell away beneath him into silence. He leaned over the banister, staring after her as if he could will her back.

Finn pushed the doors open and slipped through. She'd seen them leave and had waited awkwardly. Fitz seemed to come out of a daze when she nudged his arm.

'You all right?'

He shook his head and put his arm around her. 'Not good. You?'

Finn sighed, 'I'm still feeling seasick. The floor keeps going up and down.'

He nodded gravely as if he understood, and watched her follow Pearl unsteadily, her footsteps fading to nothing, like a rumour.

Five

There was a dim light on in Millie's office when they drew up in the empty street. Finn stared up and the window. 'Probably just left her light on. We could post the stuff through the door.'

Pearl shaded her eyes against the street lights and was certain she saw a shadow waver across the blind.

Finn tried the outer door and it swung open into the darkened hall and staircase. Somewhere above they heard a chair scrape. Pearl's mouth was so dry she couldn't whisper. She nodded towards the stairs and led the way up.

They crouched on the small landing. The silence seemed to echo and rain leaked through the windows. Finn slowly pushed down the door handle. It was unlocked. Glancing at Pearl she whipped the door open and they burst in, flicked off the light and dropped down behind the photocopier.

Sitting at her desk watching a miniature TV with the sound turned down, Millie had just upset a cup of coffee and was frantically mopping her desk with tissues.

'One of these days I suppose you might just walk normally through that door.' She steadied herself by wiping down the pages of her desk diary. The next day had run like a watercolour.

'It *is* after midnight, Millie.' Pearl sat down on Krish's desk and let her heart slow to normal.

Millie glanced at her watch and nodded. 'That makes you twelve hours late.' Her face was anxious. 'Did you get it?'

Finn put the sealed envelope on the desk. 'He was almost too perfect. Times, places, even what the boy ordered to drink. The bloke owned the hotel where they were staying. It was as if he'd read the script.'

Millie was reading, flicking through the pages.

'It is all legit, is it?' asked Pearl carefully.

Millie took a deep breath and folded the document back into its envelope.

'It's a version of the truth. It does a job and it's not breaking the law.' She was busy switching off lights. 'What happened to that phone call incidentally?'

Pearl noticed Finn had slumped onto a chair and had fallen asleep instantly. She refused to feel guilty about the gig, not on top of everything else.

She dumped her carrier bag on Millie's desk and smiled ruefully. 'Things don't always work out quite how you plan them, that's all.' She was talking about the job and thinking about Fitz. Millie switched the coffee machine back on. That just about summed it up.

Six

Maureen Jennings watched people streaming into the NUAVE Union building. She deliberately worked the outer limits of flexitime to allow herself the space of offices without people. She preferred to think of herself as John Foxton's personal assistant rather than simply his secretary; when he was out on the road she practically ran the place.

Only this morning she had got there before the sun had started to heat the glass-clad building and settled in his office with her thermos, radio and tape-recorder. By the time Foxton had arrived she had sliced through all the papers and carefully pasted together a file of all the main headline articles, features and editorials. She had also recorded his and other relevant interviews from national and local radio, all collated on the tape. It gave him an instant reference so that by the time he had consumed his first cup of freshly-ground coffee he would be perfectly briefed.

It was the sort of initiative that gave her a pleasure second only to the one she got from adjusting certain phrases in his letters which he then signed without reading.

Settled uncomfortably at his desk Foxton felt unaccountably restless after a sleepless night. He nursed a pang of resentment as he ploughed his way through the newspaper cuttings. He preferred the first-hand hit of excitement as he held the bulk of the paper with his picture on the front page. He preferred instant granule coffee and felt uneasy, as if the day was developing an uncontrollable edge to it. This anxiety had built gradually, his concentration wavering during the stewards' meeting, and now, as he waited to see Trevor, his mind wandered helplessly back to the barbecue.

Outside his door he heard Trevor Mitchell arguing with

Maureen about the right to smoke. He ushered him in impatiently. Trevor sat down, hot and flustered, rubbing his forehead.

'I'm sorry, John.' He fiddled with a disposable lighter with clumsy fingers. His nervousess was infectious. 'We might have an unavoidable delay with the strike fund money.'

Foxton looked up at him sharply. This was the last thing he was expecting to hear. Trevor dabbed his mouth with his handkerchief.

'It's Kevin Railton, our financial advisor.'

John waited, refusing to show agitation. 'What about him, Trev?'

'I'm waiting for him to get back from Brussels. No point having an expert if we don't use him. It's a matter of liquidating assets. He'll have it all in hand. Don't worry.' His watery smile was not reassuring.

John nodded. The men had to be paid strike pay every week or the dispute would lose its nerve. But Trevor Mitchell knew that better than anyone.

When Trevor had gone Foxton spoke quickly into the intercom and summoned Maureen.

'The thing is, John,' she sat down and opened her notepad, 'Trevor's phoned Railton's firm four times today. Nobody really seems sure where he is.'

'You connected the calls for him?' She nodded. Foxton phrased his thoughts carefully, his mind full of unvoiced suspicious. 'Observing total confidentiality, Maureen, I want you to get balance details of every union bank account for my inspection. You'll need the confidential list of banks and account numbers.'

'But they'll all be in Accounts, won't they?' She looked puzzled.

'Will they?' He looked away awkwardly. A small flicker of shock tightened her face. She waited fretfully.

'Get hold of our version and the banks' and check them against each other.' He went casually to the safe. 'I'll get you that list.' It was obvious what he was implying and it made him uncomfortable.

'Don't bother with the list,' said Maureen, closing her notebook. 'I can easily access it from Trevor's database.' She shut the door noiselessly after her and he heard her steps hurrying away down the corridor.

She had displayed no particular surprise at his request. Maureen, who listened in to every call she connected and tapped manicured nails on keyboards to plunder computer memories. She was a formidable secretary but he felt unnerved by the way she'd picked up on his request as if she'd thought of it herself.

He prepared for a day of meetings and an evening of speech writing. In the office silence settled like dust. He'd had no word from Pearson's management at the Nottingham plant yet. Someone had to break cover soon.

Krish clashed shut each of the venetian blinds in rapid succession. The slats shadowed the office in evening browns and golds. Pearl spun round slowly in his chair. 'We'll wait, Krish. We can lock up.'

He pulled on his jacket and tugged impatiently at the cuffs. 'No way. Millie goes straight home from the court if it runs late.'

'Surely she phones?' Finn enquired innocently, observing him carefully. She wondered who he was meeting in his pale grey suit which off-set the wild blue paisley waistcoat. She found him attractive, as she always had. The awkwardness between them had faded, a night they'd both regretted disguised by daily banter, Finn's hurt subdued by her harsh reassessment. As he glanced at her now, smiling casually, she reminded herself firmly that the person Krish loved most was himself.

He turned away officiously and started to set the burglar alarm. 'She's not even been well today.'

Pearl looked up from his desk diary enquiringly. 'What's the matter with her then?'

He shrugged. 'I dunno, not herself at all. PMT or something?'

'Don't be so sexist.' Pearl was feeling irritable and concern masquerading as condescension was more than she could take from Krish. He rolled his eyes and pocketed the mobile phone.

'Don't take that, we'll need it if there's something urgent.' Finn reckoned they had him rattled.

'No jobs, girls,' he repeated. 'Unless you're willing to lower yourselves to a little debt collecting?'

Pearl curled her lip and continued scanning the classified column in Millie's legal journal. A minder for an opera singer's daughter looked interesting. Shame it was Birmingham.

Krish suddenly snapped. 'You know your trouble don't you?' They both watched him blankly. He pointed a finger. 'You've been spoilt rotten. You think a retainer with Millie means a life packed with foreign travel and car chases.' Gulping cold coffee from a cup he glared at Pearl.

'You're dreaming. It's mostly bad debts and tacky divorces. So take your pick, there's not a real detective story in sight.' He thought of his new girlfriend Lavinia, waiting in the theatre wine bar, her perfect face poised with anger. She was probably deciding to leave about now. Edgily he felt in his pockets for the expensive theatre tickets for a play with a perplexing title.

Pearl grinned at Finn and together they broke into a slow dismissive handclap.

Later in a coffee bar Finn went methodically through their loose change. Most of it was pesetas.

'Maybe he's Spanish,' she said hopefully, heading for the counter and the Italian barman.

Watching her in the queue Pearl remembered the early days when they'd worked together on their first case.

'Applied pyschology and common sense, that's all we need,' she'd briefed her new partner.

'And a pair of wheels,' Finn had added practically, and had promptly returned with an acquired car.

Pearl smiled ruefully and dug in the sugar bowl. Her ability to edit the truth into something bearable was becoming dangerous. If she was ever going to get Fitz out of her bloodstream, she would have to force herself to remember every detail accurately.

Pearl had hired herself for her first real job. It had poured non-stop, thirty-six hours of rain. She'd crouched in a car with a stop watch, waited in a door way and stared at a lighted, then darkened, bedroom window. She'd set herself to prove that Fitz was being unfaithful to his wife. And, for the first time, unfaithful to her.

Pearl had thrown all the details, the chronology of his day and night's betrayal on his desk the next morning. Shaking with shock, almost grey, Fitz hadn't even tried to lie his way out of it. He stared at the closely typed pages and rubbed his eyes, his ebony face childish with guilt.

He had reached out to calm her and recoiled when she hurled his computer discs out of the window. They lay on the pavement below like coloured sweets. She had heard them scrunch underfoot as she strode across the road clutching his monitor. Her jealousy and anger had given her an unquenchable sense of power. She had watched herself exact the revenge she had invented like a plot in a play. Pearl had felt positively drunk as she had lobbed his screen into a builder's skip.

There had been a howl, and Finn emerged from the debris inside the skip like a recrimination. She was clutching her head, blood blotting quickly through her dark cropped hair. She'd been asleep and now she was furious. Pearl had felt shock catching up with her and thought she recognised the tough-looking girl, powdered with brick dust.

'I know you, don't I?' She had held her hand out tentatively to pull her out of the rubbish. 'Stupid place to kip.'

'Yeh, I remember, biggest mouth in the school.'

Pearl had taken Finn to Casualty, sat with her and stopped her bolting. The cut was bad and had needed stitches. In the end Pearl had had to leave and had impulsively thrust her flat keys at Finn. The angry Geordie with the thousand megabyte gash on her hairline had been impressed. Pearl was someone worth considering if she'd trust her with her home. More importantly, she had never once asked what Finn had been doing in the skip.

Finn arrived back at the table with one cappucino and sat down. 'If you're pissed off, just say so.' She scooped the chocolate powder from the froth on the coffee.

Pearl hacked at the sugar before she spoke. 'Fitz is just doing this to make me jealous, right?'

'Right.' Finn spooned the unsugared coffee awkwardly.

'Then why does it hurt? I hate feeling like this.'

Finn didn't know an answer. She'd only felt the kind of jealousy which eats at the heart once, when she still a kid, not with an adult's rage. Even then she'd thought that she'd understood how people found it possible to kill each other.

'You've been trying to get rid of him for ages.' Finn tried another tack.

'I know,' Pearl nodded. 'I suppose I just didn't expect to be so successful.' She stared moodily at Finn piling sugar into their shared coffee. 'And what do you call that?'

'It's the opposite of champagne.' Finn stirred it vigorously and generously pushed it towards her.

Seven

Millie was ironing. She was ironing everything that had been in the basket for months, discovering strata of clothes she hadn't seen in weeks. It was part of a strategy. On the draining board several bags of vegetables defrosted miserably while the fridge leaked and crashed into the drip tray.

Her largest saucepan bubbled with bones. They'd been in the freezer for weeks; making a good stock pot was something she'd had on her mind like a guilty conscience. Her mother's fault: Millie had been brought up to believe that having home-made chicken stock in the freezer was close to achieving a state of grace.

Millie sighed. What had been a perfectly presentable and comfortable terraced house had been rapidly reduced to chaos. On the floor the vacuum cleaner lay disembowelled, its dustbag removed for the first time. The replacement lay abandoned nearby after an episode of undiguised temper. On her return home that evening she'd felt the urgent need for order; for honest rationalisation of the piles of washing, and of the fridge, which had frozen so hard round the ice tray that she couldn't even prise it open with a carving knife.

The phone rang. Millie nearly didn't answer, but a sense of expectation made her pick up the receiver, trying to sound warm and relaxed. It was a reversed charge call from France.

'Mum. Hi.' Her daughter's telegram tones pattered in her ear. Only her resentment of enduring details of the birthday concerto tinged the pleasure of Laura tugging at her name. Millie began to pick her way through the fragments.

'It's the pits. Pissed down since we got here, My Docs are killing me – we have to walk everywhere. Walkman nicked on the metro. Pianist turns out to be a wally with wandering hands. Dad and Gill bicker about the price of a coffee.'

'Apart from that . . .?' Millie guiltily felt relief hit her bloodstream. She took a sip of her gin.

'Not bad. I've met a really nice guy.'

'Oh . . .?' Millie felt her recovery decelerating.

' "Oh, I expect he's a crud?" Or "Oh? I'd love to meet him – I'm sure he's delightful"?' Laura delivered option boxes down the line.

'When?' She cross-examined intuitively.

'Great. See you ASAP then. We'll collect him from the airport next week?'

'Two things . . .' Millie sipped her gin again.

'Sunday, and he's French. Knew *you* wouldn't mind. Must go, Mum. Dad's waiting. You know what he's like.'

The line hummed for some time before she replaced the receiver. She poured more gin and trawled for ice in the drip tray, feeling properly whole again for the first time in days. The din of the past suddenly stilled. She should have known better than to open even a crack in the old chaos. There was a peace levelling out again, and her daughter's trust steadied her heart.

Millie was pushing magazines under the sofa and becoming aware of the smell of burning bones when she heard the doorbell. It was nearly midnight. The house was blazing with light; with every window thrown open she couldn't pretend she was out.

She hesitated by the front door and checked the safety chain, her heart running fast.

'Who is it?' She sounded scared. There was a pause, the letterbox flapped.

'John, it's John, Mil . . .?' A slight tinge of north country, just enough to make her name sound different. She considered the wallpaper. She hadn't given him her address and she was angry that he considered it possible to turn up on her doorstep without warning, and so late. And with what intention? She was about to shout a reply when she heard him walking away.

Impulsively she opened the door a crack. He turned, looking very pale in the street light.

'Is there something wrong?' Millie felt ridiculous, like someone in a film.

He walked back and hesitated on the doorstep. 'I need your help, Millie.' He rocked slightly. 'It's urgent.'

Millie took him straight through the house and into her secluded garden. It had been hot all day and even so late it was warm and close. She opened out chairs and flicked on an outside light. She often sat out here in the dark with candles, but now she dismissed the idea. In the same way, sitting in the house was wrong. She needed time to prepare herself to see him sitting among her belongings again. And time to decide whether that was even what she wanted. A pool of light in her garden seemed suitably neutral.

Foxton's mood of anxiety excused his silence. Millie brought out the remains of a bottle of wine and a single glass. He smiled gratefully and gulped down several mouthfuls. She was waiting.

'I know it's late, Mil. But I need advice,' he faltered. 'From someone I can trust completely.' He was looking out into the darkness, not at her, almost dazed.

Millie sat down on the bench. 'Why don't you sit down and explain?' She said it simply, puzzled by his distress.

He sat down quite close to her, staring at his hands. 'I hope you would feel you could ask the same of me, Mil?'

Millie nodded, suppressing a flicker of disquiet.

He moved so that he could face her, his grey eyes bright with anxiety. 'I think we might be heading for big trouble . . .' Again, he searched for words.

Millie smiled uncertainly, 'We . . .?'

'The union.' He sighed. 'I think something's gone horribly wrong on the financial side.'

Millie concealed a lurch of disappointment. She had been expecting something personal, rather more traumatic. This was turning into an office consultation. Before she could say anything he stopped her with a rueful smile.

'I think I owe you an explanation.' He tugged at his hair uncomfortably. 'We've been involved with a few moves which were not strictly above board in the past.' He glanced over defensively. 'Sometimes it's a case of means to an end.'

35

Millie swallowed her disappointment. The intimacy between them had receded. 'You mean witholding funds?' she prompted.

He nodded. 'A few years ago we were supporting a strike by a component factory in Holland.'

'Illegal secondary picketing?' Millie pushed him to say what he meant.

He nodded slowly. 'The government threatened us with sequestration so we hid money in a variety of secret bank accounts. Even hired a fancy money-man to tackle some clever investment tricks. But now, just when we need instant cash and a lot of it, it looks like we've got problems and they may be connected with dealings we'd rather not admit to.' He sighed and finished his wine. 'Perhaps even with embezzlement.'

'What are you saying? You suspect someone?' Millie suddenly saw how serious this was.

'One of my oldest friends, Trevor Mitchell,' he said miserably. 'He's our financial secretary. I don't know what to do.'

'You'd better bring the paperwork to the office first thing. We can't discuss this properly until I've seen it.'

He put his hand on hers and frowned. 'I haven't got any proof yet, Mil.'

'Then what exactly are you talking about?' She leant back stiffly against the bench.

'I don't know, just a hunch. I may well have something more definite by tomorrow. But I'm having to think ahead, Mil, because if I'm right we're going to have to move fast and keep it all under wraps.'

Millie poured herself a drink in his glass. 'You're saying that this Trevor might have political motives?'

Foxton looked confused. 'I'm not sure, not him necessarily. But with two thousand men depending on me for strike pay, confidence and trust is everything. A financial scandal in the union would bring the strike and the union's creditability crashing down.'

'But you're just guessing, John?'

Foxton loosened his tie and looked at her seriously; a look which used to stop all her questions.

'I think someone's setting me up, Mil. I can feel it, smell it.'

Millie addressed him coolly, like any client. 'If someone has perpetrated a fraud on the union, you can't be held legally responsible, unless you were negligent.'

He gave a hopeless laugh. 'If the strike collapses, the buck stops here, believe me.'

Millie stood and gripped the back of the chair. 'And so does this consultation. I'm sorry John, you come here at the dead of night to seek my professional advice with a problem which may well not exist. I suggest you come back in office hours.'

'Not *just* professional advice.' He looked alarmed. You're a trusted friend, Mil, when I saw you on Saturday . . .'

'. . . you put me back on your contacts list.' She couldn't hold back her resentment.

He didn't retaliate, just looked rather battered. Millie checked herself.

'John . . . if you've just been using this as an excuse to come here and see me . . .'

'No.' He was sincere. 'It wasn't that, honest.'

Even that might have been more acceptable, she thought, as she steered him towards the high brick walls surrounding her garden ushered him through the door and drew across four bolts. She leant against the creosoted wood panels waiting to hear him walk away.

'Don't get me wrong Mil,' he continued. 'It was just that I thought you might know someone who could look into it for me. I wouldn't know where to start.'

Try the Yellow Pages, she thought unkindly, as she relocked the padlock, refusing to admit more hurt.

Eight

The last shift of morning cleaners drifted like a shoal of fish through the reception area and spotted Foxton shaking his umbrella on the polished floor. He smiled self-consciously and they waved.

'Saw you on the news last night, John.' One raised her clenched fist in solidarity. These were the people who relied on him. He felt hung over with worry and started to plan a list of phone calls.

He crept past Maureen's office. A transistor interrupted itself with jingles and there was a faint whiff of glue. It was only eight o'clock.

He punched coffee and dried milk, and inhaling warm plastic, pushed into his office. Sitting at his desk, Maureen was on the phone. At her side the fax whirred. She glanced up and smiled, only a little uneasily, jotted down a note and replaced the receiver.

'Did you get my message, John?' She offered him her thermos.

Foxton couldn't repress a fleeting double-take. She could have been his boss. Maureen Jennings, in her late twenties, was dressed in a loose black dress and a grey jacket, her tawny hair darted with highlights suggesting expensive holidays; she removed copper-rimmed glasses and rubbed her eyes carefully. He felt momentarily disorientated with the notion, light-headed with insomnia.

'What message?' He refocussed. 'What are you doing in here, Maureen?'

She could feel her heart beating violently. 'I couldn't take the risk of anyone seeing what I was doing.' He nodded and stared down at the mass of paperwork on the desk.

'There are only two more banks to check,' she continued gravely. 'But already there's a considerable discrepancy.'

Foxton seemed to absorb her information slowly. He slumped into the armchair and sipped his coffee.

'How considerable?' He sounded as if he were asking after an invalid.

'I've rounded off the figures.' She was flicking pages. 'But give or take . . . we're about three million pounds down.'

'Are you absolutely sure?' He felt quite shaky.

'I've been through it twice. I haven't been home, John.'

She seemed quite high, he imagined her there throughout the night, dredging through the figures, watching the terrifying truth emerge.

She stood up wearily. 'Do you want me to get Dudley over here?'

Foxton shook his head numbly. The union lawyer was the last person he wanted to alert. He shook out the contents of his case and leafed through his diary for a card.

'Phone this number,' he instructed. 'Ask for Mrs Millington personally. Say it's me phoning on business and that I've now got the documentation she requested.' He paused as if adding a postscript. 'And ask her if she can see me as soon as possible. It's become rather urgent.'

When he returned from his stewards' meeting Maureen was waiting.

'There's a taxi ordered,' she reported. 'Mrs Millington said she'll see you in an hour.'

Foxton breathed a sigh of relief.

'And naturally,' continued Maureen with a knowing look, 'I won't say where you've gone, not to anyone.'

Millie dumped the shoe box in Finn's lap and waited impatiently. She looked over at Pearl for support but Pearl was suddenly engrossed in the coffee machine.

Millie selected a paper bag with a date scrawled across it. 'We don't run to genetic finger printing here, so give me a clue.'

'They're my expenses.' Finn flushed. 'I've got a bit behind.'

'They're incomprehensible scraps of paper.' Millie was withering. 'And most of them are extremely sticky.'

'They're Spanish . . .' Finn started lamely.

'Translate them into forms, Finn. I called you both in for a case briefing, not to flood the office with waste paper.' Millie hurried back to her office.

While Finn started to wade through her receipts she glanced curiously through the partition glass where Millie was brushing her hair in the mirror. She threw the brush in her bag as Krish appeared at the door with the next client, a tall good-looking man who seemed vaguely familiar.

Finn automatically watched through the partition as Millie sat behind her desk listening grimly to the man who was pacing in front of her. Pearl left the photocopier and joined Finn, noticing how Millie avoided looking up at her client and offered no warmth when she replied briefly to his questions.

Krish tapped on the window and gestured that they should go in immediately. Pearl nodded in the direction of the client and grinned at Finn.

'Oh boy, when Millie doesn't like someone, she certainly doesn't waste any energy disguising it.'

As Millie began deftly to outline the known details of the embezzlement Foxton was carefully observing them. He barely disguised his surprise when they were introduced, and Pearl enjoyed his lack of reserve.

'I've got to admit it, Mil.' He seemed nervous. 'I was anticipating a guy in a raincoat.' Pearl registered the 'Mil'.

'You've been reading too much Raymond Chandler,' she answered evenly.

'Trevor Mitchell,' Foxton explained, 'is our financial secretary, he's directly responsible for our accounts and financial admin-istration. He's the man who could pull a stunt like this. But personally I just can't believe it.' Foxton looked physically pained. 'I've known him as friend and colleague for twenty-five years and he's a union man through and through.' He sighed. 'What would old Trev do with three million anyway?'

Millie raised an eyebrow. 'Come off it, John. People get tempted. No one's immune.' He look unconvinced.

Finn shrugged. 'Why can't you just tackle him with it? If you're sure?'

Foxton turned to her. She was surprisingly attractive although her leather jacket and jeans made her rather boyish. Her accent made him homesick.

'I can't, not yet.' They waited. He was searching for the logic. 'For a start, it would be bloody dreadful if I've got it wrong. I need proof. But it's something else. Whoever it is – I'm worried there's more to this than just a money rip off.' He looked ruefully at Millie. 'I suppose I'm starting to sound paranoid again?'

'Possibly,' said Millie, acknowledging the reference privately and seeing him again in her garden, his head in his hands. 'But shouldn't we tackle the missing money first and see where that leads?'

Foxton nodded. 'If we got the police in, the scandal would scuttle the strike. I don't know any more than that. But meanwhile you've got to find out who's got his fingers in the till. And bloody fast. We're trying to get the strike pay out this week, but if there are any hitches after that we're finished.'

'Anyone else deal with the finances?' Pearl sensed this was no ordinary case.

'There's Kevin Railton, I suppose. He's a financial consultant.' He handed them a card. 'His company are specialists. We brought him in for some sharp investment advice. But even so, nothing can happen without Trevor's say-so. It all comes back to him, I'm afraid.'

'Do you trust this Railton bloke?' Finn noticed Millie avoiding his look.

Foxton shook his head. 'Not really. He's a slick bastard and was very clever when we needed to camouflage some money in the past.' Foxton looked a little rueful. 'It was a matter of survival. As it is now.'

As Foxton got into his taxi Finn bent the blinds and watched him.

'Seems all right,' she observed.

Millie nodded. 'But he could be off the map if you don't come up with something quickly. And that would be a waste.'

She opened the NUAVE file and started to brief them on the background. 'Just get the proof so that Foxton can deal with it himself. It's a case that musn't turn into a case.'

'What about Foxton himself?' asked Pearl.

Millie blinked. 'Isn't that a rather eccentric suggestion?'

'Probably.' Pearl had leant never to make assumptions. 'We'll get started on Mitchell and Railton but what if we need anything on Foxton?'

Millie shrugged. 'If it comes to that, try me.' Finn looked at her curiously. 'My husband used to know him quite well.'

The door slammed as they left and Millie hastily rescheduled her diary. Krish was in her office gathering up the coffee cups with more than a hint of resentment.

'Your next client's waiting,' he reminded her. She nodded.

He was niggled. 'I thought we were at full stretch and that Pearl and Dean were booked for a timely spot of debt collecting?'

Millie handed him the file with a smile. 'You'll approve of this, Krish. There are crucial issues at stake, over two thousand men's jobs in the balance, not to mention the future of the trade union movement. What's more, the fee's going to be lousy and probably late. How could we possibly refuse?'

Nine

The Last Judgment was a good place to talk. It was the sort of pub which came and went with the tide. The river slapped against the quayside as Foxton paused by the door and looked inside. Trevor propped himself up against the bar reading a newspaper. Glancing back as the water bailed sunlight, he ducked into the shadowy bar, leaving the smell of the sea behind him.

Trevor smiled. His dark suit, a bright red handkerchief and faintly striped shirt made him look as if he'd been shaken out and pressed. John registered he was drinking mineral water.

'Strategic details, John,' Trevor began immediately. 'It's going to be an important week.' Foxton loosened slightly as he saw Trevor brisk and animated, ready to discuss the campaign with his old energy. A twinge of regret nagged him as he recalled his recent precautions.

Trevor casually rattled though some routine provisions and then paused. 'There's only one slight change to normal procedure.' The words sloped away, didn't sound so ordered.

'The strike was called on Wednesday, but we're going to need more than a week to raise the money. I've calculated we can pay them Monday week.'

'That's not what we said.' Foxton was instantly suspicious. 'It leaves them more than a week without money. It's a question of morale, Trev.'

'It's more like good housekeeping.' Trevor was firm. 'Unless we want to throw money away we need that time to mobilise certain stock.'

John looked at him intently; seemed about to ask him something.

Trevor shook his head. 'I know what I'm talking about. I've

worked all this out – we can eke out an extra two weeks from the same investments if we do it my way.'

Foxton nodded and let it be. There was nothing so very wrong with Monday payments and Trevor knew his stuff. He cautioned himself against over-reacting. He could have confided in Trev there and then. They might have tackled it without any outside help. But a small questioning voice still troubled him. He said nothing, finished his drink and left.

Trevor added a double gin to the mineral water and then walked slowly back to the office. He felt suddenly tired. Avoiding Maureen and her diciplinary looks he marched into his office. A striking black girl with a mane of hair tied back in a flame-coloured scarf appeared to be flicking through his desk diary.

She looked at him quite calmly and collected up two coffee mugs. 'Mr Mitchell?' She was smiling now. 'I'm Pearl Parker. Your new temp.'

'Tried to warn you, sir.' Maureen was watching through the door. 'But you must have slipped past. Can't imagine why John thinks we need more staff. Especially on a Friday afternoon.'

Trevor ignored her and started stabbing numbers into his phone. Pearl hovered. He moodily ordered black coffee, and looked up in irritation when she didn't leave immediately.

He asked for Railton sharply and was kept waiting to the plink of synthesised folk tunes. 'Well . . .?'

Pearl hovered near his desk. 'Sugar sir?' she asked.

'Mr Railton is not back in the office as yet,' said the breathy secretary.

'Damn.' Trevor threw the phone down; fine sweat dampened his forehead.

'Sweetners,' he muttered to Pearl. 'Four.'

Kevin Railton glided through Customs with matching soft leather overnight bag and briefcase. He looked attentively towards the barrier, his thin inquisitive face made bony and white by a dark beard. His pale wispy hair gave him a piebald appearance and Finn peered anxiously at the black and white photo. It was definitely him. The panic settled. Suspects in crowds very rarely look like their photographs, especially if they've grown a beard.

Finn had spent the morning sifting through the passengers from five Brussels flights. But this was it.

She had just stepped out to follow him when a short girl with blonde hair in a plait rushed through the crowd of passengers to meet him. They talked for a moment and he took her coolly by the arm as they hurried out together to the taxi rank.

Finn sprinted across the foyer, vaulting over a suitcase being trailed on wheels. She pulled up sharply by the flower stall, only feet from Railton, as he ordered a cab to Docklands.

Stationed in the Wolsey, Rufus furtively pulled down his baseball cap and watched Finn weaving through a coach queue towards him. He started the engine and revved furiously.

'Oh man – go ahead and say it,' he said as she leapt into the car. The coach pulled up and parked in front of them and fifty elderly women began to haul themselves aboard.

'Brilliant place to park, Rufus,' she said, without looking at him, her hand hard down on the horn.

Privately Maureen was pleased. Pearl was a cut above the usual temps who kept holiday brochures in their in-trays and spent all lunch break on the phone. She was definitely somebody she could engage in conversation.

'Know my theory?' she said quietly as they toured the accounts department. Pearl looked interested.

'It's all down to status. If John can fill the place with a bevy of secretaries and personal assistants it looks dead impressive when the others come for meetings.'

Pearl was wryly enjoying Maureen's vision of office politics. She followed her on the tour of the building, silently cursing the skirt which halved her stride, and the twisted tights which threatened to cut off the blood supply to her left leg. A young man with gelled hair and tartan braces waited by the photocopier and eyed her up and down quite blatantly.

Maureen caught Pearl's expression and rounded on him sharply.

'Excuse me,' she ordered, flicking a switch and opening the

huge spring-loaded machine door against his knee. He limped away down the corridor.

'It's all quite straightforward,' she said heavily as she crouched and pointed at the belly full of ink and paperpaths. 'If the green light flashes "key operator" you come to me, right? I'm the key operator. I'm also the union rep. Understand?' She sniffed in the direction of the disappeared gel and braces.

That afternoon Pearl worked her way discreetly through every unlocked filing cabinet. Wearily she scanned the wads of branch audits and reports. Whatever she was looking for wouldn't be kept here. She needed access to Trevor's personal filing system.

'Mr Railton's here for a meeting first thing Monday morning.' Maureen was at her side, watchful as an umpire. 'Unless, of course, he sends his number two.'

Pearl had plucked a small bunch of keys from Maureen's desk and was picking through them.

'Her name's India, can you imagine that?' said Maureen wistfully. 'I think it might change me if I was called after a country. Old Trev fancies her rotten, he's always phoning her.'

Pearl nonchalantly attempted to open the slim red filing cabinet.

'India? What's her surname then?' The keys didn't fit.

'Macphail, but she's not Irish.' Maureen was vigilant at her shoulder. 'The red ones are always kept locked.'

'But what if I need to find something?'

'You won't.' She was adamant. 'Temps *never* deal with confidentiality.'

Finn fumed as she and Rufus waited at a zebra crossing and watched as Railton's taxi drifted off down towards the river. They had already spent hours watching outside the exclusive Dockside flat into which he and his girlfriend had disappeared. He had emerged alone and now he was slipping out of sight through the rush-hour traffic. The lights changed and Finn rounded the corner. Railton's cab had competely disappeared.

She put her foot down and shot down the road. Suddenly every other vehicle was a taxi. She groaned and irritably flicked off the radio and pulled over. It was a perfect summer's evening. Down below a barge had been converted into a wine bar decked out with bunting and parasols. Rufus was anxiously consulting his watch.

'I know things are really hotting up, Finn, but I gotta split soon.' Finn sighed and scowled at the river. There, walking down the gang plank, self-consciously buttoning his jacket, was Railton.

'Stay here and cover him if he comes out,' Finn ordered, jumping out of the car. Rufus looked torn.

Pearl had decided she'd have to cut some corners. So when Trevor had asked her if she'd like a quick drink she accepted and endured the brief dockside journey in his smoke-filled car. Gripping the wheel until his knuckles whitened, he drove hard at corners and junctions, pulling away like a man pursued. Pearl steadied herself against the dashboard and curiously tapped a small black box studded with switches and a display panel. Trevor glanced at her and lurched into a corner.

'Try it,' he said, 'weather prediction and stress control.'

'How does it work?' She pressed some buttons.

Trevor made a late bid for a car park entrance; a car horn wailed past them. Sighing, he swerved over some gravel and tapped the box with his finger. 'Barometric pressure, not very accurate.'

Pearl saw a wavy green line predicting rain. Suddenly the box erupted with the hiss of electronic machine gun fire. She snatched her hand away.

'That's the stress control.' Trevor's eyes fixed wistfully on a boat on the river. 'Sometimes it's quite effective.'

The pub was quiet and the barge shifted slightly on it moorings on the wash of passing river traffic. Cupping a double whisky in his hands, Trevor calmed and patted Pearl's hand.

'Nice to have a pretty face round the office, Pearl.' He spoke with sincerity. 'A man in my position can do without someone who looks like the back end of a bus.'

Pearl slowly dug her nails in her hand. Trevor relaxed and smiled his melted smile. She nearly forgave him, basically he was harmless. Hopefully she could get him talking.

Trevor insisted on another drink and as he mellowed and

surveyed the river through small windows, Pearl decided the time had arrived to probe Trevor for any hints of expensive habits. He was savouring the faint rocking movement of the bar when he stopped in mid-sentence and stared towards the door.

A bearded man with wispy blond hair was striding towards them. Smiling curiously at Pearl, he slapped Trevor on the shoulder.

'Where's the fire, Trev?' His thin lips curved with amusement.

Mitchell was immediately on his feet and steering the man towards the door. 'Get us a drink, will you, Pearl?' he apologized. The man turned back with a leer, and handed her a twenty pound note. With some frustration, Pearl watched them hurry out on to the deck.

'Of all the pubs, you had to pick one on the water didn't you?' The Geordie accent was unmistakable. Finn had appeared at her side, talking furtively and staring straight ahead.

Pearl nudged her. 'Get out there, Finn, Trevor's having secret conservations with some suspicious bloke and I can hardly go out and join them.' Pearl pointed to where they were standing on the lower deck.

'That's Railton, you prat,' said Finn, slipping off her stool, 'What do you think I'm doing here?'

Pearl kicked the bar. Suspects never looked like their photos. Never.

Rufus clung to the underside of the gang plank, up to his knees in watery black mud. The rope was cutting his fingers but he could vaguely hear the two men sitting almost directly above him and he had a good view of their feet. The podgy one seemed to be shuffling backwards.

Rufus could hardly hear Railton, most of his soft, wheedling voice faded against the river. Only when he stood up and their feet were quite close, did he hear him say, slowly and with an edge, 'Don't you dare start rocking the boat Trev. All right?'

Finn peeled paint off the cabin and watched the two men reflected in the window. It was impossible to get any closer and she could guess that they were having a row. Rufus was nowhere to be seen.

Railton looked back over his shoulder nervously as he walked back up to the gang plank. Finn turned quickly and, hunching instinctively into her jacket, she turned quickly back towards the window and almost bumped into Trevor returning to the bar, his face flushed with anger.

Three pints later Mitchell was indignant. 'Bloody experts,' he moaned, his hand patting Pearl's knee. 'Never there when you need them. The strike's in its third day before he saunters back from Brussels.'

'So why's he so important?' asked Pearl simply.

'Investment. He's good in Europe.' Trev mopped his brow. 'He moves the money around, calls the shots. I'm not in that league anymore. He does the hassling, I do the worrying.'

'But you're the boss, right?'

He nodded thoughtfully. 'But it's a changed world, Pearl. He leant towards her, suddenly sobered. 'Can I tell you something, Pearl?' She nodded but drunken confessions seemed unlikely. Maybe Trevor was a complete innocent. 'I'm a lonely man, Pearl.' He smoothed his sketchy hair pathetically and looked genuinely hurt when she grinned. 'Honestly, my wife's away a lot.'

Pearl slid off her stool and finished her drink. There was only so far she was willing to go with this boss and secretary scenario.

Trevor was staring mistily at the river. 'We've got this villa in Spain, she spends most of her time there these days.'

Pearl sat down again, suddenly interested. 'A villa, Trev?'

He looked embarrassed. 'Breeze blocks and whitewash I should say, more like a double garage with a patio.' He laughed. 'My dad fought in the Spanish Civil War you know, died last year, a union man all his life.'

Pearl seemed to have lost the thread. Trevor was almost tearful, he pawed her arm. 'What would he think to it? Betty and her pals soaking up the sea, sun and sangria half the year.'

'He'd think you must be a rich and successful man.' Pearl squeezed his hand. Trevor had just put himself back on the board.

'And they've squandered every penny the old man left us,' he muttered grimly. 'It's indecent.' She stared at him blankly. Back to square one.

'You're a really nice girl, Pearl.' Trevor fumbled in his pockets. 'Could you possibly remind me where I left my car?'

The chrome-trimmed Cadillac glided along the river towards a landscape of glass and metal. Fitz stared straight ahead, then wrenched himself around in his seat. Glancing back to the road, he slowed down and checked his mirror, steadying it with his hand. He was not mistaken. Holding the car door open and laughing, Pearl was helping a lumpy man into a Ford Sierra.

'Tell me I'm seeing things,' he said to his passenger.

Denzil turned the tape down. 'Nope.' He checked his wing mirror with a sigh.

Fitz rubbed his tight black hair, almost groaning. 'I was sure little Sally might help to concentrate her mind. I thought it was working.'

Denzil was phlegmatic. 'Blew her mind more like it, man. He must be forty if he's a day.'

Fitz stopped the car with a lurch and stared at the water which seemed to boil and lash up the bank.

'Please, I'll drop Sally, talk to my wife, anything. But just bring that girl back into my life,' he pleaded to the river and the sky.

Ten

It was Saturday lunchtime by the time Pearl and Finn arrived at Millie's house and walked through the open front door. The hall was full of groceries and a box of ice cream was collapsing onto the carpet. Finn scooped it up and found Millie on her hands and knees in the kitchen stacking the fridge. She smiled vaguely and rammed the mishapen block into the freezer.

Finn handed her the vegetables scattered on the floor – coloured peppers and a bundle of asparagus.

'Grab yourself a glass of wine.' Millie splashed black grapes under the tap and tore off a small bunch for Finn, dropping them into her hand.

'Laura's coming tomorrow.' she explained. Chewing grapes and putting the pips on to Millie's white porcelain plate Finn felt a sense of loss.

Pearl wearily dumped a sheaf of photocopies on to Millie's glass table. She held out no real hope of clues from any of the correspondence or invoices.

'I'll get Krish to comb through his lot on Monday,' said Millie, flicking on the television and killing the sound. 'What else have you got?'

Finn frowned. 'I spent all day yesterday following Railton.' She was going to make it clear how complicated that had been.

'And he turned up to meet Mitchell,' interrupted Pearl. 'But I can't believe Trev's our embezzler. He's just not capable.'

'You're just sorry for him because he's a drunk.' Finn was harsh, robbed of the only worthwhile piece of news she had. 'That doesn't mean he's not thieving.'

'He could be just a pawn?' suggested Millie, slightly distracted by flickering pictures on the lunchtime news. 'Perhaps Railton's pulling the strings?'

Pearl looked unconvinced. 'But robbing the till's quite crude, isn't it? It was bound to be discovered. Wouldn't an operator like Railton have covered his tracks more cleverly?'

'What *is* his game then?' demanded Finn. 'They seemed to be having some sort of heavy row.'

Pearl remembered Mitchell's helpless face. 'Maybe Railton's know-how kept Trev in his job, and he's been charging a commission for his services. Could be why Trev was petrified to make a move until he got back from his trip.'

Finn was decisive. 'We need to start crossing some people off the list. We'd better get some gen on this Railton character.'

Pearl nodded. 'We'll go and see his assistant at his office on Monday morning when he's due for a meeting with Trev.'

Millie suddenly turned up the volume. On screen was an angry debate between John Foxton and Nigel Pearson. She sat down on the floor sipping her wine as if she had been waiting for the item. Pearl noticed a pile of newspapers on the floor; most of them had the dispute on the front page with pictures of Foxton speaking at the plant. Millie had been buying at least four papers a day.

The camera closed in on Pearson sitting confidently, fingertips tensed together like a priest. Foxton raised his voice insistently and the picture panned round to catch him dragging his hand through his hair and interrupting the interviewer. 'We're being misrepresented. Our union is not against change, we're not against modernisation. It's just not true.' He stared at Pearson, breathing hard.

'Then why won't your union accept the need for modernisation?' Pearson's inclined head suggested fatherly irritation. 'If British car manufacturers are going to compete successfully in a world market, there will have to be some sacrifice.'

The interviewer, a dark-haired, bobbed woman with a bland smile went to preface Foxton's reply with a question, but he swept past her, glaring into the face of management.

'I presume you'll be taking a cut in salary yourself, will you, Nigel? Come on, let's tell it like it is. You're not a British car manufacturer anymore, you're a multinational. Profit comes before Britain in your calculations. Rationalisation doesn't mean a plant full of new technology. It means two thousand men on the scrap heap.' Foxton moved his hands expansively as if to hold the moment. 'You say you want to negotiate, Nigel; let's fix the time here and now.'

The camera swerved past Pearson looking tense and petulant, before the presenter filled the screen with her awkward conclusions, the signature tune starting almost before she had finished.

'Good stuff.' Finn liked Foxton's fire.

'Yep.' Millie switched off the television and Pearl watched her curiously. 'Do you mind if I ask you something personal?' Millie shrugged and passed her more wine. 'He's not just another client to you, is he?'

Millie rubbed a mark on the carpet. 'It was a long time ago.' She looked straight at them. 'And it's not relevant now.'

Pearl looked uncomfortable. 'It is easier to do the job if we know where you stand with him, that's all.'

Millie poured the remainder of the wine into her glass, catching the last drop, for a wish, her mother used to tell her. 'OK. I'll do a deal. When *I* know where I stand with him I'll let you know, all right?'

Monday morning saw Finn and Pearl parked outside Kevin Railton's office block staring moodily through the dirty windscreen. The car reeked of river mud and stagnant water. Rufus' jacket still lay in a muddy pool on the back seat.

'You don't think he's drowned, do you?' said Pearl.

'No chance,' Finn was scornful. 'He must have fallen in the river, used the car as a changing room and scarpered.'

Pearl was confused, 'How do you know that?'

'Deduction.' Finn sniffed. 'And the tide was out, and he had an appointment with Fitz. He may be your brother but he's a dead loss as a detective.'

Pearl watched the main entrance to the building. She planned to divert the commissionaire so that Finn, in her blue overalls and carrying a bucket, could slip unnoticed through the reception area.

'Do you reckon Millie's having it off with Foxton then?' Finn wasn't sure she could cope with her boss suddenly being so vulnerable.

Pearl grinned. 'Such an elegant turn of phrase.'

'Well, why else would Millie care so much about some rip-off in a union?'

'Because it's important if someone's trying to start a scandal so that Foxton and all he stands for will be discredited. I agree with her.' The car windows were steaming up.

Finn gathered her bucket and scrubbing brush and rolled up the enormous sleeves of her uniform. 'I've never really seen the point of unions myself.'

Pearl grinned. 'You've never really seen the point of having a job though, have you?'

Pearl straightened her tailored jacket and marched into the marbled reception area. Maintaining a safe distance across the car park and watching her through the thick smoked glass windows, Finn saw her chatting with the commissionaire.

Pearl had shown him the photos of Rufus and her mother from her wallet, and was signing the visitors' book, when the commissionaire, gloves folded on his shoulder, leant past her and shouted angrily.

Finn froze in panic by the open lift doors and was about to bolt back to the entrance when he gestured sternly for her to use the stairs and sat back down wearily.

'Domestics used to have some sense of hierarchy,' he remarked heavily. Pearl agreed, and with her heart pounding, pinned on the identity pass.

India MacPhail was petite but muscular, with shoulders like a swimmer. She looked at Pearl suspiciously. Her office was blocked into corners containing monitors and keyboards. A fax machine scratched intermittently behind a perfect bunch of golden freesias in a jamjar.

'John Foxton phoned,' she began briskly. 'He explained you want the familiarisation routine. Is Maureen OK?'

Pearl nodded, 'This was her idea. Said I'd work better for Mr Foxton if I know exactly what's going on, that sort of thing.'

'Or just do it all for him?' smiled India. 'Maureen's quite an anarchist on the quiet.' She handed Pearl a thick file.

'If you read this you'll get a good general briefing on our investment strategies for union funds, and I'll give you a quick run-down on Mr Railton's handling of NUAVE if you want.'

Pearl opened the file. India's heavy perfume drifted round the room. She seemed to think all this was perfectly routine.

'So where do you fit in?' Pearl had to gauge how important Railton's assistant really was.

'I set up most of the transactions.' She was dismissive. 'It's quite usual. I do background research on prospective buying and selling, chart the market and profile the financial climate. Railton's at the sharp end doing the deals and meeting the clients. And taking all the credit of course.'

Pearl picked up her tone. India noticed and smiled ruefully. 'Don't you like him?' Pearl risked it innocently. It was also important to establish how much she could trust her.

India shrugged. 'He's a real shit if you really want my opinion.'

She seemed to have surprised herself and went to get the coffee, starting a small retraction. 'He's welcome to the limelight. It gets pretty vicious at times.'

Flicking through the file, Pearl found press cuttings about a recently discovered set of Picasso sketches sold in New York for over a million pounds.

'The union buys paintings?' Pearl looked up in surprise. 'Do the members realise Trevor's investing in Old Masters?'

India shrugged. 'Who knows anything? Stocks and shares, art, buildings; it's all money in the end. We're established in this field because it can bring very high returns. The union hired us for a routine problem a while back and we persuaded Mr Mitchell to take on a more adventurous portfolio.'

'You mean it's risky – the union could lose money?'

India shrugged. 'It's all risky. Look at the stock market – everyone got caught last year. Art can be a little unreliable but it's my speciality. Kevin feeds me good contacts. The pension fund has done very well out of it. So far.'

Her final remarks sounded a defensive note. Pearl suddenly wondered how much of her apparent openness was selective.

'What are these figures?' Pearl ran her finger along monthly debits against individual paintings. 'Looks like hire-purchase.'

'Insurance. It's quite phenomenal.' India glanced at her watch. 'I mean you can't just hang a Van Gogh in the typing pool, can you?'

Pearl suppressed a smile. She didn't imagine that Trevor appreciated the condundrum of making a fortune by keeping paintings in cupboards.

'I wonder if I could have a complete set of figures for a painting you've bought and sold so I can see how it all works?'

Pearl smiled eagerly but India frowned.

'I think Mr Railton would have to oversee that,' she said. 'It can be rather sensitive information.'

Pearl was suddenly very aware that India, sharp and perceptive, could simply pick up the phone and check on her authorisation. But she didn't. Unperturbed she gave a little gesture dismissing protocol and went straight to a computer terminal, accessed a file, and started to copy it.

'This floppy disc will give you a detailed breakdown of art account figures direct from Mr Railton's database. Perhaps you'd wipe it when you've read it?

Pearl curbed her instinct to hurry away clutching the disc. 'Do you mind me asking?' India turned, Pearl smiled. 'We were wondering . . . about your name?'

'Oh, that.' She looked relieved. 'It's from the company's telex code. It sort of stuck.'

Pearl followed her down the corridor and stepped into the lift with her. They descended in silence as if their scene were over. India got out after a couple of floors, frowning as the cleaner pushed in past her. She left behind a strong draught of freesias. As soon as the doors closed, a disgruntled Finn struggled out of her overalls.

'I spent the whole morning being trained by a supervisor to clean Railton's office. She never took her eyes off me.' She smelt strongly of lavender polish.

'No chance to snoop around then?' Pearl was disappointed.

Finn pulled a thick a wad of paper from her T-shirt and flicked through it triumphantly. It was a photocopy of the entire contents of Railton's desk diary.

'I don't think India was hiding anything,' Pearl explained as they hurried across the car park. She waved the disc. 'And this should tell us where the figures get massaged. Here or back at the union.'

Finn suddenly stopped dead. 'Hang on. *That* was India in the lift?'

Pearl nodded. Finn had just placed her.

'She met Railton yesterday at the airport and then they went back to her flat for a smoochy lunch. For several hours.' she added.

Eleven

Finn leant heavily against the red filing cabinet and edged a thread of fine wire into the lock. It was after ten o'clock that evening and she and Pearl had made their way through the empty corridors of the union building for a closer investigation of the offices. The lock gave a soft click and after turning forty-five degrees allowed the drawer to slide open.

'Haven't lost your touch, then.' Pearl grinned as she accessed the file on Maureen's computer. The screen filled with figures. If you find anything interesting in there, the photocopier's next door in the reception area.'

The documentation scrolled through a financial year: poetic titles, famous names and rows of noughts. Pearl rapidly cross-checked the figures with the bank accounts and Trevor's official version. All the figures from Railton's department tallied with the bank's. Trevor's sheets looked like a lonely fiction. He fooled me completely, thought Pearl. I even bought the villa story.

Finn waited for the photocopier to warm up. The deserted building creaked, and somewhere down the corridor a phone rang, and stopped. An anxious wife looking for a husband leading another life. She was positioning a list of European removal firms on the glass when she heard a chair creak in the next room, Mitchell's office. Light was leaking around the edges of the closed door. Holding her breath she inched it open. An elegant woman with glasses on a chain swung round, stared at the figure in the leather jacket and screamed.

Pearl was more than a little shocked to see Maureen installed at Trevor's desk glaring at Finn. How were they going to explain themselves to someone they couldn't trust?

Maureen tucked her hair behind her ears. 'I'm not stupid. I

know exactly who you are.' She looked quite menacing, almost desperate, thought Finn edgily. Pearl glanced at her partner and then back at their new suspect. Maureen pointed angrily at Pearl. 'I spotted you on your first day. You're journalists digging for dirt and despicable anti-union stories, aren't you?'

Pearl decided to see what the truth might do. 'We're private detectives working for Foxton.'

Maureen looked disappointed and she sank back into her chair. 'That's what I'm doing. On a purely amateur basis of course.' She pointed at Trevor's electronic organiser on the desk. 'Have a look at this, I sneaked it out of his briefcase, I've been at it for hours.'

Maureen had printed out most of the contents, addresses, four years of diary appointments, ferry timetables. 'He's mad about gadgets.' Her commentary was comprehensive. 'I reckon if he's got anything to hide, he'd file it in here.'

Finn looked quizzical. 'You reckon he's behind the embezzlement then?'

Maureen looked grieved. 'It's Trevor all right. How else do you think he runs his hacienda and a sizeable drink problem?'

Finn looked at Pearl triumphantly.

Maureen was tapping away on the organiser again. 'The thing's got a locked file and we can't get into it without his word key. Any ideas? I thought it would be really predictable.'

'Double whisky?' Pearl wasn't hopeful.

'I've tried that already.' Maureen stared round the office like a child playing a game, trying out possible pass words under her breath.

Finn wandered around the office and examined a photo of Trevor on the beach with his wife. She grimaced and eased the newspaper off a large parcel next to the desk. Inside was an elaborate sign made from lacquered wood and wrought iron.

'Who's Daphne?' she asked.

Maureen was scribbling a list. 'His wife.' She walked over and examined the sign irritably. 'Isn't that typical, after all that moaning, he goes and calls the villa after her.'

Pearl quickly tapped the six letters into the organiser and watched the red 'S' flash on and off as the file was accessed. 'Maureen, how would you like to extend us the use of your services for a very small fee?' She observed the whirring electronic memory of Trevor's bank statements.

Maureen stared with admiration at the new data and nodded. 'I started yesterday, remember.'

Trevor's entire financial statement scrolled through the organiser display.

'How do we know we can we trust this stuff?' said Finn uneasily.

'What's the point of keeping a secret file full of duff figures?' Pearl switched off the display panel thoughtfully. 'But it looks like Trev's been been collecting peanuts. No more than a few measly grand every few months.'

Maureen snapped her glasses into their case and sighed. 'Thank God, I was wrong.'

'But who's got the rest?' Finn suddenly felt very tired.

Pearl picked up the organiser and they followed her back into Maureen's office, where she re-accessed the art file.

'India's given us a clean bill of health for Railton, a man she says she hates, but in reality beds at lunchtime.'

'She may have very good reasons for concealing her private life from you.' Maureen looked at her defensively. 'But that doesn't mean she's involved in all this.'

'She could be running the whole thing.' Pearl glanced at Finn.

'She's certainly capable of it.'

Maureen stared intently at the figures on the screen and a fiery flush crept up her neck. She extracted the disc and examined it carefully. 'This is *India's* software, not the central system. So this disc orginates from *her* database, not Railton's.' She hesitated and took another, wider disc from her drawer. 'When Railton sends reports and account sheets his secretary uses the mainframe – a different system. I have to get them reformatted. But India's gear is compatible with ours.'

'So these aren't Railton's figures at all?' Pearl felt the pieces slipping into place. 'She's given us her sanitised version to throw us off the track.'

'I can hardly believe it,' said Maureen unhappily. 'But it's possible she's given you this version to fool you.'

Twelve

It was almost light by the time they reached the scruffy car park outside the council flats. An opaque moon hung over a wasteland where a small bonfire smouldered. Finn turned off the engine, disturbing a swirl of seagulls.

Finn caught her breath and bit back something she couldn't find the words for. There was something about this light – the shiver before the dawn which caught her, reminded her of those first mornings after she'd run away. Sleeping rough; waking near strangers; drifting between bridges and meals.

Pearl caught a look she didn't understand and decided not to intrude. They walked towards the tower block.

Their flat had been systematically turned over. The door was swinging open, and where the stairs dropped down to the sitting room, clothes were strewn over every step. Drawers gaped, books, records and even the meagre contents of the fridge were scattered all over the floor. Pearl snatched up a small ribboned bundle of letters lying with the dumped contents of a drawer and kicked open the bathroom door. Finn sat at the top of the stairs and simply stared, eyes wide with disbelief.

Throwing herself down on the sofa Pearl fingered the letters numbly. She'd walked into dozens of rooms like this, picked over people's lives torn out of cupboards, and looked for the reasons. Now she felt sick and angry.

Gingerly, Finn sat beside her. 'Who do you think?'

'I'd recognise that perfume anywhere.' Pearl was coming back together. 'Whatever she's up to, she's getting serious.'

Finn was suddenly aware of the cloying scent of freesia.

The next morning the Bond Street auction room was busy with

the preliminary viewing of paintings and small pieces of statuary. Pearl and Finn separated and started to comb through the crowd. Clutching a catalogue, Finn made her way through waves of buyers staring intently at small watercolours and cast bronze birds and animals. Visibly off-balance in these surroundings, she searched for India. She suddenly spotted her talking intensely to a young man in a blazer and spotted cravat who was working on a pocket calculator and looked under pressure. He made quick, agitated movements with his fingers and then walked briskly along a line of large paintings which featured shoals of luminous fish glowing in darkening skies.

Finn had positioned herself close to the end of the row. India solemnly considered the final painting and nodded briefly before diving back towards the auctioneer. The young man scribbled notes, bobbing in her wake.

Bidding had started by the time Finn caught up with Pearl. They watched the sale start with India in crisp combat with the spotted cravat, making tiny movements with her catalogue. Within less than a minute a luminous pike achieved three thousand pounds and belonged to the young man. The entire shoal seemed to be following.

The final fish was gold and silver and flew above water with fins like wings. India bid earnestly, moving both hands rapidly, and was beaten. She had lost the lot.

Finn had been watching her closely and was puzzled to see her shoot a brief indifferent glance at her opponent as she closed her catalogue and disappeared into the crowd. They pushed after her and watched her feed a card into a wallphone and start dialing. When she turned she saw they had covered both exit doors. Her face contracted and she turned back to dial another number.

Finn instinctively moved up behind her and heard the end of her instructions, her hand nervously touching her hair, caught in a knot like a charm.

'Yes, Door B, thank you. Two girls, outbidded, they've been hassling me, picking some sort of fight.'

Pearl cut her off unceremoniously. 'What the hell are you playing at?'

India suddenly looked scared and pushed past them both. 'I'm not playing at all.' Her voice wavered. 'You've had one warning already.'

She turned and pointed. Three uniformed security men grabbed the two girls roughly, and dragged them the length of a warehouse where men were packing priceless porcelain and pitched them out on to the street.

Two plate glass doors melted back like water and John Foxton followed Millie out of the sunlight into the shadows of a small Italian restaurant. They sat down at a table surrounded by small screens which were covered with postcards and positioned like windbreaks.

The waiter lit their candle with a delicate movement, spreading intimacy like linen, and after positioning glasses discreetly, he left them.

Millie felt uncomfortable. She had accepted the invitation for a working lunch but hadn't intended this. They had not spoken since the office briefing on Friday – which she had kept deliberately contained, down to the detail of getting Krish to call her to the phone as soon as she wanted the meeting to finish. She had bid him the briefest of goodbyes, already holding another client's problems to her ear.

The union had developed into an extensive project for the practice as she and Krish had prepared strategies to defend the past financial tactics of NUAVE. Already they had the best possible defence prepared against the event of a sudden public disclosure. Foxton shrewdly prepared for every eventuality. So typical of him. She watched him pour her wine, remembering the way he had plotted their meetings. Already separated from his wife, his lies had been minimal, whereas Millie had embarked on a mass of fictions with Roger, always on the edge of discovery. She ran her finger down the menu and ruefully remembered that she had suspected his business might have been an excuse for renewed intimacy.

'The old days.' Foxton touched his glass against hers. 'We had some good times, didn't we?' She drank reluctantly, almost angrily, feeling relegated to some dispensable section of his life.

Snapping bread sticks, she recovered and waited for the briefing to begin.

They ordered. Foxton put his hand over Millie's and held it there. He cleared his throat and looked at her intently as if trying to read her response.

'I've really missed you,' he told her simply.

Millie felt her heart lurch. Like losing her footing. It had been so long since she had let that feeling in. She looked up suddenly and betrayed herself. It was possible, if she wished it, to gather up distance and time and make a circle. Without thinking she pulled his hand towards her.

He looked uncertain and offered her bread. The meal arrived, the waiter rained pepper and parmesan and brief suggestive smiles. Wiping his mouth with a white napkin, Foxton looked at her seriously. Millie was overwhelmed with the memory of having loved him.

He paused as if waiting for courage.

'I think perhaps we should call the girls off, Millie. I'm sorry, I've been trying to think how to talk to you about it. I've been a bit of fool and, well, you're the last person I'd . . .'

Picking individual grains of salt from the table cloth, Millie felt a hot pulse like pain.

Steam was rising from his spaghetti like cloud across his face.

'You see, I had a long talk with Trevor this morning.'

'You mean you *told* him?'

'No.'

Millie's relief was for Pearl and Finn.

Foxton looked over. 'I pushed him hard, well obliquely, you know, about the missing money. He's explained, Mil, it's a temporary hitch and . . .' He smiled and put his hand back on hers. 'I'm not stupid and I can see there's been a balls-up somewhere, but nothing more. He says he can handle it. Trevor's got – integrity.' He said the word like a secret and shrugged. 'As long as he can get himself out of it, I'll be satisfied.'

He smoothed his hair and pushed his chair out as if the distance would help. 'He'd confess if we were in real trouble, I'm sure. If I don't give him a chance . . .'

Millie folded her napkin carefully and leant over the table. For a moment he moved slightly nearer, but her tone was icy.

'You've hired detectives to find out the truth, John, and that's what they're doing. Make your judgments, however bizarre, after that. Trevor may well *need* that truth to get him out of whatever he's in, guilty, half guilty or bloody stupid. And your friend's precious dignity apart, you need your money back, not vague promises. Whose integrity are you fighting for exactly?'

Her words bruised him and locked in skilfully to all he'd said. It was a lawyers' logic but the anger was hers and she drew on it liberally.

Foxton was subdued; he nodded. He didn't notice a small man in a donkey jacket push into the restaurant. Millie was about to leave but hesitated as she watched the odd figure approaching, knocking into waiters. John looked up suddenly as he arrived at their table. Suddenly the man smashed his fist down on the cloth, knocking Millie's glass to the floor. It shattered on the bricks and she felt the wine splash her legs.

'You would be here, wouldn't you, John?' The man glared, his wiry black hair against the light giving him a jagged look. Foxton was on his feet, then he slowed, vaguely recognising the man, noticing the familiar blue overall under the jacket.

'Fancy lunches, speeches on the telly . . .' The man was shaking. Millie smelt drink: he was a blur of grief and wild movement.

'They say they'll have to close the plant altogether if we lose.' He slammed a handbill on to the table so the candle guttered a pool of wax.

'What's the point of fighting? We'll lose out and get no redundancy.' He paused, almost gasping for breath. 'Have you thought about that, John?'

Foxton heard his own name like a curse. The man took one last stare at them and as he turned away he caught on the table cloth. The remaining glass rolled in a slow curve across the cloth fell and shattered.

He swung back, his face doughy with despair. 'Sorry.'

Then he lumbered away through the door. No waiter attempted to stop him.

Millie swallowed and picked up the handbill. It was from the management, detailing a list of accusations against union activity and explaining how a new age of progress was threatened by working-class mythology.

Angrily she made John read the harsh heading. 'YOUR LEADERS MAKE PROMISES WHILE YOU DO WITHOUT.'

'Don't you start on me, please,' he said quietly, staring at the accusing stain of wine.

'I was about to stop completely,' she said, 'but that man's just changed my mind.' She held the leaflet. 'You've got a strong case for defamation here so we'll need to get proof of management distribution. But forget softly, softly, John, until we've got the full facts. If you can't pay that man his strike money . . .'

She looked towards the door as if he might still be standing there.

'. . . I'd never live with myself.' He said the words as if he were used to sharing his sentences with her. He looked up at her gratefully. 'I think it's about time we talked properly, you and I.'

Millie shook her head. 'Let's just forget the old time stuff, John. I get the distinct impression that as priorities go, "we" are not even on your agenda.' She shrugged. 'Be honest about that for once at least.'

As Millie walked down the pavement she was aware of keeping her steps regular and slow. She had torn herself away from him and was superstitious about the danger of looking back.

She nursed a loss which had no logic.

Thirteen

Finn drove them swiftly away from the auction rooms through the concrete and glass landscape of Dockland.

India's flat was on the top floor of an old bonded warehouse on the edge of the river. The harsh brick frontage hugged apartments with wide windows, all double glazed and secure as banks.

Finn carefully selected tools from her bag and got out of the car. She and Pearl hurried to the door as a young woman punched in numbers while three small twitching dogs braided their leads around her feet.

Pearl smiled as she quickly followed her through the door. 'India MacPhail.' She nodded reassuringly at India's name on the inner listing. 'She always says it's like coming home to a wall safe.' The young woman smiled faintly and the dogs' yelps ricocheted around the brickwork.

'You never seem to meet anyone,' she said, distantly trawling back the dogs. 'Not even in the lift.'

Pearl and Finn hurried up the stairs set into a deep glass well next to the lift shaft. They heard the high-pitched yelps glide past in their cage and found India's door. It was solid steel. Finn put her tool bag down carefully. 'Trust India to live inside a metal box.' Pearl felt a flicker of panic. India had demonstrated she had something to hide but they still had nothing definite. Another concentric circle. They were in danger of floundering, of falling. Footsteps clanked on the stairs and impulsively Pearl pushed down the door handle. The metal swung open noiselessly as the footsteps faded through a door on the floor below.

They closed the door behind them and stood in a dark hallway slashed with light from venetian blinds covering wide windows.

Dappled with blues and greys, the blinds shuddered continuously like water.

Finn looked at Pearl and shrugged. The apartment was totally silent apart from the muffled throb of boats on the river. Finn walked down into the main room with its polished boards. On a glass table, almost suspended in the gloom, was a bunch of drooping tulips with flurorescent blue petals. She switched them on.

Pearl was pulling on thin cotton gloves. 'We'll give it a quick once over and get out.'

'Better find the fire escape.' Finn tugged back thick drapes from a door fitted with metal rods. As she kicked the last bar loose, the door opened and the afternoon sun blazed through the gap. From the shadows came the sound of someone clicking their tongue with disapproval. They each swung round to a laugh and a dry throat-clearing, as though someone were about to speak.

Not waiting to hear more, Finn grabbed Pearl's arm and threw herself at a battery of light switches behind a huge sofa. The apartment whirred like a machine as the mechanised blinds opened their slats and thin metal hawsers resonated and clicked into place. Sunlight flooded in but the room, all wood and skeletal furniture, was as empty as ever.

'Who's there?' Finn heard her voice, unfamiliar with fear.

A large grey and blue parrot cocked his head in their direction and cleared his throat self-consciously. Sitting on a wooden branch planted in tank of sand, he suddenly gave a shriek and flapped clipped wings.

Pearl felt her heart slow with relief and she stood up uncertainly. Finn grinned ruefully and headed for the back of the flat.

'Let's get this over with.' She glared at the parrot moodily. 'Don't push it. You're only here because you match the blinds.' He fidgeted sideways and laughed.

The room was almost bare, apart from rows of paintings in beautiful wooden frames ranged along every wall. The furniture seemed to be made from reclaimed materials, with unsettling results. Pearl ran her finger over thick rope handles on crates used for seating. A great scooped block of wood serving as a table had been a butcher's slab, from Smithfield probably. The bevelled, varnished wood surface was marbled with blood. There was no comfort anywhere.

The parrot chortled and clinked, minute links of a silvery chain holding him to his branch.

The pictures were puzzling. Sequences of sketches and water-colours hung in regimented rows like a geometric exercise. Pearl peered at sepia riverscapes, slowly deciphering the artist's signature. They seemed to be Renoirs. Further down, a blue pencilled Picasso nude hugged herself, and a grainy etched Jacob wrestled with a Chagal angel, his muscles knotted hopelessly against the heat of folded wings. Pearl ran her finger along an inlaid walnut frame. It was like wandering into the Tate.

So this was it. India was salting away art like pemmican. Finn went through the last door and bad-temperedly looked round a high bedroom lined with hessian. Rough sailcloth hung on booms across the windows and flapped with the draught from the door.

There was something she resented about this woman, her colour-coded parrot and her expensive jumble of ideas. She grudgingly admired a mesh of knotted rigging above the bed. Her own room at Pearl's had a square of window covered by a paper blind which boiled with light in the morning and smoked with frost in the winter. It was something she loved privately, and she glared at India's showy display. Her auntie had had a room full of souvenirs made from shells. Every seaside resort had yielded ashtrays, vases, plates and encrusted bottle-lamps. She remembered a small wooden weather house driven by a strip of seaweed, and a pebble which looked like a farm egg. When the police had caught up with Finn that distant morning, soaked through and terrified, they'd taken her back to that room. The inspector had grinned as he picked up a bottled snow storm with his stubby red hands. Soon they were all laughing, carelessly picking things up, making a mockery. Finn shuddered remembering her auntie's face, pinched with shame. It was all part of the way Finn had conspired to hurt her.

She wrenched the sail away from the window. So what made the difference between a sail and a shell, the nod and the sneer? Only purchasing power. She wanted India to be as guilty as hell.

Laid out like a body across the coverlet on the bed was a man's suit. A selection of silk ties laid against one lapel. Two pastel sweaters were stacked near a pile of striped shirts still in stiff cellophane packets. On top of these lay a silver hip flask with initials engraved on the side. Finn ran her finger over the etched letters: KR. In the top pocket of the suit was an envelope addressed in computer script, to India. From KR presumably. Kevin Railton.

She was ripping open the envelope when she heard the parrot shrieking maniacally. There was something unhinging in its cry which sent Finn slithering along the polished boards and crouching back at the doorway.

At first she couldn't see anything in the bright sunlight. The parrot had quietened and now sat curiously cocking its head towards the fire escape. Finn was about to creep forward when she saw Pearl walk into the light.

Pearl contemptuously dropped her hands and glared. India inched forwards from the hallway, her hand holding the shape of a gun underneath her shawl. Finn moistened her lips; if she moved quickly she could probably reach India before she turned. She calculated how she could bring her down with a sliding tackle, scudding along the polished wood.

But Pearl's gesture had made the woman angry, she pointed aggressively and motioned Pearl nearer the window, further away from Finn.

'Where's your partner? Call her.'

Pearl was deliberately low key. 'She's not here.' She smiled knowingly. 'She's fully occupied following your boyfriend.'

India motioned Pearl towards a chair.

'You've over-stepped the mark this time. I could call the police right now and that would blow things right out into the open, wouldn't it?'

'Oh yes,' said Pearl evenly. 'It certainly would.'

'Listen to me.' Unaccountably India's tone became less threatening. 'I'm telling you for your own good to get off whatever case you think you're on. Tell the union they'd better forget it.'

'I think they'd be very reluctant to forget three million pounds,

India.' There was a certain obtuse relief to see a suspect confirming suspicions so graphically after all the shadowplay. Pearl felt almost relaxed.

India gave a sudden laugh. 'You think I've got it?' Pearl faltered slightly, it hadn't occurred to her that she would bother with the pretence of innocence.

'You and Railton. And you've been feeding Trevor crumbs from the table.'

In her agitation India let the shawl slip and Pearl saw she was clutching a clasp purse. Niggled by the deception, Pearl pressed on. 'Come off it, this place is piled high with paintings.'

India laughed again and sat down. 'They're just prints, Pearl – reproductions, all of them. They're the best – but worthless. My collection only contains sketches and lithographs, so a print provides an almost indistinguishable replica. I wouldn't have an original in the place. Buying pictures is nothing but materialistic lust, the desire to own. It's loathsome; I despise it.'

Incredulously Pearl took a painting off the wall. 'So you wouldn't mind if I tore this one up, just as an academic excercise?'

India looked startled and nervously took it away from her.

'What's the problem? I'll buy you another one.'

'The frames *are* worth something.' Her hands trembled as she loosened the picture. 'I thought it was a nice irony to invest in carpentry.' She smiled distractedly as she slid out the picture of the angel wrestling and flipped it over. Stamped on the back was the name and address of an art shop in Venice.

'And I suppose you're going to tell me that you're entirely innocent as well?' Pearl was scathing.

'Not that you would care either way about that.' India turned on her aggressively, her face draining of colour. 'You've been hired to frame me and Kevin. He said the union would try something like this. Trevor's been helping himself and that's embarrassing, especially now. So you've been told to get it pinned on us, right?'

'Is this what Railton's told you?' Pearl was thinking fast, another circle was emerging with bewildering speed.

'He should know.' India abandoned caution. 'Trevor's been almost hysterical since they've had to get the strike money flowing. He's trying to force Kevin to help him cover up what's happened.'

Something wasn't making complete sense. Pearl stood up and looked around the room, searching for the clue.

'That disc you fed me – the art account figures – who compiled it? she asked.

'Kevin. He gives me the basic data and I do the presentations for the clients.' India remembered something triumphantly. 'In fact that's exactly how I detected that Trevor had been creaming off large sums every month.'

'So you reported it to Railton?' India nodded. 'But *he* gave you the data in the first place – so he must have wanted you to find it.'

'No.' India was insistent. 'It happens to be the truth.'

'So why turn our flat over?' Pearl was aware that Railton's assistant was giving a convincing performance.

India looked surprised, then she shrugged. 'Survival. It's not just Kevin's career on the line here, you know.' She shook her head. 'I thought I could find out what you were doing.'

'Did Railton put you up to this?' Pearl gave a shiver as she placed her hand on a marble table, cool as a fish.

India walked over to the window. 'No. He doesn't know about you. He'd probably blame me for giving you too much information.' She turned, her eyes were remembering something from the past. 'He might well over-react.' There was something close to terror in her voice.

'He sounds too dangerous to be innocent.'

India recovered herself angrily.

'How the hell did you break in anyway?'

'I didn't. Didn't you realise the flat was left unlocked?'

India looked genuinely distressed. She turned her back on her and rubbed the windowpane as if clearing her view to the sky. Pearl didn't give her time to think. 'Presumably you believe Railton's story because you're having an affair?'

India gave a hopeless laugh and in the corner the parrot echoed it. 'Good theory, but as I told you before we don't even like each other.'

'So why did he bother to write you a leaving note?' Finn

stepped forward and dispassionately handed her the opened envelope.

India maintained utter composure as she read the sheet of perforated paper. Then she walked slowly to her bedroom. They found her lying on the bed amongst the beautiful clothes, unshamedly weeping.

'These were presents.' She was touching them as if he were still wearing them. Pearl sat down next to her, something registered too painfully to withold compassion.

India turned her tear-stained face to Pearl. 'It was only a half-lie I told you.' She stopped crying abruptly. 'He never really loved me, not the way I thought I did him.' She looked down at the sheet of paper screwed it up bitterly. 'Couldn't even be bothered to hand write it. Probably got this on file.' Pearl held her arm as if keeping her head above the water. 'So, you see I meant that part, he's always has been a bit of a bastard, but it didn't stop me caring.'

'You can't trust him, India.' Pearl said it softly. 'Not him, nor his figures, nor his story.'

India nodded miserably. 'No. But that makes me even more certain. Don't you see? I know categorically that he hasn't got that money. I've had my own suspicions and this morning I went right through his private records. He's absolutely clean.'

Fourteen

John Foxton spent two hours after his lunch with Millie going through correspondence in his office. Letter after letter from different branches all over the country offered advice and support. A five pound note folded into a perfect square fell out of one envelope: a pensioner had sent his drinking money for the week. They would all have to be answered. He stared blankly at the wall.

His head ached with a small conversation which had probably lasted no more than three minutes. He had completely misjudged a situation he had been advancing with the utmost care. Millie's hurt had been so palpable that as he went back over it, he moaned softly, his head in his hands. He had wanted to explain, properly; let her help him through his confusion. Reaching for the phone he struggled to think of what he might gracefully say. As he dialed, he imagined Millie instructing her assistant to say she was busy with a client. Replacing the receiver he called Maureen's name into the intercom.

She appeared a few minutes later, reading through notes on her pad and looking up impatiently over her spectacles.

'Dictation, if you would, Maureen.' He picked up the first letter wearily.

'Just a suggestion, 'she looked at him briskly, 'but do you have any objection to using the dictaphone this afternoon?' She placed the slim black recorder on his desk.

'Why?' Foxton was exasperated. He wanted the company, her prompting when he faltered and her unerring sense of tone. 'Is this going to become a permanent thing?'

'Only when I'm busy.' Maureen dispensed an instruction manual and spare batteries and stacked a pile of mini tapes on the desk. 'And you'll be abroad more now of course.' She seemed rather preoccupied.

'What's so urgent?'

'An important enquiry for Mrs Millington.' Her look was confidential. 'Should have it cracked soon.'

The reference to Millie had startled him enough to let Maureen go without further questions. He had started to write her an oblique letter of apology when the phone rang on the direct line. He grabbed it hopefully.

'John? Nigel – Pearson.' His clipped voice smiled, the Christian names a warning. Foxton tightened the phone against his ear.

'Been thinking, might be helpful if you and I met informally. Completely off the record of course.'

'Would there be any point?' Foxton held back.

Pearson sounded weary. 'Just a thought. I'd rather hoped we could save a lot of . . . unnecessary carnage.'

Foxton was baffled, thinking fast. If there were some opportunity to avoid the deadlock, it was his duty to try it. There would be nothing lost if he were careful.

'Just you and me, Pearson?'

'Absolutely. Let's make it neutral territory. There's a club I go to in South Ken.' Foxton wrote down the address and calculated the nearest tube. He felt nothing but distrust.

The late afternoon sun was fierce on his face as Foxton turned into a small mews stranded on the edge of a demolition site. He looked along the brass numbers, past the troughs of geraniums and gloss front doors. Searching for thirty-seven he realised that all the odd numbers were missing. Angrily he stared down the street, oddly sensing he had walked straight into some sort of humiliation. A small hovering man with a cough like a bark looked up from a new-stand, and seeing Foxton, turned quickly and shuffled away.

Foxton was convinced he was being followed. Looking back he noticed the man had reappeared and was placidly filling the stand, his back firmly turned. Foxton caught his breath and cautioned himself. He was getting jumpy and Millie had been right, all he had was a hunch. Every workman in overalls reminded him of the questioning voice cutting through his speech, of a table turned over in a restaurant, the curving red of the wine glass. The heat made him feverish with doubt.

Thirty-seven was a large modern hangar built on the wrecked site between the houses. Foxton checked the address as he scanned the grey windowless panels broken only by a smart front entrance guarded by a man in combat uniform.

Ignoring the cocky salute he hurried into the foyer, jostling with well-groomed young men looking as though they had stepped straight from banks and dealing floors. Waiting by an entrance leading through the building a large group in combat gear gathered noisily, glancing up at the red light over the doors.

Seething with anger he pushed to the front of a queue. If Pearson thought that meeting him in some ex-service men's club constituted neutral ground he'd soon put him right.

He refused to sign the visitors' book and demanded to see Pearson.

'You can't go in without him anyway,' sniffed the receptionist, dressed unendearingly in khaki.

Pearson led his guest up steep stairs into a comfortably furnished replica of an officers' mess. Catching the crease in his trousers he sat down and poured tonics into two vodkas. He smiled considerately. 'Not really your sort of thing, John?'

Foxton refused the drink and looked round dismissively. 'I was what you would no doubt have called a conchy, Nigel.'

'So was I, actually.' Pearson pursed his thin lips. 'My family was desperately cut up. I managed to swing reserved occupation. Been in it ever since in a sense.' He smiled wryly. 'Let me get you some tea.'

Foxton braced himself against warmth from a man he despised and followed him over to a fifty-foot observation window set into the wall opposite the bar. It was a gallery looking on to a full-size battlefield.

The warehouse had been landscaped like a Vietnam assault course and dozens of players in US combat gear brandishing rifles threw themselves behind sandbags and into craters. Pearson was explaining the game, pointing through the soundproofed glass. As two groups met head-on he flicked a switch and an impassive blow-by-blow commentary issued from recessed speakers. Foxton watched bodies drop into the mud, splashed with red paint.

'I find it quite fascinating,' Pearson observed as a man threw a smoke grenade and lunged for the enemy flag. 'It's pure escapism of course.' He met John's eyes. 'Unlike golf.'

They walked the length of the hangar and its mock battlefield with trenches and dug-outs, hills and shell craters. A referee blew a whistle occasionally.

'People pay money to do this?' Foxton leant his forehead against the glass.

'Think of it as squash with bullets.' Pearson handed him a pair of headphones with a pleasant smile. 'If you get killed you just wait for the next game.'

Foxton listened to a headful of gunfire and shouts and watched ghoulish players in visors stain red and crumple to the ground.

Pearson flicked off the sound and turned back to the armchairs. 'We send our all management boys here. Very good for team dynamics – must be something about the intensity.'

'Or the fear.' Foxton was cold again. 'Let's get to the point, shall we?'

Pearson leant forward. 'I want a deal, Foxton. We're in a hole and we can't both win.' He gave a small gesture of submission. 'I'll split the difference with you. Half the skilled jobs can be saved – at a price. I could just about get that through the new board, providing I have your word that you'll vouchsafe union co-operation in the future. We'd have to draw up precise terms, naturally. A prototype contract.'

'No. Thank you.' Foxton shook his head. 'I gave those men my word.' The tea he'd been served burnt his throat but he drank it down deliberately.

Pearson poured another cup thoughtfully and stirred a piece of lemon. 'I want you to think about it.' He glanced at John casually. 'You see, your men will lose it *all* if you refuse. I must warn you.'

The only way you can break our strike is with a fair offer, not a sell-out.'

Foxton pulled at his tie and loosened his shirt collar. It was hot and airless, disorientating without daylight.

Pearson stood up with him. 'Be realistic, Foxton. Less bloody for everyone to do it now, rather than later.' He followed Foxton slowly down the room and held the door.

'I'll take my chances.' He raked his hand through his hair.

'Didn't realise you were such a gambling man.' Still smiling, Pearson took a card out of his wallet and scribbled his home number. 'You would of course be rewarded for your years of public service. I'd certainly see to that.'

Foxton absorbed his words slowly. 'What the hell are you talking about?'

Pearson offered the card confidently. Give me a ring when you've had time to think about it properly.'

Turning it over in his fingers, Foxton deliberately tore the Kensington telephone number and the embossed letters of Turnbull Motors into two neat pieces. He handed them back bitterly. Pearson observed him stiffly and glanced down at his watch.

'A great shame. We could have called the war off.'

Foxton hurried across the foyer and barged through the front door. As he turned back he saw Pearson step out after him, chatting to the doorman.

'I thought you were a pacifist, Nigel.' His shout echoed between the bricks and empty windows.

'Not any more.' Pearson didn't raise his voice, but Foxton heard him perfectly.

Fifteen

The drive back from Docklands had been slow and hot. Pearl's flat was stuffy and she threw windows open uselessly to a hazy evening of city heat.

Finn looked into the fridge and scrutinised a piece of dried-up cheese and a yoghurt carton. 'Trouble with this job is that you never get time to do any serious shopping,' she muttered, thinking of Millie's block of ice-cream. She made a jug of instant coffee and emptied an ice tray into it.

'What's that?' Pearl sat moodily on the sofa, which was still strewn with India's handiwork, and prodded the steaming brown iceblocks.

Finn shrugged. 'Iced coffee. Couldn't find anything else.'

Pearl had been preoccupied since they'd left India; hadn't spoken a word in the car.

'Do you think she's telling the truth?' Finn started to flick through one of the files of cuttings she'd lifted from Maureen's desk.

Pearl nodded. 'As far as she knows. But I'm not convinced about Railton.' Somewhere under a heap of newspapers the phone rang. Finn went to answer it but as she pulled it out by the flex the answerphone cut in. They had dispensed with the message and a single bleep cued the caller.

'It's Millie.' The voice paused with irritation. Finn was about to intercept when Pearl waved her to stop.

'Perhaps you could see your way to make contact? Maybe even tell me what's happening? Our client needs to have a proper showdown with Mitchell and he can't wait much longer. Ring me at home tonight.' There was an exasperated pause. 'Put it on your expenses.' The line went dead.

Finn winced and picked up her copy of Railton's diary.

'It's not going to take long to update her.' Pearl unplugged the phone miserably and headed for the bedroom. 'Got a call of my own to make first.' The door slammed.

Railton's diary was blocked and cross-hatched with meetings and lunches and meaningless references. Then suddenly Finn noticed a name. She turned to Maureen's file and went back through the cuttings taking a page out triumphantly.

'Pearl, I think I've got something here.' She went into the bedroom.

Pearl was sitting on the floor holding the phone numbly. 'I'm a stupid fool,' she said. 'I dial his number and *she* answers, and I hang up, *again*.' Finn looked apologetic. 'That's the last bloody time. I mean it.' She plucked the duvet angrily. 'Give me a moment? Millie can wait.'

Sitting down beside her, Finn opened the file. 'This won't take long, just tell me what you think.'

Pearl looked away. 'The trouble with you, Finn, is that you have no idea about what's happening to me. You just don't understand.'

'I do.' Finn was stung.

'I'm talking about serious relationships, not one night stands,' Pearl lashed out and regretted it immediately. It was crass and clumsy and guaranteed to hurt.

Finn stood up and threw the file on the bed. 'If you want to cop out on a case, that's up to you. Give me the phone – I'll talk to Mil.'

Pearl held on to it stubbornly, wanted to say sorry but ached too much to make the effort. She looked vaguely at the newspaper photo. It was a line-up of management leaving the Nottingham plant on the day the strike was called. Nigel Pearson was smiling icily and a square-featured young man was standing stiffly beside him.

'That's Mepham, the assistant director,' Finn read the caption and stabbed his picture angrily with her finger.

'So?' Pearl didn't recognise him.

Finn threw down Railton's diary. 'So it's pretty odd that a Mepham is playing golf with Kevin Railton tomorrow afternoon, isn't it?'

Pearl connected and stared at the diary entry. 'Top brass management socialising with the union finance advisor? You're right, it stinks.' She looked up at Finn guiltily. 'Maybe we're getting somewhere at last.'

'We've got to be there and find a way to hear what they're talking about.' Finn was jotting down a list. 'And that means borrowing sound equipment from Fitz's studio.' She stopped. 'And problems, right?'

Pearl looked uncomfortable. 'You'll have to leave me out of it. But go down to the studio – Denzil's working late there this week, he's dubbing a compilation album or something. Maybe he could lend us some gear on the quiet, without Fitz knowing. See what you can manage.'

Finn listened without looking at Pearl and doubtfully fingered her hair, leaving a wake of small spikes. Catching her uncertainty Pearl went to touch her shoulder but she stood up abruptly. When Finn reached the door she turned, her voice was small and hard. 'And don't forget to phone Millie this time.'

Pearl decided to wait. She felt badly about Finn and then blamed her for increasing her misery. All day she had been fighting Fitz from her mind. He had no right to unpick her life after all this time.

Her wrecked room was still off balance, with posters hanging off the wall. She picked up her calendar and touched the red ring around the day's date. It seemed to burn. The anniversary of the day she and Fitz had met. It was an act of madness to make it special when they had never owned one complete day or night between them. She tore away the whole month and crumpled it in her hands.

A broken vase lay on the table, split into petals. She started to gather up fragments. The call could wait. If Millie was bad-tempered she wouldn't appreciate the maze they'd already been through to get this far. If she waited she might even be able to detail how they proposed to tackle the next day. Slowly she started to subdue her demons one by one, mechanically.

Finn had been away for about an hour when the doorbell rang. Pearl stiffened. If Finn ever forgot her key she always beat a tattoo on the door. Pearl had always found it irritating but suddenly she felt alarmed: it had to be someone else. India's eyes had been hard with fear when she had talked about Railton over-reacting. Pearl couldn't believe she would have blabbed to him, not now, not after what he had done. But still the bell rang, longer and more insistent each time.

She slipped off her shoes and crept up the stairs. The bell burred and then stopped as she looked through the spy hole.

An empty corridor. Whoever it was had obviously given up and gone away. She leant her hand against the wood with relief. Suddenly there was a rustling against the door and the eye piece was filled with red. She recoiled with fright and then looked again, her heart hammering.

Standing in the corridor was Fitz clutching a huge bunch of roses.

'This is the rifle mike, you aim it just like a gun.' Denzil picked the long boom out of its padded box as if it were a child. Framed in the yellow cube of the sound box window, Finn watched anxiously, her face pale and concentrated. Denzil's long fingers ran along his explanation, the black notes on a keyboard.

Standing in the darkness of the studio floor Rufus watched them through the thick plate window and smiled. Liberated by the new assurance of his first big gig, he felt a great surge of belonging to a life where musicians and artists dispensed with the tight manoeuvring of the outside world. He had never wanted anything else. The colours were more vivid here and he couldn't imagine settling for less. Denzil, hearing silent notes like a wild animal, shared the touchstone which set him apart.

Rufus walked across the muffled studio floor and remembered Fitz gratefully. Changeable as the weather, doing deals, fretting about money, Fitz had pulled him out into the light. Rufus glowed with his new being, rap fluency, network radio and something powerful like second sight.

'It's no good.' Finn panicked, hopelessly pushing the boom back to Denzil. 'They're bound to see us. There's no way we'll hide something as bulky as this.'

Denzil's face was abbreviated in the shadows as he walked away patiently with the boom on his shoulder. 'You can be up to thirty metres away – I could be out in the street and still hear your heart hammering.'

Finn grinned, coaxed it on to her shoulder and swung it round. It was surprisingly light, but the favour weighed a fortune. She moistened her lips; they would have to be careful.

Denzil was instructing her on the earphones and portable tape recorder as Rufus joined them. The acoustic door slid shut behind him. Finn's look was sharp and accusing.

Hugging Denzil, Rufus glanced guiltily at Finn. There was something about her sometimes, almost a magnetic field; he felt the current bowl against him. She looked away.

'He'll kill you man – this is his best gear.'

Denzil nodded. 'But he's not going to find out, right, Finn?'

Finn snapped the case shut. 'When you're on a job with us Rufus, you don't just split when you feel like it.'

Rufus' smile contracted. 'I fell in the river.'

'We know, you left most of it in the car.'

Rufus grinned at Denzil. 'Sorry. I had to chip, that's all.'

'And we were relying on you, that's *all*.' Finn found it easy to be hard on him.

Rufus nodded ruefully. 'I nearly tore my fingers out under that ramp.' Finn looked surprised. 'Old Railton was giving it to him all right. The sweaty guy was on meltdown by the time they'd finished.'

Finn stared. 'You mean *Railton* was threatening *Trev*?'

'Course. Clever Trevor was squirming and trying to back out of something. Railton had him pinned. He told him not to rock the boat.'

'What else?' Finn was trying to piece this together.

'Nothing. I fell in the mud.' Rufus grinned. 'Anyway, you knew they were at each other?'

She was thinking. 'But not *how*. You've just put someone else's story in a very different light.' Finn was missing Pearl. 'So what boat might Trevor rock?'

Rufus picked up the miniature camera and focused it on Finn's worried face. 'The one they're both in, I suppose?' He pressed the shutter.

Finn locked the equipment into the boot and avoided offering

Rufus a lift. It was raining again and the dark street was already running with water. She wanted time alone to think before she got back to the flat.

'Where's Pearl then?' Rufus was leaning on the driver's door hopefully, his baseball cap pulled down to his nose. 'Finn?' He casually put his arm around her. 'Tell me all about it?'

'It's nothing.' Finn didn't have to be polite, not now he was being clumsy. She shrugged him off and unlocked the car.

'Hey, if it's that's sister of mine . . .' Rufus was vaguely conscious of the danger. 'She can be really heavy, really feels things, you know?'

'Yeh.' Finn shut the door and reluctantly rolled the window down to him. *And I suppose you think I don't.* She didn't say it.

Rufus leant through the window cautiously.' You should get out more, Finn. Be good for you. I could fix you up with someone?'

'Thanks a lot, Ruf, but an eighteen-year-old agony aunt I can really do without.' She started the engine.

If she hadn't had to stop at the next traffic lights she would have lost him. But as he ran up spattered with spray she relented and let him in.

'Thanks.' He was sheepish. 'I've got this big break lined up tomorrow so I've got to look after my vocal cords.'

'Stop talking then,' Finn advised.

He nodded. 'Right. Fitz has got a recording session tomorrow afternoon with this guy, session musos and backing vocals, the works.'

Finn gave no sign of being interested, she appeared to be lost in thought. 'Anyway, if they have time left, I can use them to lay down a few tracks for a proper demo.'

'And if they don't?' Finn pulled into the car park outside the flats.

'They will, I can feel it in my bones, and that's always a sign.'

Finn smiled at him wearily.

Rufus had his face pressed against the window. He had just spotted a silvery Cadillac parked across the tarmac. And now, so did Finn.

Pearl opened the door on the safety catch. Fitz anxiously looked at the roses and back to her. 'Happy anniversary Princess?'

She made herself angry. As he leant through the crack, she smelt sandalwood and noticed a tiny smudge of talcum powder on his neck.

'You've forgotten.' he laughed hesitantly. 'You said you'd be first.' Her look reminded him of the river, offering no solutions. He asked again, 'Please P, open the door?'

She released the catch and stood stiffly to one side, keeping herself separate. 'Just for the record, Fitz, I remembered.'

He smiled and offered her the flowers.

'This is a bad time. Please go.'

He clouded and lowered his voice anxiously. 'Have you got somebody here?'

'Trust you to think that.' Pearl's bitterness allowed her to walk away. He followed her down into the sitting-room and stared vacantly at the devastation. He walked across the room, gathering up a heap of magazines, and noticed a pile of letters on the table in his handwriting. Pearl followed his questioning look and scooped them up carelessly.

'Occupational hazard.' She frowned at the flat. 'All of it I suppose,' she said, looking directly at him.

He tried to lead her to the sofa. 'Relax P, I just want to talk.'

The sense of scenes stolen from films overwhelmed her. 'I don't want your roses, or your explanations, or your promises, right?'

She went angrily into the kitchen just to escape. She could hear him talking to himself, still standing there, saying 'I hate being without you.'

'I've noticed that, Fitz.' She returned to wound him while she still had the strength. 'How dare you come here. What is this, some sort of male pride thing?'

He flushed. 'Look, Sally, she's nothing.'

Pearl almost hit him. 'Nothing but recreational sex you mean? And what about your wife, *what* exactly is she?'

Fitz flinched. Black stubble stippled his brown chin. 'Sally was about getting you off my mind. Do you understand? You told me we'd finished and I couldn't stop thinking about you. She didn't work, nothing works . . . What am I going to do, P?' He looked at her helplessly.

She turned away bitterly. 'I think you'll go on doing everything the same. And then years later we'll meet, and you'll give me that same old smile, and get a kick out of still feeling something. But that's *all* it will be.'

He shook his head and grabbed her hand. He pulled her into the bathroom. 'I can't think straight in all that mess.' He shut the door and faced her. 'Look, I got married at seventeen. We had babies. Well, you do, don't you?' He looked somewhere distant. 'And then eleven years later I fell in love.'

Pearl splashed water on her face and stared at herself almost calmly. The beaded brown water could have been tears, but without the pain. She felt that she had nothing left to tell him. 'All I know is you make me miserable a lot of the time.' She dictated her words to the mirror. 'I hurt people I care about. Nothing's good while I feel like this, and I blame you.'

When she turned back he was quietened. He looked rather lost. 'So you do still love me?'

In her room padded by darkness and far away in a sleep of being held, Pearl heard the familiar tattoo on the door. Her heart flickered. She tensed and waited for it again as Fitz moved against her in his dream.

The noise went away. She had to let it go. She allowed herself to be carried on fast currents, away from regret or anything that tethered her to the real world.

Sixteen

Railton sat in the garage waiting room and stared with irritation at the breakfast television chat show without the sound. A square-jawed interviewer in a red sweater which flared and fuzzed as if he were catching fire talked solemnly to the camera. Railton put down a cup of coffee which tasted distinctly oily and chewed indigestion tablets against whisky and a sleepless night. This thing with India was making him feel uneasy.

He'd had no option but to close the relationship down when she'd stopped being indifferent. Walking away from her apartment the previous morning he had reflected that their almost contractual affair had involved dangerous clauses and loose ends which would have to be tidied. He had calculated her angry reaction to his departure and shrewdly anticipated some sort of necessary mutual agreement. To this end he had privately set aside yesterday evening, judging that to be when her assault would start. But when he was still alone at midnight he had left for her apartment with increasing annoyance. Having decided to see her, he had been determined to get it over with.

He had punched in her number and leant against the metal door, soon realising the combination had been changed. He had shouted into the voice panel, the door ringing like the slab of a tomb as he had slammed the flat of his hand against it. The whole thing had unsettled him; her behaviour had been uncomfortably unpredictable.

Railton's fitful sleep had been was interrupted by an alarm call at four-thirty that morning. The operator was calm and insistent and at his request checked the number. It had been booked the night before; it was on her sheet. He had burrowed back beneath the sheets, cursing the telephone system. A dull headache had throbbed against his eyelids.

It was six-thirty when his doorbell had rung, someone's finger jammed down hard, a long scorching note. Railton grabbed a dressing gown and disengaging his complex security system furiously confronted a special delivery.

'Don't blame me,' said the courier. 'I just deliver.' Railton signed, grabbed the parcel and headed for the kitchen. Crunching aspirin, he dug a carving knife through the padded envelope and opened it impatiently. It was full of newspaper.

Two hours later when he couldn't start his Jaguar and found the carphone severed, he became fractious. A wild thought of a vengeful India crossed his mind and lingered just long enough to be unpleasant. It was not possible. She didn't possess the imagination.

When the mechanic had diagnosed sugar in the petrol tank of his new car, Kevin experienced a small wave of panic. He'd have to scrap the morning in the office and go straight on to his golf course appointment. But first he must speak to India.

The payphone was in the garage main office.

'India?' Railton scowled at an inquisitive girl hunched over the till. India was curt and distant but calm. She sounded genuinely surprised about his car and the other incidents.

'India – if you . . .'

She gave a bitter laugh. 'If I wanted to express my disgust for you, Kevin, believe me, I would be operating on a far grander scale.'

He was shaken by her acerbic tone but curiously relieved. 'So who the hell is it then?' He demanded, pumping in another coin.

'I'm the last person to ask.' India hung up abruptly. Railton was sure she was mocking him.

Wiping his face with a tissue he angrily dialled his company again.

'Strictly speaking,' the garage girl drawled, shooting price stickers on to pot plants, 'it's emergency use only, and not long distance.'

Railton demanded India and was told by an assistant that she'd left only minutes ago for the Paris fine art auctioneers. 'Exactly. It's tomorrow's sale I want to discuss with her,' he snapped. 'Get her to phone me from the airport. I'll be home for one hour.' He slammed down the receiver and redialled for a taxi.

John Foxton had left the office late to get to Nottingham. With the car windows open and the evening sun softening fields and gasometers, he had experienced a sudden surge of release. Pearson's back-street wargame and the confusion with Millie were postponed in a city growing more distant with every mile. He had felt again the charge of returning to the front line where he might make some real difference. Stopping for petrol at a service station, a crowd of lorry drivers had recognised him and had whooped encouragement across the forecourt. Foxton had smiled and felt he was coming home.

The city-centre hotel had been bland and impersonal. Even with the windows open on to the park, the room was stuffy and smelt of polish. He had selected two bottles from the mini bar, flicked on the television and debated phoning Millie, before settling to script the next day's impromptu speech.

Breakfast was served in a thickly carpeted dining-room. Waiters crept past tables with cold toast, and coffee cooling in silver-plated pots. Foxton noticed a couple talking in whispers, the woman stroking the man's shoe with a stockinged foot.

The taxi dropped him half a mile from the plant and he walked briskly past identical houses towards the factory gates. Breakfast television flickered noiselessly through net curtains and occasionally a pale face stared out: men lost at home, and their wives marooned with them.

The picket line saw him coming and put up a shout. A small line of men was raggedly guarding a NUAVE banner and a series of hoardings around the gate. Two shop stewards were sitting in deck chairs nearby and rose to their feet stiffly. Lurching forward a press photographer caught Foxton smiling triumphantly as he shook mens' hands and accepted their hope.

Walking over to the stewards he quietly ran through the revised schedule. A woman with a toddler threw a coin in a bucket containing mostly coppers and half an inch of rain. They laughed and passed round a fresh brew of tea, an oldish man with a stoop rolling a cigarette in a tin lid, carefully catching every wisp of tobacco.

'How did they take it?' Foxton stared at the factory yard through the railings where he had made his speech only a week before. He seemed to hear the roar go up again, the walls of the building buckling with its power.

The steward mopped his face and squinted at the sun. 'No real problem, John.' He slapped his shoulder. 'If you say money'll be there, they don't mind waiting, not at first like.' He frowned as he saw a red car nosing towards the gates. 'Won't take long though, before there's some real hardship, even with support.'

John banished the memory of his stifling hotel room and his uneaten breakfast, solictiously borne away on a tray. He felt anger well up against Trevor and his mismanagement, for allowing these men to wait so much as an hour longer. He marched back to the main gate where the official pickets were haranguing an elderly grey-haired man through the closed window of his car. The man stared stolidly ahead and tried to inch forward, sounding his horn. Foxton reached their ranks and bent down against the reflection on the window. The grey wavy hair moved into shadow and he suddenly saw the runnelled face clearly. Freddie Jones, his opposite number at the Automated Technical Engineers, known floridly by union gossip as 'the dealer'.

Foxton's blood beat faster. In the bright sun the car seemed to throw off metalled heat. The men shouted angrily, some thumping the car sides. John knew he had to seize the moment for them. He saw the scene before him as if it were already a news item; an image accomplished to raise his men's morale.

Pushing past, Foxton went to the front of the car and leant towards the driver with both hands on the bonnet. Jones saw him clearly and his chiselled chin slackened with surprise. Without prompting, the men went silent as Freddie Jones opened the door and extended his hand towards Foxton.

John glared and beat the car with a fist. 'Good to know you're on our side, Freddie.'

'I might be, lad.' Jones was displeased with such open hostility and very aware of the dangers of anger in crowds. He lit a cigarette. 'There's negotiation to be done if you've got the stomach for it.' He inclined his head towards his car. 'Must be fate this, Foxton, I was about to ring you.'

A man behind him spat on the pavement. It was a sound like poison. John glanced at their suspicious faces and made a decision.

'Forget it, Freddie, we're fighting this one on our own.' The men cheered and called out his name. Someone beat the bucket with a spar of metal.

'You can't John, not this time.' Freddie Jones shook his head, as if foretelling a death.

Finn sat in the car outside the country club near Greenwich. The afternoon simmered with heat, and the impossible green of the course dissolved into distant mirages of men playing golf in water. All the surveillance gear was under a blanket on the back seat and Finn was waiting behind the steering wheel, knotted with growing anger.

Last night now seemed worse. After seeing Fitz's car she had hesitated. When Rufus had told her she was being too sensitive she had gone in and knocked on the door out of irritation as much as anything, and exhaustion. All she had wanted that moonless night was the invisibility of sleep.

Finn was always forgetting her key and had felt sick when she couldn't find it as she rummaged through her pockets. 'It is your home too isn't it?' Rufus' voice was in her head and out of weariness she had tapped out her knock on the door. Unaccountably she felt a jolt of hurt remembering how she and Pearl had left each other; she knew that her anger was still there to be dealt with. The flat had been silent. Nobody had come. Finn had walked back to the car park and saw Rufus still standing next to the Wolsey, the white leather on his baseball jacket burnished with street light.

And now Pearl was dismantling the whole thing. Hadn't answered the phone all morning, wasn't with her here on the job which needed them both and might turn the whole case round. They never did that to each other, not for any reason. Finn refused to want to understand.

A matt-black BMW drifted into the car park and parked near

the clubhouse entrance. Almost immediately a cab lurched up and Railton pushed out a bag of clubs, waving briskly.

Finn frowned through small field glasses. It was definitely Mepham, looking oddly casual in a citron sweater with dark green tartan trousers. A rap on the window nearly stopped her heart. Rufus squashed his nose against the glass.

'Thought you might need a caddy.' He climbed in beside her.

Still watching the two men unpacking their golf bags she tried to sound unconcerned. 'How did you know?'

He examined the rifle mike busily but didn't answer. Finn grabbed his wrist. 'What's going on, Rufus?'

He looked evasive. 'All I know is that you said this was crucial and you can't carry all this gear by yourself, right?' She nodded reluctantly. 'And, if you drop any of it, my recording career's over.'

He balanced the boom on his shoulder like a javelin. Finn pulled it down out of sight quickly. 'What do you want, a flashing light as well?' She loaded the camera, checked the tapes and swallowed hard. 'This time Rufus, I'm giving orders and you're listening, OK?'

Railton and Mepham were leading away their clubs on trolleys. Finn carefully slid the mike into a golf bag and stepped out on to the course.

The men were laboriously starting their eighth hole as Rufus and Finn slithered into a small damp ditch near the green.

Rufus' face glistened with sweat. 'Bor-ing.' He shook his head with disbelief, 'And we're killing ourselves to listen to all this stuff about con-tin-gencies.' He raised his eyebrows quizzically. 'Who is this Freddie Jones character anyway?'

Finn looked at him with alarm. 'Hang on, aren't you meant to be in the recording studio?' He nodded dismissively.

'Your demo?' she whispered.

'Only a maybe, nothing definite.' He looked back to the golfers.

'And you're missing it because of this?'

'Yeh, looks like it.' She touched his shoulder and he put his hand over hers without looking round. The men were almost opposite.

Hearing her own heart thumping Finn adjusted the earphones. Railton straightened his co-ordinated blue checked sweater and adjusted his eye shade. Rufus grinned and lined up the rifle mike menacingly.

Mepham watched his opponent's drive soar down the fairway. 'I'm under a lot of pressure, Kevin. In fact I'd call it an ultimatum.' His voice was accusing. 'We've made a big investment in you and we're looking for some returns, and fast.'

Railton wiped down his club. 'Don't worry. I've got it all in hand.' He handed his partner a tee and smiled. 'I'd say Foxton is already as good as finished.' Finn sat bolt upright and checked the tape was running, signalling urgently to Rufus.

Mepham's taut face turned fleetingly towards Finn's camera. 'Then perhaps you'd tell me what the hell's going on?'

Railton took some pleasure in making his partner wait until he'd chipped on to the green, before releasing his concentration to talk.

Breathless and muddy, Finn held the headset until her ears rang. She heard Rufus' knees crack beside her. They looked at each other and caught their breath. John Foxton's suspicions were breaking cover.

'Mitchell's in deep trouble,' grinned Railton.

'And how does that help us?' Mepham moistened his lips and rehearsed the perfect execution of his putt.

'He hates my guts.' Railton pulled at his beard with amusement.

'And when he presents the strike pay strategy in full tomorrow, I've advised him to report that we took a knock during the stockmarket crash last year. Even Foxton will see that's a blatant cover-up.'

Mepham damped his face with a handkerchief white as a flag. It flapped and muffled his voice. The microphone fizzed with static and Finn strained to hear.

'But how does that get us *Foxton*?' He was getting hot and testy and Railton was unpleasantly smug. To his discomfort his partner abdicated from the discussion again to hole a long curving putt. Mepham glared.

'I want Foxton to sack me.' Railton's voice was systematic

now. Then I go to the president of the union and tell him that Foxton and Mitchell have been lining their pockets to the tune of three million pounds. I'll tell them that Foxton's sacked me because I'd rumbled them.'

Mepham suddenly looked interested. 'Go on.'

Railton smiled lazily. His lips looked very red against his beard. 'The union will have to hold an enquiry and the whole thing will be whipped up into a sizeable scandal.'

Mepham was frowning against the sun. 'But what happens when Foxton clears his name?'

Railton filled in his score card with a flourish. 'First rule of politics, Vincent: throw enough mud and some of it is bound to stick.'

Seventeen

Millie gripped the receiver like a bone she might break. 'Are you absolutely sure?' She noticed her daughter critically thumbing through her record collection, and nodded vigorously. 'You're right, Finn, I'll call Foxton, we should meet here in about an hour.' Millie rehearsed asking Maureen calmly for a quick word with her boss and frowned. 'No? Pearl *didn't* call. Never mind that now, you've done really well, both of you.'

The phone went dead abruptly and Millie smiled. Finn usually avoided making any calls and if she ever got the answerphone would leave her name bluntly, like a reprimand, and hang up. Her news about Railton changed everything. '*I keep thinking this must be more than just a money rip-off.*' John's ellipitical remark at the briefing ricocheted back. She tidied her work papers with irritation. If she hadn't let herself feel so emotionally entangled with him she might have picked up on that and maybe made sense of it. She shivered as if she had just walked from sun into shadow. She felt a sense of direction shaping, one that shrugged off old weather.

Her daughter looked up with some dismay. 'Please don't tidy up too much,' she pleaded. 'I don't want Eric thinking you're some kind of bourgie.' Her mother looked blank. 'You know – bourgeois – as in scatter cushions and napkin rings. Mum, please?'

'Eric doesn't sound very French.' Millie deflected the slur by pronouncing his name like a deodorant.

'His family's ancient. His grandfather was Foreign Legion or something.'

'Légion d'honneur?' suggested Millie hopefully.

Laura nodded dismissively. 'Don't tell him I told you. Would it be possible just to leave these coloured ribbon things on your desk?'

'Briefs,' said Millie. 'They're confidential briefs for court, not dried flowers.' Laura smiled and fanned them out carefully, throwing down some law magazines on the table.

'And shall I get a few bottles?' she suggested casually. 'Some red wine maybe? Dad usually has something decent in the cellar; I know what to get.'

Millie was always vulnerable to this tactic. 'Out of interest, Laura, why did you ask Eric Neuf du Pape to come *here* and not up to your family seat and well-stocked cellar?'

Laura looked startled. 'Eric's mother's a feminist.' She put the remark down like a card.

'Yes – ?'

Her daughter straightened a photo of Millie in her gown. 'She's quite famous and really radical and divorced. She and Eric have loads of interesting friends who drop in at all hours and the coolbox is always stacked with sour milk she's forgotten.'

'So you're saying that your father's tidy fridge might give your Eric the wrong impression?' asked Millie with a slight twinge.

Laura shrugged. 'It wouldn't work. And Gill's *so* English. She can't help it.'

'No . . .?' Millie thoughtfully untidied the letter rack. 'Laura, you wouldn't be saying you're marginally proud of me, by any chance, would you?'

She dialled the union number and waited anxiously. It was already quite late, he might already have gone home. Home. She had no idea what that meant to John any more.

Maureen answered and switched from efficient secretary to conspirator. 'Tell the girls they should phone me, Mrs Millington. There's something brewing for tomorrow. India's been phoning all day and Trevor's not been in.'

As Millie waited for John she replayed the alarm in Maureen's voice. Foxton should have phoned her himself, and she had a shrewd idea why he hadn't.

'Millie?'

She nerved herself. 'We've come up with something, John. We need an urgent meeting, my place? As soon as you can.'

'I'm on my way.' But his voice was hesitant. 'Would you prefer to meet here at my office?'

'The venue's not a problem.' Laura looked up curiously. 'And maybe you'd consider briefing us properly on developments your end?'

She was still vaguely holding the phone after he'd rung off. Disconcerted, she noticed Laura watching her.

'Sometimes when you're on the phone, you sound like someone else.'

'Good,' said Millie.

Finn arrived an hour later in the middle of an argument. She looked as tired as Millie felt.

'Finn will agree with me,' said Laura, appearing out of the kitchen. Finn smiled back, slightly uneasy with Laura, dizzy, educated and tweaking her mother like a magpie. Millie seemed different, slightly defensive with this confident girl who looked so like her.

'My boyfriend's coming to stay,' she explained, 'and Mum wants to put him in a separate room.'

Finn swallowed a mouthful of wine and turned to face Millie.

'We are still negotiating it, actually.' The last thing Millie needed was to discuss this with Finn.

'So what do you think?' Laura gauged her mother's discomfort and pushed it; she obviously needed a new perspective.

'Your mum's pretty reasonable on the whole.' Finn shrugged and headed for the high-walled garden and fresh air.

'But you're still quite young, Finn?' Laura went for one last score. 'Someone else can't possibly make these decisions for you, can they?'

Finn looked quite grave. 'It might be better if they did, believe me.'

Millie was watching Finn, not her daughter. She had grown surprisingly fond of her. She had been difficult to get to know. She had even distrusted her at first, her police record always close to the surface in times of doubt. But Finn was fierce with instinct, invariably true as a line on motives. She had an inside track on breaking the rules, but her toughness swayed like a reflection if she were challenged.

They had never discussed the day after the office party, when Finn had turned up late at the office looking for Krish. Millie had been working late and had pulled Finn back before she bolted down the stairs. Finn had wept solidly, head down on the desk, tears flooding off paper, shoulders shuddering. She hadn't explained anything but Millie knew she must have spent the previous night with Krish and then been discarded. She'd almost seen it happening – Krish, resplendent in a crimson waistcoat and drunk on vodka. Finn disarmed by drink and transparently joyful with his arm round her. Twenty-four hours later Millie had hugged her, and Finn had clung as if she were falling, and had trusted her never to mention it again.

The doorbell rang and Laura looked repentant. 'Mega over-reaction, Mum, right?' Millie kissed her gratefully and headed for the front door.

John Foxton had planned to have a private word with Millie. She obviously wanted to settle the harsh words between them. He had been restive and had found himself rehearsing lines. He was intrigued by the way she had put him back on course to handle the problem with Trevor. Momentarily weakened by an automatic loyalty to his old friend, her anger had stung him back on course. It was a capacity for passion which he remembered accurately.

Standing near the table was a young girl in a mini-skirt and a man's shirt. She stared at him curiously and then apologetically headed for the stairs. Her smile turned his heart over. 'Laura, isn't it?'

She looked puzzled. He shook her hand rather formally and wryly registered her amusement. 'I think your daughter must think I'm a little old-fashioned, Mil?'

'Not at all.' Millie glanced at Laura. 'But rather bourgie perhaps.'

She noticed Finn setting up the tape at the table in the garden, checking a wad of photographs. Her smile faded.

'Come on, John, you'd better listen to this tape.' He was surprised to hear something more than efficiency to her voice.

*

When Finn's note had come through the letter box, Pearl had let in bright daylight, opening windows on the heat of a summer's afternoon. She ran a bath and unfolded the paper cautiously. Finn's rounded hand was brief and heavily underlined.

'Hole in one. Millie's at six. Be there. Please.'

Pearl closed her eyes and tried not to think. She confined herself to the smallest details. Finn wasn't into punctuation but the full stops were full of hurt. She didn't want to explain anything.

Fitz knelt by the bath and traced a finger over her wet brown shoulders. She shivered. He smiled rather hopelessly, suddenly puzzled that after their intimacy, his touch was an intrusion. He was dressed and about to leave.

Pearl pulled herself up out of the bath abruptly, and stepping past him, grabbed a towel. He pulled her to him, suddenly alarmed that she might slip past and disappear. She shrugged away.

'Give me a chance not to have your arms around me, Fitz, before you walk out. Understand?' Her voice had become hard with the future.

Fitz followed her into the bedroom where she pulled clothes out of drawers and got dressed hurriedly.

'P, listen to me.' He tried to slow her up but it was as if she were running. 'While you were asleep I was thinking.'

Pearl pulled on socks angrily, so he really thought she'd been sleeping.

'No more promises, P, no more vague ideas. I'll just admit it to her, tell the truth. You see until I do, I won't be able to leave her . . . my wife.' He used the word clumsily knowing how it displayed his disloyalty to them both. 'It's a question of making it real. I can see that now.'

Pearl heard his rush of words with a numbness and turned away, suspending immediate reaction, avoiding the danger. She felt illogically shut out of his decision and her faith wavered for the first time. *His wife*, a woman he lived with, and two children; was he going to leave them for her and then arrive with wounds she could not heal? She had reminded herself how much she still needed him. His words were racing ahead as if she were making them up.

Fitz spoke carefully as if breathing in a high altitude. 'I'll do it, this weekend, I promise.' He held her shoulders and made her look at him. 'What do you think, Princess?'

She refused to meet his eyes.

'What can I say to convince you?' Fitz wanted her to be all reassurance and make him stay longer. He wanted her to believe.

'Nothing. There's no point.' She frowned and grabbed her jacket. 'Just give me a lift round to Millie's. I've got an important meeting and I'm going to be late.'

Fitz dropped her a few doors down at her request, and as Pearl hurried towards Millie's terraced house she felt almost weightless. She didn't attempt to prepare excuses, she just wanted to be back on the case, somewhere nearer solid ground. As she hesitated by the front door she saw Millie's daughter look through the window and wave.

Laura ushered Pearl in and nodded towards the garden. She admired Pearl's careless eccentricity with clothes: blazer, baggy shorts and a running vest. And Finn intrigued her with her striking, watchful looks.

'What are you doing at the weekend?' Pearl looked preoccupied but Laura went on hopefully. 'I've got a friend here, so drop in anytime, OK?'

The weekend. Pearl frowned and looked doubtful. 'I might have something on. Not sure yet.'

Finn had just finished explaining about their investigation of India and was now passing Railton's desk diary entry over to Foxton. Pearl stood awkwardly in the doorway and Millie automatically waved her through to a seat.

John flicked through the photos of the two men and angrily slammed down two close-ups of Mepham. 'Top exec with the company for less than a year. Fancy suits from Milan and believes in nothing better than the main chance.' He sighed wearily. 'Him and Railton, the new breed, playing with companies and men like kids with Monopoly.'

Finn loaded the tape and carefully avoided looking at Pearl.

She pressed the play button and they leant forward to the static and breathing and the unmistakable voices of Railton and Mepham. '*Foxton is as good as finished*,' Millie glanced anxiously at John. Pale and staring at the tape he logged the conspiracy word by word. Pearl's mouth was dry, she gulped orange juice and tried to concentrate. Finn clicked the tape off and sat down.

Millie turned to Pearl. 'Are you sure they had no idea?' Pearl was surprised. It hadn't occurred to her that her partner would have covered for her.

'We're sure.' Finn was definite, only looking at Millie.

Foxton sat like a man in the silence after an explosion. He was talking almost to himself. 'So Trevor is collaborating with them against me?'

'Not necessarily.' Finn had been working out the possible scenarios. 'About a week ago Rufus heard Railton threatening him.'

Pearl looked surprised. 'He never told me that.'

'No, he only remembered last night,' said Finn tightly.

Foxton fleetingly looked relieved, then angry. 'Stupid bugger.' He banged the table so that the photos slithered onto the grass. 'So he got caught up in this somehow. But why didn't he come and tell me? Am I really so unapproachable? His friend?' He tailed off and stared into the shadows.

'Perhaps he couldn't face you?' Millie's voice was softer. 'Thought you would judge him?'

Her look was brief but Foxton felt blatantly accused. 'Well, I'm not such a righteous lefty that I haven't got a few tricks left up my sleeve.' He was almost shouting and then suddenly looked embarrassed.

'OK. So now you can stop this scandal,' Pearl was thinking aloud, 'But you still don't know where the money's gone.'

'I've got a bloody good idea though,' said Foxton grimly. 'And I want it back with interest.'

Finn looked up quickly. 'We're still on the case then?'

Foxton nodded. 'I've got to handle this carefully. I won't confront Trevor until Railton's made his move and pushed me to sack him. But I'm going to nail that bastard for the money, and more, if it's the last thing I do.'

'Right then.' Pearl stood up and nodded at Finn. 'We'd better get you some evidence.'

'Don't need much more than this, do we?' Finn waved the tape aggressively at Pearl.

'Inadmissible, I'm afraid.' Millie looked at Foxton. 'You can use the tape to put the frighteners on Pearson but it's very unlikely it would do the job in court.' She turned to Pearl and Finn. 'We're going to need something rather more substantial.'

Foxton watched the old Wolsey pull away and drew the curtains to enclose Millie's sitting room. As darkness began to fall a cool breeze had sprung up and they'd come in from the garden shivering. On her hands and knees, Millie was starting to lay a fire in the patterned grate.

'A fire on a summer's evening with the windows wide open, it's very restful.'

She turned. 'So have we nearly finished, John?'

He was startled, had assumed he might stay, but was now being referred back to the agenda. He lingered thoughtfully on his final point. 'Railton's playing it both ways of course. He's milking us, and getting a fat fee from management, no doubt.' He clenched his fist and cupped it against his hand like a blow. 'It's bloody ironic. Mepham and his masters asset-strip good companies and throw men on the scrap heap, but who'll be depicted in the papers as greedy and selfish?'

'The unions naturally.' Millie put a match to the kindling.

He turned on her bitterly. 'Trade unionism is being turned into a dirty word.'

'Then fight,' Millie said simply. 'You've got the showdown with Railton tomorrow for starters. Let's hope Trevor comes out of hiding.'

'How do you know about that?' His tone was almost indignant.

Millie fed small pieces of wood on to the flames and felt equaninity flowing back. Perhaps it was true – relationships were nothing but power struggles after all.

'One other thing,' she was taking him insistently down her list, 'when you contact management with your bombshell, as a condition of your silence, get them to stop distributing the smear pamphlets. Maureen's unearthed where they print them so I'm going ahead with defamation.'

'Maureen has . . .?' Foxton felt distinctly disorientated.

Millie nodded. 'Do you want a drink before you go?'

He held his hands out to the fire and smiled cautiously. 'I hoped you might want to talk sometime.'

Millie selected a bottle of good red wine from the newly stocked rack and brought in a tray from the kitchen. She watched him struggle with the cork and then register the three wine glasses. Laura came down the stairs in a flowing black dress sewn with small Indian bells; she made ringing noises as she moved.

'Only one glass, Mum.' She looked nervously at her watch. 'We've got to be at the airport in an hour, remember?'

Eighteen

Kevin Railton drove his ice-blue Jaguar over Vauxhall bridge and through tinted sunglasses watched the tarmac shudder. The engine laboured and stuttered, still ragged from the sabotage. He turned up the volume of the tape deck; the slow persuasive love song made him feel detatched and cheerful. Rewinding the track, he listened again, swinging round corners and accelerating through amber traffic lights. All along the Embankment the traffic shimmered in lines. Car radios yammered. Another day of sun and pollen dropping on the city like a punishment. Kevin lit a menthol cigarette. The smoky sunroof slid back noiselessly and gave him a square of blue sky with a cloud like a comma.

Beyond Greenwich the streets became narrower and more crowded and he divised small impromptu shortcuts down side streets. Waiting at junctions, he smoothed the lapels of his grey jacket and straightened his tie in the mirror.

He thought back to the long green fairways of the golf course and Mepham's gratifying reaction. Railton despised him. Their first meeting in the exclusive club restaurant had swiftly presented an agenda of ruthless behaviour, finely detailed for swift execution. Mepham had gone through it point by point, ordering food and Foxton's removal as surely as he handled the sharpened silver cutlery. Selecting wine without pleasure, he had presented the terms of his ultimatum. Railton had allowed himself to be hired like a mercenary.

Trevor Mitchell had already been a soft target but Foxton was a challenge. Kevin had set up intricate series of trip wires and enjoyed the bloodless Mepham's dependence on his expertise. The adrenalin fired him – raised his game. He smiled privately;

yesterday had been the first time he'd gone round below his handicap.

He pulled into an empty parking meter outside the union offices and flattened his wispy hair in the mirror. The street was airless and busy, and struggling to find change he broke into a light sweat. He dropped his newspaper. An attractive black girl in a light dress and with a tangle of curls bent down close to him and picked it up.

'Morning Mr Railton.' She was strangely respectful.

He juggled with his briefcase and searched his pocket for a coin. 'Do I know you?'

She smiled but lingered for his response. 'Mr Mitchell.' She nodded at the building. 'Remember, at the pub?' He smiled back at Pearl vaguely.

Suddenly down the street, violently scattering shoppers, came a black boy on roller skates zigzagging along the pavement and ripping a route through the crowd. Railton wheeled with alarm when he heard the screams, glanced off the boy sideways and fell heavily to the ground.

Rufus rode the collision, and dipping low, curved round to scoop up Railton's bunch of keys. Swerving sideways to clear his body, he glanced over to where Finn crouched on the far side of the car. Like a pitcher he skimmed the keys to her, and kicking off against Railton's shin powered off down the street.

Sprawled on the pavement and shouting, Railton caught the briefest glimpse of a young girl scrambling into his car, her white face tensed as she started the engine. Behind him a woman had been thrown backwards into a stall of oranges and was babbling hysterically about a boy wearing his cap back to front.

'It's all right,' said Pearl, leaning hard against Railton as he clutched his ribs, 'he didn't get your briefcase.'

Finn kicked the car out of the space and lurched into the traffic. The powerful engine hardly purred as she accelerated away and drove it hard over the cobbles on to the wharfside. The sunroof opened at the touch of a switch and the suspension barely sighed. Finn smiled with pleasure as the new tyres squealed softly down a ramp onto the old barge bays.

The engine cut out to the sound of seagulls and Finn examined the keys carefully. A series of unusual mortise locks and a yale would be for his house, and the small toothpick-style for the burglar alarm. An older key with a long bevelled shaft was less obvious. She unclipped three others, the car keys, the only ones they wouldn't need.

Finn took a deep breath and steadied herself, she hadn't been here for a long time. Knocking firmly on the cut-out door in the railway arch, she pushed it open. The acrid smell of welding filled her lungs as she struggled against the gloom, dazzled with acetylene. A small stumpy man hunched over an old car which was stripped back for respray. He peeled off a number plate and it clattered, glowing, onto the concrete floor.

Closing the door, Finn waited for her eyes to catch up with the darkness. The man left the torch hissing on the floor and came over with the protective visor flipped up like a mask.

'Got 'em?' She nodded and placed them in his outstretched hand.

The fluorescent strip hummed and flickered as he scrutinised the keys between stubby fingers. Then, selecting the correct shape of metal blank, he tightened it into a vice. Working on quickly, and licking cracked lips, he occasionally checked the contours of the keys by touch, as if feeling for a pulse. The bevelled key was the most exacting, its worn teeth difficult to fix for the mould. Muttering, he filed the metal patiently, glaring at it through a watchmaker's eye glass, his face screwed in a scowl.

Smithy had done the work for the jobs all those years ago. Her other life: Finn used to do the key runs whenever her uncle could get them. It made life easier; made the jobs cleaner and more efficient. The knot in her stomach reminded her of an old sick feeling.

There were times when she had nearly talked to Pearl about it, then shrank away, vaguely dreading her disapproval. The day they'd both been broke and she'd come back with pockets bulging from the supermarket, Pearl had said hard things. And Finn had indignantly scattered frozen food from their seventh floor window and flinched with the accusations.

Now Finn watched Smithy holding up the new keys against the

originals, making small adjustments. Coming here wasn't helping the confusion.

'Thought you'd retired, Finny?' He grinned and a tiny crack in his lip bled vividly.

Finn nodded, faint with heat and shadows. 'Strictly business, this.' The lamp lit up his face like a gargoyle. 'I'm on a case, private investigation.'

'Is that so?' Clearly Smithy didn't believe her. 'It's nearly done any road.' He held the new keys briefly in a flame to clean them then doused them in cold water. They hissed angrily.

Finn paid him notes, peeling off each one on to the top of a metal bench still hot from welding. He scooped them up and stuffed them into his shirt pocket, then looked at her properly for the first time.

'You've changed,' he said abruptly.

'I was only a kid.' Finn shrugged, wanting to be gone.

He nodded, 'You had quite a talent.' She watched him pull out a large locking mechanism from under the bench, stripped back, probably from a wall safe.

'Go on, have a try, it's good but I bet you can hear your way into it.'

Finn smiled reluctantly. She knew this was a compliment, but Smithy's invitation was all about the old world and people she had made decisions against. She shook her head and carefully bound up the warm keys in greased sacking.

'Detective.' He pushed out his bottom lip. 'Is that so?'

'Yes.' Her cheeks burnt like a kid accused at school.

'So you wouldn't be interested in small family reunion?'

'No thanks.' She pushed together a smile and set off for the door, almost dreading he'd follow her, drag her back, and remind her how impossible leaving could be.

When she'd pulled the door open and could feel the sun blazing on her back again, she paused.

'Terrible waste,' remarked Smithy. 'You were quite something.'

The curved door clicked back into its perfect fit. 'And now I'm something else,' Finn said over and over as she walked back to the car. '*I am.*'

She flicked the radio on as she drove back. The sun span off the water and a warm breeze from the river reminded her of a seaside beach where she'd been with auntie. She caught her frown in the mirror and straightened it out.

She was all right: now she knew she could walk through shadows. The only thing she allowed to go on hurting was the argument with Pearl.

She swung into a side street, just in sight of the union building and watched the fourth window on the fifth floor. When Pearl closed the blinds she would know it was safe to return the car. She settled down to wait and polished small shreds of hessian from the keys.

Nineteen

Pearl helped Railton to his feet and handed him his jacket. He stared woodenly at the space where his car had been and glared at Pearl.

'I just don't believe this.'

He swayed on his feet, and glassy eyed, put his hand to his head expecting blood. Pearl snatched his briefcase and headed firmly for the door. 'You look a bit rough, Mr Railton. Better not be late for your meeting with Trevor. I'll phone the police if you like.'

Maureen made coffee while Railton retired angrily to the wash room to salvage the appearance of his light-grey suit. After careful adjustment of the intercom in Trevor's empty office, Maureen anxiously steered Pearl towards the stationery cupboard. Ushering her in, Maureen followed furtively and locked the door behind them.

'Not a word from Trevor all day yesterday,' she shook her head. I tried everywhere and it's the auction this morning. He should be here. India's been calling him urgently, the strike fund distribution has to be finalised, he's got a meeting with John and Railton, and his wife's called three times from Spain.' Maureen punctuated each item as if dictating to a typist. 'You don't think he's gone and disappeared do you?'

'No, he wouldn't,' Pearl said uncertainly, trying to sift through the fragments of information logically. 'Why was India so desperate to get hold of him?'

Maureen looked rather glazed and took her glasses off to concentrate. 'She wouldn't say.' She was replaying the conversation again in her head. 'She was very secretive, almost rude.'

'Go on.' Pearl wa interested. 'What did she say exactly?'

'When Trevor hadn't turned up by late afternoon, she asked me whether the money from this morning's sale was needed immediately for the strike fund, or for later distribution.'

'And what did you say?'

'I didn't know.' She looked rather hurt. 'Trev doesn't seem to tell me things like he used to.'

'But why could it matter so much to her?'

Maureen searched for an answer, holding on to the shelving as if the floor were shifting. 'I should be able to work this out, shouldn't I?' Her face looked crushed. 'I'm not really much good, am I? Perhaps you'd prefer me to resign – as your associate?'

Pearl suppressed a smile. 'Come off it, Maureen, *we* haven't got a clue what's going on half the time.' She took the keys firmly from Maureen's hands and started to search through them. 'Just let me out of here. I've got to pretend to phone the police in front of Railton or Finn's going to be back in gaol.'

'Pretend?' Maureen looked concussed. '*Back* in gaol?' Pearl sighed. 'We stole Railton's car to get his keys.'

'But you didn't tell me.' Maureen's face went flat with shock.

'No, I'm sorry.' Pearl picked out the key and unlocked the door. 'Confidentiality, Maureen. It's for your own good.'

Trevor Mitchell had just arrived in the reception area and was putting his overnight case onto the desk. He looked up warily at Maureen and raised both hands. 'Went away to concentrate.' He patted her tentatively on the shoulder. 'No good giving you the phone number, you'd only have rung me.' His smile flickered unconvincingly and he flattened down his hair as if preparing himself for a dive. 'Brief me on any immediate problems, and tell Railton to wait.' He looked at his watch, breathing heavily.

The door to the corridor burst open and Railton marched in. Still clutching a towel and dabbing at the wet patches on his suit, he acknowledged Mitchell contemptuously and brushed past him into the inner office.

Maureen met Trevor's helpless look. 'He's just had his car stolen,' she explained, 'he's a bit upset.'

Trevor followed Railton slowly into his office, requesting no calls and shutting the door firmly. Maureen flicked on the intercom, and with her hair falling over the desk, put her ear to the speaker. She started to make rapid shorthand notes. She had to strain to catch at Trevor's soft defensive replies, and when her phone interrupted, her heart hammered with guilt.

India was nervy and evasive. She wanted to speak to Railton and said it couldn't wait. When Maureen asked her to phone back there was a desperation in her voice that she'd never heard before. Maureen put her through and noticed how India waited for the click as she replaced her receiver. Turning down the humidifier she at first heard nothing but a crackling silence. She was just fiddling with the equaliser when Railton barked, 'Just tell me what the hell happened, and very slowly.'

Maureen nerved herself for a lead and decided it was a justified risk to lift the extension. Pressing down the silent button, she lifted the receiver and heard India telling Railton that they'd lost nearly a quarter of a million pounds. Her voice wavered only fractionally as she started recounting the disastrous resale of the *Electronic Shoal* pictures in the Paris auction only an hour previously. Picking up the dictaphone already loaded with fresh tape, Maureen held it to the receiver and recorded the entire story.

Trevor watched uncomfortably as Railton's shock turned to silence. Railton put the receiver down slowly and sat quietly tugging at his beard as if small self-inflicted shots of pain were preferable.

'You're in trouble, Trev,' he said eventually, 'big trouble.'

Trevor illogically remembered the garden in Spain, parched all summer, crazed without water. He saw the earth opening up in large cracks, trees leaning sideways with their roots exposed. He waited anxiously for the aftershock.

'That was India,' said Railton, springing to his feet and pacing the room. 'She just phoned to let us know that she's made a complete and utter balls-up. In fact, her timing's quite exquisite,' he added as an afterthought, and then as a query to himself, 'she couldn't have chosen a worse moment.'

'How does that affect us?' asked Trevor.

'The sun beat through the window on to his back. He glanced edgily at his watch; they were both due to see Foxton within the hour and there was a great deal to discuss. They needed to get their story straight. Trevor needed time to manoeuvre if he was going to stall John any longer.

'Today's sale was a disaster; we're down by quarter of a million.'

'But that's the strike pay money.' Trevor felt sick.

'It happens.' Railton trudged to and from the window. 'That's why art's risky, you've got to get the timing right. It's not like cashing in a postal order.'

'What do we do? And what do we tell John?'

'The truth for a change.' Railton twisted an odd smile, 'Add it to all the rest and see what he makes of it. Matters have got a little out of control unfortunately.' He raised a quizzical eyebrow at Trevor's sunken face. 'Ironically, this is exactly the sort of event we might have invented ourselves as a very credible excuse for losing money.'

'We should at least go in with a plan?' Trevor was unnerved and anxiously opened a battered file. He'd been carrying it around with him all the day before, and fallen asleep reading it in the hotel where he'd stayed overnight. The pages were creased and scribbled with notes, the cover was dodged with coffee rings.

'Too late for that now.' Railton shrugged carelessly, almost impatient for the storm. 'Let's go in there and brazen the whole thing out. It's about time he gave us some of his good advice. He's been leading a rather sheltered life, don't you think?' Only mildly irritated now by the wet patches mapping out his trousers, Railton savoured the moment. 'I'm sure he'll promise to stand by us Trev.' He loaded the sarcasm. 'He'll give us his word, no doubt.'

Gathering his papers cheerlessly Trevor followed Railton into the reception area. Silently he composed a speech to a crowd of workers, their white upturned faces dazzling within a sea of blue overalls. He rubbed his eyes. Anxiety gnawed at him like an ulcer and he chewed a peppermint to take away a taste like rust. He had never meant it to come to this.

'The *real* bastard hasn't even occurred to you yet, has it?' Railton propped himself against a filing cabinet and watched Foxton through a square meshed window finishing a phonecall.

Trevor looked up blankly. 'What's the matter with you, Mitchell? Your brain's gone to mashed potato these days.'

Trevor lunged towards him and then pulled up, holding his fist to his mouth, breathing hard.

Railton looked at him with pity. 'If you stopped mooning over your bunch of striking no-hopers just for a minute, Mitchell, you might remember that the *profit* margin this morning was pretty bloody crucial.'

Trevor looked away, dazed. 'It was going to pay our outstanding bill to Customs and Excise, remember?' He frowned. 'Bloody India,' he reminded himself. 'I think she owes us a favour.'

The filing cabinet rang out as he kicked it, and Foxton looked at him quizzically as he opened his door and nodded to Pearl for coffee.

'Sorry about your car, Kevin,' he said seriously. 'Pearl mentioned some kid on skates and something about a skinhead?'

Railton nodded ruefully. 'Sounds unbelievable I know.'

Foxton held his look steadily and ushered them in. 'The police will sort it out I'm sure. They usually do.'

Pearl laid out a tray and counted measures of coffee into the machine.

Maureen brooded over her keyboard. 'It was you who stole my cuttings file, I suppose?' She swung round in her chair accusingly.

'We only borrowed it.' Pearl noticed Maureen was shredding a tissue. 'It was really useful. It gave us a great lead.'

'Glad to be of some service, even if it's only for filing.' Maureen sulkily watched the screen colourise her first menu.

Pearl perched on her desk and observed Maureen carefully. 'So you heard the auction's gone wrong, but didn't India explain why?'

Maureen shrugged and quickly retrieved a tape from the dictaphone. She was busily displaying indifference. She sealed the tape in an envelope and pedantically locked it in her desk drawer. 'I couldn't listen to her. You can hear if someone picks up the extension, there's a sort of loss of volume, it's a dead giveaway. Couldn't risk it really, could I?' She clamped on her headphones apologetically.

The office was stifling, and as Pearl watched Maureen's fingers sprinting over the keyboard, fresh suspicions started like prickly heat. Maureen locking drawers and not listening in to phonecalls was worryingly out of character.

Checking the street carefully, Pearl eased down the blind.

A hot summer wind was eddying around the office block. A window in Foxton's office banged and the blinds swayed and shivered; the heat was thundery. Foxton looked up from the sheet of figures and absently tore an old blotter off his desk pad, covered in reversed signatures and old decisions. He crumpled it, dropped it in the bin, and looked across at the two men.

Trevor looked like a man who'd just struggled out of a wrecked car. Staring at the floor as if it gaped, he clutched a file to his chest and rocked slightly. Railton challenged John's look with a smile.

'So, Kevin,' John paced himself carefully, 'you'd agree with Trevor's assessment of our losses?'

Railton's hair lifted in the draught. He pushed it back briskly. 'Absolutely. The stock market's been like Russian roulette, everyone's taken a pasting.'

'And you advised Trevor to camouflage the figures?'

Trevor wiped his face in sections and prepared to speak but Foxton silenced him. He wanted their consultant's version.

Railton stood up and picked a tiny fleck of tarmac off his jacket. 'Yes, I advised that exactly.'

Trevor stared uncomprehending at the inexplicable lie but remained silent.

'No point in starting a stampede.' Railton peered at an old framed photograph of the Jarrow marchers and sniffed. 'Money markets are all about nerve. If rumours had got around, it could have weakened your position.' He shrugged. 'Much wiser to keep it in the family.'

'Especially if you know you're three million pounds down, Railton.' Foxton's voice was suddenly hard. 'Especially if that money should have been safely under cover and perfectly placed to administer for the strike. Especially as you know we would be very vulnerable if we were to make a fuss about its loss *if* we don't accept your explanation?'

Railton smiled. 'Honest John . . . Skeletons in the cupboard, not really your style at all, is it? Not quite how the world sees you.'

Foxton looked at him a long time. 'What is your game exactly, Railton?'

He didn't answer.

'You might as well tell me. I'm going to get to the bottom of this if it kills me.'

Railton barely disguised a sneer. 'Why don't you ask Mitchell? He's your treasurer, I simply advise him, as you know.'

Trevor shifted uneasily in his seat. 'I'm afraid that's not our only problem, John.'

As Foxton listened uneasily to the art sale losses he felt a thin thread of control visibly fraying.

Railton lounged in his chair. 'Unaccountable blip in market prices,' he remarked lazily, 'genuine losses can happen if the timing's out.'

Foxton glanced at Trevor hopelessly. 'This one's *genuine* is it?'

Trevor's cheeks blotched red as he leant forward and placed on the desk two sheets of closely-typed paper from his battered file.

'I've been working a strategy.' Trevor avoided looking at Railton. 'Minor liquidation options. They were for emergency use only, sort of safety net, but they could raise cash quickly for the strike pay.' He tailed off. 'It's not ideal.'

John stared at the figures, something in Trevor's voice sounding like the last desperate lunge at the finishing tape. 'Can it be ready for Monday? That's all I want to know.'

Trevor shrugged. 'It's just about possible, but our losses would be larger.'

'Just do it, Trevor.' Foxton met his watery eyes. 'And get onto it immediately.'

The door closed behind him, blowing papers off the desk. Foxton closed the windows and glimpsed a shimmer of sheet lightning across the city.

Railton lit a menthol cigarette and exhaled mint. 'I expect you're blaming me for this.' His target watched the lightning and the heavy rain which began to spatter the window. 'Under the circumstances, I assume you'll be dispensing with my services?' He watched Foxton deliberately return to his desk.

'Under the circumstances,' Foxton leant back in his chair, 'that's the last thing I'm going to do Kevin.'

Railton sat up. Leaning forward in his seat, he watched Foxton jotting notes with increasing incredulity.

'I accept your explanation,' Foxton continued. 'The situation has been *less* than ideal and no doubt you'll be helping Trevor to rebuild?'

Railton stood up in confusion. 'That's very reasonable of you, John.'

'I'm a very reasonable man,' Foxton smiled.

Pearl came in apologetically with the coffee.

'Good news, Mr Railton, we've just noticed out of the window that your car's back.'

'Thank God.' Railton diverted all his anguish towards his means of escape. He needed to get away fast and think himself through the shock. There'd be a way round it: resignation was an option he'd nearly offered but it lacked the drama he needed for his plan. He needed time to advance a counter-attack.

'Unfortunately,' continued Pearl, passing the milk to Foxton, 'there can't have been any money in the meter because the police have clamped it and now they're towing it away.' She passed him his cup sympathetically. 'Shame about the rain too, your sunroof was open.'

Railton thumped the arm of chair, his eyes distant with visions of revenge. 'Bastards, bastards.' He privately named the people who would soon regret crossing him.

'I can understand just how you feel,' said Foxton.

Twenty

Pearl went straight home at lunchtime with a sudden sick headache, as arranged. She walked across the car park past their old Wolsey, dust and must splotched with rain. She looked up at the tower block and saw the lights were on in her flat. She had some bridges to build. Cold drops fell on her face.

Lying on the sofa, Finn idly flicked through the channels and settled on the racing. She remembered playing a game as a kid, standing waiting for her uncle at the bookies. The winning game, a secret thing – she almost smelt the cigarette smoke as she went back into the memory – picking a horses's name, sometimes encouraged by the jockey's silks, bright flame, red for fire and luck her auntie said. She'd pick a name and repeat it over and over. Right through the race she'd drum the name inside her. With a hot certainty, she knew she could will it, she could make it work, and if she got it right, the horse would win. Small amongst the jostling men at the end of the race, pushed sideways by the crowd, she'd hold the secret tightly like a pebble in her hand. Finn leant back and read the names as they tumbled through the electric scoreboard, and curiously held on to one. She closed her eyes to bring back the feeling and heard the key turn in the lock.

Pearl came slowly down the stairs, threw off her shoes, and briefly checked the red zero simmering on the answerphone. Slightly surprised, she slumped onto the sofa. Finn shifted up without a word, intently watching the horses nudge into their stalls.

'Got a bet on?' Pearl checked her silence anxiously.

'Kind of.' Finn was turned into herself, her face set with concentration, and she watched through to the end of the race.

The camera swung back to a results round-up. Finn sat up and hugged her knees.

'Did you win?' Pearl wanted to talk, wanted to tear down the wall Finn always bricked herself behind. Finn nodded. 'How much?'

'Didn't put any money on.' Finn flicked the picture into near silence. 'But that doesn't matter.'

Pearl sat awkwardly next to her listening to the rain sweeping against the window. Two more races went by. 'Hang on a moment.' She jumped up decisively. 'Don't go anywhere, OK?'

Walking quickly to the bedroom she pulled off the suit jacket and skirt and dropped them on the floor. She felt like somebody else – like a secretary. She shed black tights and pulled on a vest. Opening the wardrobe she curiously faced herself in the mirror. Her burnished skin gleamed with heat; she casually pushed back her tumbling black hair. Suddenly glimpsing something she slammed the door, Pulling on her shorts she cursed herself out loud. She had walked in and compulsively checked the answerphone for his message: promised and broken. She'd even been searching her own reflection for him, for his feelings. Pearl turned away angrily and marched back to Finn.

Finn was asleep, her arm round a cushion. Pearl turned the racing commentary off and cleared her throat. 'Finn. I'm sorry. I didn't mean any of it. I was upset.'

Finn opened her eyes. 'Right then.' All she could think of was backing away into more silence, but Pearl was waiting. Finn looked at her awkwardly. 'So, what do we do next?'

'We could try talking to each other.' Pearl sat on the coffee table and made Finn look at her.

'I meant with the job – Railton.' Finn was still burning with resentment. 'Or do you want me to carry on by myself?'

Pearl walked away to the window. Finn stared bleakly, her tightly bunched anger like a blow about to fall.

'I can't explain about the other night, Finn.' Pearl watched a solid line of windscreens flashing on the dual carriageway down below. 'Or about not turning up for the job. It wasn't about letting you down.' She met Finn's look. 'I'll never do it again. That's almost a promise.'

Somewhere in the hallway children squabbled over a skate-board and their voices echoed away into silence. Below them the traffic hummed like the tide. The look had softened as Finn put Railton's keys on the table.

Pearl examined them carefully, running her finger around each one. 'They look perfect.' She looked up curiously. 'He must be good?'

'The best.' Finn nodded. 'He'd have to be, only an artist could get those right. They're designed not to be copied.'

'Artist?' Pearl grinned.

'That's what we used to call him. It was meant as a compliment.' Finn looked away and shivered, then took the keys, thoughtfully examining the one with the bevelled edge.

'You didn't really want to go there did you?' Pearl watched her partner carefully.

Finn pursed her lips and held up the key. 'This one doesn't belong but I got it done anyway.' She attempted a smile. 'Going there wasn't as bad as remembering it.'

Railton's home address was a new development on the Isle of Dogs and Pearl thumbed her way through the *A to Z* looking for the street name.

'Can't you tell me about it, Finn?'

Finn was staring at the television. 'I don't know.' She watched the cameras pan round the race course and felt Pearl trying to close the distance. Finn wished she could reach back, but she froze. Something she hadn't yet discovered was stopping her.

Millie crawled home through the mid-afternoon traffic. Piled on the back seat were hours of reading, briefs and research notes and Krish's television. She needed quiet and an absence of phones to get through the work for the next day in court. Waiting at the traffic lights she double-guessed when to accelerate and ran through a mental list for clearing space. She would ring John and check the results of his showdown with Railton and discuss the next moves. The case was unwinding nicely, and with the work on past sequestrations completed, very soon she and John Foxton would have no reason to meet at all.

Her front door appeared to be jammed. Balancing the files on her hip, she turned the key until it threatened to bend. Then she rang the doorbell.

Somewhere within the house she heard a door slam and someone running down the stairs. Her heart raced slightly and a file slithered on to the step.

She was bending to pick up a client's scattered letters when her daughter answered the door sheepishly in Eric's shirt.

Laura looked at her mother with a glazed smile. The memory of a book she had just read on sexual infidelity swam around in her head. It had stated categorically that clichéd behaviour automatically becomes your destiny if you embark upon a secret affair. She had dismissed that section in favour of the chapter on strategic pyschology, but now, it was with no real surprise that she heard herself say unconvincingly, 'Hi Mum, you're home early.'

Millie stowed her papers on the desk, put the kettle on and dialed John's number. Maureen moodily informed her that Mr Foxton was in a meeting and she would give him a message. Millie replaced the receiver, irritated that she couldn't normalise herself by dealing with something else. She grabbed the kettle, which was boiling dry without a lid, and called loudly for Laura.

Her daughter, restored to her own clothes, sat on the sofa and smiled uncomfortably. 'Thanks Mum, that's really kind.' She was searching for the aerial socket for the portable television.

Millie gave her a cup of tea and sat down opposite her with nothing to say. If this had been a defence or a prosecution she would have advanced the facts along the elegant curve of argument. But now she was all emotion and didn't trust herself.

It was Laura, sobered with the silence, who spoke. 'There would have been a massive loss of dignity, you see.' Millie tilted her head. 'If you'd found us in bed. Mostly for you. I didn't want that.'

'Thanks.' Millie sipped her tea and thought of Laura's father. They might have been dealing with this together in a different scenario and it might not have felt so difficult, like breaking bad news.

Laura shifted in her seat and dropped all her quick confident movements. She reached out and stroked her mother's foot rather hopelessly.

Millie's imagination re-engaged. Roger, of course, would have been appalled, broken things, threatened Laura with punishment and damnation, would have sent her into retreat. And Millie knew she would have defended, have wanted to shelter her in the face of anything. Roger would have burnt to a cinder before daybreak, taking them all with him if necessary. Millie shivered.

'Do you trust Eric?' she asked eventually.

Laura smiled. 'Is that a trick question?'

'No,' said Millie, 'extremely serious. And apart from the other more obvious ones about making you sure you don't get pregnant or diseased, which I assume you've catered for along with my dignity, it's the one I want you to ask yourself.'

Laura looked at her solemnly. 'Is that all you're going to say?' Millie nodded. 'Are you going to tell Dad?'

'Would he tell me?'

'Expect so. He'd want you to sort me out and tell how immorally I'd been behaving, wouldn't he?' Laura was hoping to make her mother smile.

But there was something like misery in the way Millie couldn't face her after that. She gathered up her work and took it up to her bedroom.

Millie had heard them go out noisily an hour later. She'd listened for the call up the stairs, and later looked around desperately for a note. Sometimes Laura left odd messages constructed with difficulty from the incomplete set of magnetic letters clustered on the door of the fridge. She looked and saw only a meaningless jumble. Millie suddenly realised that Laura might have interpreted her sudden withdrawal as judgment.

Feeling quarrelsome she dialled through to the union office, fully aware that it was probably too late for anybody to be there. Maureen morosely informed her that John Foxton had picked up her recent message and gone out, urgently, to see someone. Millie poured herself a cup of cold tea and closed down the thought automatically.

An hour later she shrugged on a raincoat and left the house on an impulse. Driving to Greenwich she pulled up at a wine bar she and Laura had visited on her last stay. Wandering through the crowded rooms hanging with lifebelts, nets and ships' figureheads she scanned the tables fruitlessly. A young man in black with a scarf tied like a pirate winked at her, a petite girl no older than Laura clung around his waist. Millie left hurriedly, feeling mocked; feeling old.

A vague thought became a mission. She was searching for Laura, wanting to explain, willing her back. Reversing the car into the traffic and driving along the trail of river pubs overflowing with young evening drinkers, she slowly understood how the stakes were raised between them. Millie suddenly felt in danger of being alone.

Finn pulled up outside Rufus' mother's small terraced house. Pearl leant over and sounded the horn impatiently.

'I don't know why we need Rufus anyway.' Finn looked at her watch. 'Railton could be home to greet us if we don't get a move on.'

'Exactly. We need back-up and I'd rather not rely on Maureen this time.'

Finn looked over. 'Don't know how we can afford her anyway?'

'We'll just put her on expenses.' Pearl felt uneasy.

Rufus appeared in socks at their mum's front door and waved. 'So why don't we use her?'

Pearl frowned and recalled the scene in the office. 'I'm just not sure if she's being entirely straight with us.' Finn looked startled. 'But that may come in handy.'

Rufus had cracked a roller wheel and sprained an ankle when his getaway had taken him down a ramp and wedged him in a storm drain. He levered himself gingerly into the car and waved wearily to Rose watching him from the doorstep.

'Mum took me to Casualty.' He sat back and groaned.

Finn glanced at him anxiously. 'What, in an ambulance?'

'No.' Rufus pulled his cap over his face. 'On my skates, man. She sort of towed me there, holding my hand.'

Pearl grinned and started laughing for what felt like the first time in weeks.

Finn parked the car near to Railton's house and Rufus slipped into the driver's seat, angling the mirrors to cover the approach of any car. A heavy shower suddenly blurred the windscreen and he switched on the wipers. The street was wide and lined with mock-Georgian houses with white porticos, stubby pillars and latticed windows. The entire estate looked as if it had been assembled from a kit. Each house had a shrubbery of identical conifers, white chipped drives and panelled garage doors. Rufus beat his fingers on the dashboard and experimented with rap rhymes for Legoland.

As they headed for Railton's front door through the rain Finn tapped a small moulded plastic case. 'Carpet samples,' she explained, 'a full multi-coloured range from shag pile through to twisted wool. Stay out of sight until I make sure no one's in.'

Finn rang several times on a doorbell which played the first bars from 'Jerusalem'. No one answered. They started to go through the keys methodically. Wiping the rain from her face, Finn nervously tried the first mortise and it turned through a circle and then back a quarter before obediently releasing the lock. She held her breath and quickly executed the remaining two. Now finally the yale: she slipped it in and turned. The lock yielded sweetly but the door remained firmly shut. Pearl tried it and leaned against the door. Poring over every surface Finn extracted the other keys and looked for one they had missed. The odd bevelled key was the only one they hadn't used. They had released every possible lock and the door still remained firmly shut. Finn swiftly started to lock them all back up again.

'What are you doing?' Pearl tried to stop her.

'Something's wrong.' Finn felt the old sick feeling starting. 'And he'll go on red alert if he gets back and finds them like this.'

They hurried round to the back of the house. Finn examined every door. 'I don't understand the system.' She shook her head. 'I must be getting out of date.'

Pearl was staring up at the windows running with water. 'Maybe India can help us after all. She must have been here.'

They were both creeping beneath the large ground floor window when an opaque blind moved across it noiselessly. A light glowed behind it. Suddenly the clubbing back-beat of black disco throbbed through the glass and shadowy people filled the room, some dancing, some holding glasses. A crescendo of voices and the odd high laugh rose and fell. Finn instinctively yanked Pearl back into the soaking bushes. They stared incredulously at the empty house holding a party. Pearl's mouth felt like sand; Railton had been in there all the time, might even have seen them.

They crept forward and were slithering through damp waxy flowers when they saw Rufus limping towards them. He was totally visible, walking directly past the kitchen windows.

Finn lunged towards him and pushed him backwards angrily. 'Can't you see the place is crawling?' she hissed.

'Wrong.' He grabbed his ankle painfully and then limped to the main window and observed the party carefully. He appeared to be counting. Pearl grabbed his arm and tried to pull him away.

'Relax, P.' He didn't bother to lower his voice. 'They're only holograms.'

She let go of his sleeve and stared.

'Lights and music going on and off never fooled anyone.' He pointed at the dancers moving tirelessly. 'But invent a few people and you've got the ultimate deterrent.' He watched approvingly. 'A mate of mine is really into this. It's the latest thing. He's making an absolute fortune.'

Finn still stared suspiciously. 'How much would this lot cost?'

Rufus pulled his cap down against the rain, mentally beating out syllables. 'Arm and a leg, minimum.'

'OK,' nodded Pearl, 'so this isn't to protect his poxy record collection. So what *has* he got to hide?'

'India's got some explaining to do,' said Finn grimly, hurrying back to the car.

Twenty-one

Swathes of rain beat across the car as John Foxton drove into a wide, gracious street and parked in a space reserved for the Malaysian Embassy. A small party of diplomats in ceremonial robes, brilliant greens and yellows, like tropical plants, were huddling under black umbrellas. They swayed in twos and threes for limousines and silently slid away. An embassy official in morning dress picked up a small scarlet scarf in their wake and carried it back inside like a broken flower.

Checking the map again, John pored over the tiny interlocking streets and traced the name of Trevor's road only about half an inch away, buried in a smudge of green.

He drove on slowly looking for the side street, peering through the curve made by windscreen wipers. Large stylish houses ascended from wide stairways to pillars and bay trees in white boxes. John sighed. When his friend had moved last year it seemed he had bought into a neighbourhood of tall and elegant windows.

Lodge Walk led into a subway. Cautiously he drove through and emerged into the murky light of what appeared to be a small leafy park. He left the car on the edge of the yellow brick development and checked Trevor's address against the plan tastefully etched on a sheet of steel.

The cage of trees was locked, so he walked round the edge of a complex of apartments, their wide balconies brimming with plants. The rain made the colours run. Gusting wind bent the leaves over and turned them silver. John let the rain soak into his shirt and guiltily wished he had come here before, as a friend.

Shamefully he spared himself his excuses and walked slowly up the stairs, rehearsing his lines. Trevor had apparently left the office abruptly after their meeting with Railton and had not returned. John hoped against hope that he was working at home and developing his proposed rescue plan. But his phone had rung unanswered.

Foxton needed to discuss the financial plan urgently, but more than anything else he steeled himself to get to the heart of the truth. He had to know.

In the corridor leading to a row of front doors his footsteps mimicked his hesitation. John pressed the bell and waited. Every apartment seemed to be muffled and empty. He rang again hopelessly and suddenly heard a noise beyond the door. He pressed against the wood and listened. He could hear definite sounds. Rapping on the door he called through the letterbox. Listening again in the silence he realised the noise had stopped and footsteps hurried towards him.

'I'm the domestic assistant.' The young woman who opened the door smiled shyly. 'I'm a char really.' She smiled quizzically. 'It's a feminist agency you see, less demeaning imagery, that's their line.' She smiled and plucked at her personal stereo around her neck. 'Sorry I didn't hear you. I was ironing. When I'm wearing these I go right off.' She led him down the hall.

'I didn't know Trevor was a feminist.' John searched for small talk, needed her on his side.

She laughed. 'You're kidding. It's Daphne.' John felt like a stranger at the wrong address. He'd known Daphne for years. Loud and round and flirtatious, she mixed her time between the hairdresser, shopping and bingo nights. She'd never struck him as a feminist.

'You don't *have* to wear a boiler suit,' she said adeptly, reading his thoughts, it's about non-dependency.' He nodded and her stare told him that she recognised him. 'Trevor came in and went out again about an hour ago. And I'm Nelly.' He shook her hand. 'He didn't say when he'd be back.'

'He's got a file we need urgently, I'll just take a look.'

She looked at him cautiously. 'Trev won't mind, will he?'

Foxton smiled. 'No love. He knows I'm looking.'

She went back to her ironing. The music tinkled against the steaming of Trevor's shirts, they hung garishly round the kitchen, disembodied, like bad jokes.

John walked slowly round the apartment. Exclusively furnished in lavender and pink, it was the opposite of Trevor. Copies of *The Financial Times* were stacked in piles next to the sofa, and video tapes lay scattered on the floor. John picked them up and read the spines. Recent recordings of business and money programmes had cuttings clipped to their boxes, – city articles from investment magazines. Recent financial surveys and analyses were ranged according to country in box files, each one with scribbled notes detailing the contents. A stranger would have deduced that the treasurer had been a workaholic for the union.

John sat down at the small writing desk and dragged at his hair in a daze. The apartment was comfortable but small and not extravagant. He picked up a photo in a clipframe: Trevor's wife in a sundress standing in front of a small bungalow. 'Hacienda with a palm tree.' Trevor hadn't thought much of it; said he hated the sun. John felt instinctively that Trevor couldn't have the money. If he could find him he felt sure he could make him tell the whole story.

'Daphne's still away.' Nelly had her coat on. 'Found what you want?' There was nothing but unopened bills and football coupons on the desk top and the answerphone had been disconnected. He found a bunch of keys and opened the small cupboard below. Getting on his hands and knees he pulled out a small boxed frame containing medals with brightly coloured ribbons. Campaign medals from the Spanish Civil War, and a small bronze cross for outstanding bravery in action. A small photograph in a leather frame showed a handsome man in the uniform of the International Brigade, smiling through a brush moustache and casually holding a black revolver. Foxton placed them back carefully and remembered all the stories; Trev was more than proud of his dad.

Nelly watched him steadily. 'To tell you the truth,' she seemed to be gauging whether she could trust him, 'I was rather worried about Trevor.'

'Do you know where he's gone?' he was alarmed.

She shook her head. 'He'd got his briefcase.' She met his eye and hesitated. 'But he'd had this phonecall. And when it was over I thought . . .' she stopped herself, almost glaring at him.

'What?' His anxiety reassured her.

She shook her head. 'I thought I heard him crying.'

Outside it had stopped raining and Foxton ran through puddles to his car. He went into every pub near the union offices. Trevor might have gone there to be anonymous and to think. He would hope John would come looking for him. Perhaps he wanted to be found, like a child. But he was nowhere.

Going back to the union building was a final chance. Pulling up wearily in the carpark, John looked and noticed a light slatted by blinds on the fifth floor. Water stood like shadows all over the tarmac as he splashed towards the security window.

'Someone waiting for you inside, John.' The guard at the lodge was watching football on a miniature TV and nodded carelessly towards the main entrance.

Foxton hurried across the echoing foyer. Maybe Trevor had hoped that he would track him down here. He almost ran across the space and stopped abruptly. Waiting for him by the lifts was Millie.

'We've been trying to reach you.' Her voice uneven.

'I was looking for Trevor.'

She walked to meet him. 'Isn't that why you hire detectives?'

He noticed her coat had soaked up rain in a dark tide line.

'I wasn't even sure he was missing.' He grabbed her arm and closed the lift door. 'But I am now.'

They stood awakwardly in the lift. Millie composed the beginning of two sentences and abandoned them. Foxton punched a fist against the palm of his hand nervously and, as soon as the door opened, sprinted down the corridor.

He ran into Trevor's office. The lights were blazing and there was a faint smell of cigarette smoke, coffee and office flowers. The blinds swung against the breeze. Foxton looked into the darkened reception area.

'He's been here recently.' Putting his hand on the glass of the photocopier, he noticed it was still warm. He hurried back into the office and sat at Trevor's desk. Millie watched him find a pile of files neatly stacked, the top one battered and covered in rings from a coffee mug.

A white envelope addressed to him was propped against the phone. He slit it open and silently read through the contents.

'He's left detailed plans for a liquidation of certain parcels of stock. It looks meticulous and could be implemented tomorrow.' He glanced anxiously at Millie. 'It's ready to go into action if I give the go-ahead. He wants India to handle it.'

'Really?' Millie was looking at the tiny bunch of golden freesias wiring the office with scent, and vaguely remembered something. 'Why can't he do it himself?'

Foxton looked back at the letter, ran his finger over the print and looked up at her miserably. 'I rather get the impression he's resigned.'

Millie dialed Pearl's number, left an urgent message, and slumped into a chair. John broke out of his thoughts and looked at her in confusion.

'What are you doing here, Mil?'

'I needed to talk to somebody.'

Millie suddenly looked back at the freesias. 'Why's India bringing Trevor flowers?'

He looked startled and smiled. 'India and Trev? That's just not possible.'

'Nor was your oldest friend embezzling.' Millie was thinking back to Pearl's face as she had described the wrecked flat. 'I have a feeling India's more involved in this than anybody has realised.' She looked out into the dark where strings of lights mapped out the city.

'What should we do?' Foxton was nervously at her side.

'Nothing. Just hope Pearl and Finn get back safely.'

Foxton opened up the filing cabinet and found a bottle of scotch and two glasses. 'Is that the only reason you came here?' He tried to make her meet his eye.

'I was passing and saw the office light on.' She took the glass and turned away, remembering how she had been fruitlessly looking for Laura. He placed his hand gently on her shoulder.

'I really don't mind, if that's just an excuse, Mil?'

She wheeled round and slammed the glass back on the desk. 'There are times when you really piss me off.' He recoiled fractionally. 'You're forever coming to me for free advice at any time of the day or night. You're compulsively playing some kind of cruel game with the past, completely on your terms of course. And on the one occasion I come to you because *I* really need someone,' she faltered, her voice shaking, 'you think I've come to talk about *you*.'

Millie was trembling. 'Always selfish, and I used to love you so much I made the mistake of not minding.' She stared at him, waiting for some reaction, then grabbed her drink and hurried out into Maureen's office. She was still sitting in the dark, spinning on the chair when he dared to follow her.

He drove her home. Millie let him out of weariness and complete absence of feeling. He was teaching her in steady steps how to forget she had ever felt anything. She stared blankly at busy streets, groups of kids sitting inside wine bars and wondered if Laura might desert her for good. *Massive loss of dignity*. How like her daughter to understand how much that could matter, as an excuse for hurt.

She watched John's reflection concentrate on the traffic, and tightened her watch strap until it bit into her wrist. She wanted to let out her panic about Laura, and particularly to him.

As he pulled up in front of her house Foxton switched off the engine and fiddled with the keys in the ignition. Their silence had thickened and he felt oppressed, almost frightened. Whatever it was between them, it was going wrong. He hardly dared to look at her, knowing it must be over, and not wanting the end. Drearily he stabbed the mileage counter, watching the digits flick through.

'If anyone's claiming mileage it should be me.' Millie had been watching him.

He smiled. 'But it's my car.'

She got out and leant back through his window, 'That's completely irrelevant.'

Obediently he went to start the engine and she stopped him. 'Come on in John, I'll be honest: I need some company.'

He locked the car and followed her into the dark house. She switched on a light and looked at him.

'It's nothing to do with us. Perhaps I should have said. So you can leave now if that doesn't sound quite so inviting?'

He picked up Laura's scarf and it rang with tiny bells. Staring at it bleakly, Millie automatically stabbed the answerphone.

Two messages from Maureen unable to locate John, and one from a call box, punctuated with traffic. It was Laura. 'Mum. It's me. You must be working.' A hopeful pause waiting for an interruption, then, 'Hoped you were in monitoring mode. Eric and I are dossing at a friend's. Hope you don't mind. Need some space for Question Time.' She sighed. 'Like you said, Mum.' Another faltering pause requiring another coin and more silence. 'You would answer wouldn't you, if you were there?'

Laura's voice sounded strained and strangely tearful, fretting at the space between the message and what she needed to say. The receiver went down suddenly. Millie rewound the tape. She heard John sit down.

'What is it, Mil?'

She turned ruefully. 'Laura. I was worried she'd . . .' She suddenly wondered what she would have called it. Not running away, she didn't even live with her. Angrily Millie remembered that if she had not run away herself she would have been there to take the phonecall. She should have talked to Laura before; she might have rescued the moment if she hadn't been so immediately weighed down by her own guilt: this thing in her life which Laura only knew through rumours and vague memories.

Millie smiled. 'I don't know what I thought. She didn't tell me where she was going, that's all.'

She went out into the dark garden, and taking her shoes off walked through the wet grass.

John followed her cautiously. 'Do you two always talk in code?' He searched for a bridge.

Millie nodded and regretted lashing out at him. 'Sometimes it's quite effective.' He accepted her smile.

They carried out deckchairs and staring up at the sky he started to tell her about the showdown with Railton.

'The look on Railton's face when he realised I wasn't going to give him the push.' He replayed the memory. 'I must admit I did enjoy it.'

'What about Mepham and his managing director . . . ?' Millie searched for the name of the ruthless elegant man who picked through television interviews like a sniper. 'Pearson, isn't it?'

John had a sudden memory of men shooting to kill in a shed in the back streets of South Kensington. He nodded grimly. 'They'll be getting a nasty shock, any minute now . . .'

Millie listed to his voice falling and rising and must have dozed for a few minutes. She woke with a start. John had slumped to one side, his face slackened by sleep, unprepared.

Something toppled over inside the house. Millie listened; she must have heard it earlier to have woken up so suddenly. As she touched John's arm there was a crash of breaking glass. He stood up straight out of his sleep and hurried into the kitchen. Millie followed him as he crouched behind the worktop. He looked cautiously over it into the sitting room but could see nothing. Huddled like an intruder in her own house Millie heard someone wilfully breaking her possessions.

John rushed forward into the sitting room and stopped suddenly, looking round helplessly at Millie. Flying round the room was a swallow, a smudge of black and feathers fluttering against curtains, into windows and the glass of picture frames, brushing vases and sweeping low against a wine glass in the grate.

Small piles of soot spilled out over the rug and spattered over the sofa and walls. Millie made an instinctive lunge at the bird, and passing like a shadow, it hovered and darkened the room. Terrified, it flew against the window with a thud. Millie felt its wing against her face and, touched with its panic, she grabbed at the curtains. Part of the material came away from the hooks and swung sideways. The bird toppled to the floor, and lay shivering behind a chair.

Millie froze, her head pounding, unreasonably unnerved, waiting gratefully as John crept towards it.

John missed the bird. It flapped along the floor and vanished into the kitchen. Rushing into the garden, John almost expected to see the shape shaking off soot in the darkness. But all was quiet, with no sign of the whirling bird.

Millie was pale and leaning with her back against the wall. She held her hand to her head fervishly.

'Has it gone?'

He squeezed her hand briefly and looked at the wreckage round the room. He was aware that exhaustion was letting him cast the bird as messenger.

Millie's shock was evaporating and she scooped some marigolds back into a spilt pot. She was apologetic.

'I always get spooked. My grandma used to say, if a bird dies in a house . . .' she stopped. He waited for her to finish. 'It means a death. Ridiculous, I know.'

Millie's childhood superstition disarmed her. John leant his face against hers and held her closely. She held him nervously at first, then kissed his face all over like the rain.

Twenty-two

It was nearly midnight when Finn and Pearl gave up watching India's empty flat and went home. Pearl flicked on the television and rewound the answerphone which had clocked up nine calls. On the television screen three women and two men sat on uncomfortable chairs in a badly-lit studio and semaphored an impassioned debate. Suddenly they were frozen and a commercial break wiped them out like a dream. Pearl rubbed her eyes and dismissed two calls without messages. Then there were three from Millie, all timed and building up in anxiety, followed by a fourth, her voice sounding different, explaining suspicions about India and sounding fearful.

Finn listened from the kitchen and brought fish and chips through steaming on the paper.

'It's only a hunch.' She started to eat. 'Trevor *would* leave it to India, wouldn't he? He's got no reason to distrust her.'

'Doesn't explain the flowers.' Pearl frowned. 'Millie's right. It is odd.' This small detail disturbed her, or perhaps she was still associating perfumed flowers with broken furniture. 'And it doesn't explain Trevor just taking off either.'

'He's done it before.' Finn switched to another channel and an old gangster movie hurtled round corners on two wheels.

Pearl went through the other calls, one from Rufus, then two more without messages. A total of four attempts from somebody to say something, but not bothering, or not daring. She dialled Millie but her machine answered curtly. Pearl clocked in obediently, relieved that her boss's anxiety had clearly subsided.

The doorbell rang briefly, then again almost immediately.

'You go, Finn.' Pearl kept her eyes on the screen, but felt her heart suddenly accelerate. 'Whoever it is, I've gone to bed.'

Finn looked unwilling but got up. 'What if it's . . ?' They were back again with what they had never really talked about.

'The same. Please.' She touched Finn's arm and retreated to her bedroom.

Finn opened the door to a subdued Fitz. He slouched against the wall on the opposite side of the hall. For a moment he could have been a stranger, his dark skin paled in the artificial light, his slight eccentricity, a red cumberband, around his waist. His soft leather jacket was silent when he moved, sleek like an animal.

'You alone?' He smiled, pleased to see her.

Finn liked him, simply and warmly, even when she wanted to resist. She saw the misery Pearl harboured, but remembered his face, that night at the club, staring hopelessly after her into the dark.

'Pearl not around?' He didn't attempt to pressure her.

Finn shook her head and he pushed off the wall. 'That's probably a good thing. Can we talk?'

She led him inside and down the stairs in some confusion. He put his arm around her briefly, affectionately, like a brother. He smelt faintly of talcum powder as if he'd bathed to come out, and his shirt was clean. Finn was oddly nervous; she felt she was hiding something. He sat back on to the sofa gratefully and noticed the fish and chips.

'Where is she?' He wasn't insisting.

Finn decided the truth was the only option. 'Gone to bed.'

He stared at the television; a man in a floppy mac crouched on a roof ready to ambush another.

'It's a difficult time, Finn.' He looked back at her asking for sympathy, wanting to explain and enlist support.

Pearl opened her bedroom door and walked into the room fully dressed.

'It's not easy for any of us.' She looked strained. 'So leave Finn out of it. It's not fair.'

Fitz stood up and smiled nervously. 'I don't blame you, Princess.'

Pearl glanced helplessly at Finn stranded in front of a car crash on screen. The black and white wreckage flew in every direction, a man ran towards the police with his clothes on fire.

'I came to tell you something.' Fitz said softly, moving towards Pearl and steering her towards her room. 'Please just give me a few minutes?' Pearl hesitated and then decisively walked up the stairs towards the hall. He looked confused, then followed her out through the front door. She closed it behind them.

Finn collapsed back on the sofa still caught up in the confusion which held them both, and made herself try to understand part of it again. Clutching the cushion she fell into a shallow sleep which echoed with the voices in the corridor.

Fitz paced up and down the hall, then broke their silence. 'What is this, P, back to talking on staircases?' He was suddenly upset, his leather jacket flapped around him.

'It's safer, I suppose.' Pearl was calm. 'Please Fitz, no more talking, no more anything until . . .' she broke off angrily. 'Oh I don't know, you tell me.'

He walked towards her as if what he had to say might be overheard. 'I'm leaving Saturday night. That's definite.' The words came separately. 'I had to come and tell you, so I couldn't let you down.'

A woman clattered down the stairs and stared curiously. Fitz smiled, leaned over and kissed Pearl's cheek. 'Sorry, P, I should have phoned right? But leaving a message, well . . .'

She watched him walk to the end of the corridor. He turned as if he'd forgotten something. 'You'll be here, yeh?'

Finn was fast asleep on the sofa, clutching her cushion. Pearl sat down next to her gently and pulled her arm. 'Finn?' She could have talked all night; all those things she'd been holding under. Fitz had looked grey with certainty, all his excitement was nervousness, as if he was facing a reality. Finn slept on restlessly and Pearl simply stayed next to her, sharing her warmth.

The summer sky was already pale with light and the curtains flapped through the wide-open window. Pearl thought she could smell the sea.

When Finn woke the phone had been ringing through her sleep for some time. Pearl was slumped against her, an arm thrown round her, deeply asleep. Finn moved her gently, picked up the receiver and squinted at her watch: five forty-five in the morning.

It was John Foxton. 'Sorry to phone so early, Finn.' She didn't answer. He carried on awkwardly, 'I hoped I wouldn't need to wake you, but your machine's not on.'

'We go live during sleeping hours, in case it's urgent . . .'

Foxton smiled, her Geordie edge was a relief, he didn't want anyone to be kind.

'Look, I'm in meetings all morning. But Trevor has definitely disappeared. He has to be a priority, Finn. I've been through the papers he left. I'm sure this financial plan of his won't work without him to drive it. And, there's something else besides.'

He paused so long Finn thought he'd changed his mind, but he appeared to have walked into another room, his voice sounded so different when he spoke again.

'I think Trevor's in some sort of danger.' He cleared his throat. He sounded tired, less assured. 'He may be vital to the union right now, but he's also my friend.'

'Is this another hunch?' Finn wanted the odds.

She heard Foxton understand. 'Sort of. But his letter mentioned his wife, as if she might be alone soon. I'd been trying to work out what he meant and I suddenly woke up frightened.'

Pearl stirred and sat up stiffly, rubbing her neck.

'Where do you suggest we start?' Finn picked up a pen.

Foxton gave him Maureen's home address. 'She might have some idea. If you'd get on to it now, I'd be grateful.' He hung up abruptly.

Pearl limped to her feet and hugged her ribs. 'You must have the sharpest elbows ever.'

Finn grinned and stretched her neck. 'At least I don't snore.'

Pearl's bag had spilled on to the sofa and Finn had been sleeping on the contents. Replacing the receiver, she painfully removed a hairbrush and a micro-cassette from the small of her back and put them on the table with a groan.

Pouncing on the cassette, Pearl rummaged through a drawer for their miniature tape recorder.

'What is it?' Finn watched her snapping the tape into the machine and switching it on.

The tape appeared to be blank until Pearl realised it wasn't moving. Dud batteries.' She raided the calculator and loaded them quickly. 'Maureen's dictaphone. She was behaving very suspiciously so I pinched a tape I saw her locking in her drawer.'

'How?' Finn asked curiously.

'I picked the lock with a hairgrip.' She grinned. 'It wasn't so difficult.' She rewound the tape to the beginning. 'It may be nothing, probably her memoirs.'

Finn looked crumpled, Pearl could see the line of her jacket creased on her cheek. Sun streamed through the windows. They listened to India's uneven telephone voice explaining how the union had lost a fortune. Railton's voice angrily cut through the static. Together they sorted through the events which had followed, the show-down with John and Railton's rage.

'I don't get it?' Finn looked at the tape accusingly. 'This art thing – is India playing games or not?'

'If Railton thinks she is,' Pearl was remembering India's fear and Railton's face disfigured with anger, 'she could be in more danger than she imagines.'

She turned the tape over thoughtfully. 'And it's about time Maureen told us the whole story.'

Under a huddle of sheets Millie watched John walk back into the bedroom with the telephone and plug it back into the wall next to her. He padded back out, placing each step tentatively across the creaking boards. She clutched the pillow and roused herself from sleep, surfacing towards the light. She considered getting up and following him.

The kitchen door slammed and she heard steps coming back up the stairs. John came back into the room less carefully and placed two mugs of steaming coffee on the bedside table. The china chinked together and he stirred the spoon vigorously, letting it hit the side.

Millie stirred and he sat down on the edge of the bed making a shape which included her. He bent over her face, his skin was cold like a swimmer's.

She held him close. 'Who were you phoning, John?'

'It wasn't private,' he stroked her cheek, 'I just didn't want to wake you.'

Millie turned over and pulled the alarm clock towards her.

Six-o-six moved on a digit. She looked back. Preoccupied, he was counting his way through the squares on the quilt, suddenly nervy, the night fading. He seemed almost opaque with leaving. Millie lay still, waiting for his answer. She knew he wouldn't lie to her now and it frightened her.

'It was Finn.' He tried to smooth down his rumpled hair with quick uncertain gestures and attempted a smile. 'I had to ring her. I was worrying; I couldn't sleep. I suddenly had this idea about maybe Maureen knowing . . .'

Millie watched him laying out his thoughts, working out his theory excitedly with his square hands. She dragged a pillow over her head and tightly bunched the sheets and blankets around her. He stopped in mid sentence and laughed, feeling the relief again, letting the weightlessness of the night wash over him. He tugged at the blankets. Millie still lay with her face against the sheet. He bent over, kissed her back, still brown from a holiday he knew nothing about, and traced the freckles.

'Don't you care, Mil?' She lay very still, not answering, not responding to his touch.

Anxiously he made her turn towards him and kissed her closed eyes. 'You do understand, don't you?'

Millie rolled over with the bedclothes and studied him. She felt suddenly self conscious, aware that nobody had pulled her out of her sleep for years. His blond hair looked windswept, he leant on one arm towards her, his face clouded with concern.

'What's the matter?'

'Just a bad dream.' She excused herself and turned him towards her, catching his hair round her fingers, almost wanting to awaken a hurt in him, like a memory, as warning. Smiling, he fought her away easily and then held her tightly against him. They were back with the closeness and he was waiting for her reply.

'Obviously, I wondered who you were phoning.' Millie talked into his body. 'We've got bad memories of waking too early, or pretending to sleep, just waiting to hurt each other when it got light. For a moment, I couldn't bear it, not even the thought of it.'

She could hear his heart beating, his cool palm stroking her back, and was reassured he didn't answer her. She didn't want to rouse any of those bad memories, although it was the chill of a premonition which made her certain that they would always ghost her.

She kissed his frown. 'I've really missed you.'

He looked shaken. 'It's not that simple though, is it Mil?' He bolted down the feeling as he said it. She saw how he had turned his back and made himself forget.

She had already known; would never forget that day she had retraced her steps to his office and watched him through the glass window as he had dictated a letter to a secretary. The girl had made a mistake and he had laughed and returned to his desk smiling. His grieving had been different. Millie had carried a shadow inside her. She shivered now as sunlight came through the curtains, and abandoned the memory. You could colour all the past with blame and guilt. She moved towards him for warmth.

He watched her bleakly. 'You were the one who did the walking out, Mil.'

Millie reached for her coffee and drank it down; it was already cold.

The truth so bluntly described felt like a blow. When she replied, the words sounded stark, like a statement. 'I had to.' She imagined that someone might read her words back and ask her to sign for them. 'For the sake of my child who is now nearly grown up, and my husband, who left me anyway.' She heard the bitterness in her voice and smiled. 'So much for family life, eh?'

He shrugged uncomfortably and reached for her again, vague reassuring touches almost checking she was still there.

'You did it in the right order, John, no lies, no guilt. You'd left your wife, it must have seemed so straightforward.' Millie pressed her face against the pillow.

'How do you feel about second chances?' He sounded wistful, but he had that way of saying things as if they had already happened.

Millie got up quickly and hurried down into the kitchen in her dressing gown. The fridge was artistically stacked with food and she dislodged home-made lasagne verde and pyramids of peppers and fresh herbs to find the bacon.

She had planned to cook Eric and Laura breakfast every

morning and had stocked up with mushrooms and sausages. The food still towered and sloped on the shelves.

Eric had suddenly converted to vegetarianism on the plane as a shock reaction to reading an inflight magazine feature about quail farming. The next day he had explained the revelation in expressive French and then again, flatly, in English.

Millie had been preparing a lunch of beef and Yorkshire pudding, rising golden as clouds in animal fat. Laura had been obliviously sipping coffee with the brief, bony young man half-inflated by a blouson jacket, and brown-legged in tartan shorts. A small stitched hat crouched like a bird in his black wavy hair. Millie thought irresistably of Tintin, his oval white face led by an upturned nose. She had begun to grate cheese and whisk eggs.

The bacon had remained neatly folded. Now Millie set about making breakfast with no will to eat. The coffee had only just started to drip into the jug when John came into the kitchen dressed and knotting his tie. His quietened hair lay flat and wet, his body reclaimed by the suit. Millie found herself staring and turned away, cracking eggs with concentration into the pan.

'Sorry. I really am.' He kissed her neck. 'I'm no good to you like this. I can't get any of this mess off my mind until I've done something about it. Today's going to be crucial.'

'What are you doing about Trevor?' Millie caught his anxiety reluctantly.

'If Pearl and Finn can find him I'm positive he'll tell us now how to prove Railton took the money.'

'What about the strike fund?' He was aware she was reading his thoughts consecutively.

'The first payments were just about possible until the auction disaster. Now I don't know. But I've got a plan.' He picked up his briefcase. 'I'll call you.'

She nodded. 'I'll brief Krish. He'll link for you with Pearl and Finn.'

He sensed her change in mood and put his briefcase down. 'Millie? You're still going to represent me, aren't you?'

She pulled away and nodded. 'That's what I think we should concentrate on. Keep things separate.' She looked at him calmly. 'After all, this case will be wrapped up soon enough.'

'One way or another.' He seemed subdued, his face was papery with lack of sleep. 'And what then, Mil?'

I don't know. She didn't say the words, just let him hurry out to his car. But she said them over and over again to herself after she heard him drive away.

Millie fell asleep in her bath. She woke with a start; the water had cooled and she was unbearably cold. The front door slammed and she heard Laura and Eric's voices in the sitting room. Shivering, she wrapped herself in a towel and dried herself back into reality.

Hovering indecisively on the landing she heard Laura's laugh, and the smell of breakfast wafted upstairs.

Marooned in her bedroom she made the real world seep back. She had taxed her daughter with matters of morality and trust and then spent the night with the man who had admitted unlimited chaos into her life. She dried her hair until her head ached. She was suddenly painfully aware that John had told her hardly anything about his life since their separation.

Millie descended resolutely through the living room into the kitchen. Eric and Laura were curled up together watching a cartoon and eating bacon sandwiches. A thin pall of blue smoke from fried bread hung in the air. Laura turned round happily.

'Just amazing, Mum.'

Millie ignored the cooker and the brown sauce bottle. 'Good time last night?'

Laura patted Eric's white face. 'Really brilliant. Eric's friend is a variable vegan. The whole thing's based on the positive collision of opposites.'

Millie took that to mean that bacon was once again ideologically sound. She threw away the two cold breakfasts.

'You look really rough.' Laura grinned approvingly and went to give Millie a hug. Her mother's nod was non-committal.

'Must have been some wild party.' She looked proudly from the soot spattered walls over to Eric. Millie swept a broken glass off the worktop and dropped it into the bin. John's black finger marks were all over the wall.

'Expect all sorts of unbelievable people just dropped in?'

Millie was vague. 'Yes. Something like that.'

Twenty-three

Maureen had a strict routine in the morning which varied only at weekends when she built in swimming and weight training on alternate weeks. Her radio alarm woke her at six with the farming programme and the latest prices for cut flowers and artichokes.

By six fifteen she had decaffeinated coffee and a notebook and was watching her portable television. Half an hour later she lay in the bath with her headphones and an advanced French conversation course.

The pluperfect was labouring through a weighty set of exercises and Maureen longed to be reunited with husky Yves and perky Florence of the question-and-answer sequences. An insistent female voice, steely with interrogation skills, grilled Maureen ruthlessly until she dismally switched off the tape. As she applied her vitamin cream, she parsed verbs and considered a career in Europe. It would probably entail changing her Christian name at least.

The door-bell startled her, and as she hurried down, retying her dressing gown, she saw Pearl and Finn swirled through the glass panels of the front door.

'Safer to talk privately.' Pearl was unsmiling. 'If we're going to be completely honest with each other.' The kitchen was spotless and tiny, with a rack of foreign cookery books and two hot-plates.

'Breakfast meetings are becoming almost routine.' Maureen nervously made toast for Finn and put the lid back on the museli.

'Why didn't you tell us what you'd overheard on the phone?'

Maureen poured hot water on a herbal tea bag. 'I don't know what you're talking about.'

'Who are you working for, Maureen?' Finn turned over Railton's keys in her pocket.

She sipped her tea resentfully. 'You, of course.' Finn unnerved her; there was something complicated about her, harder to answer than questions. Unrepentant, she glared at Pearl. 'It's your own fault anyway.'

Pearl put the tape down on the formica with a click. 'How's that then?'

Maureen coloured pink and hot rash prickled her neck.' You went and did it to me just like everybody else. I get really hacked off.' She was so close to tears she was shaking. 'People giving me orders when half the time . . .' She shook her head. 'Secretaries are a sexist anachronism. You began to treat me just the same, just using me.'

Pearl looked awkward. 'It wasn't meant like that.'

'That's what they all say.' Maureen chewed her lip. 'The point is that I was coming up with good leads for you and you couldn't even be bothered to tell me what you were doing.' She grabbed the tape. 'I decided to go it alone. I wanted to show you.'

Pearl sighed and glanced at Finn. 'Maureen, we apologise.'

'Yeh.' Finn looked unusually sympathetic.

'Trevor's disappeared and it looks as if India's vanished too. Could there be any connection?' Pearl looked worried. 'She may be in some sort of danger.'

Maureen hooked her hair behind her ears dismissively. 'India's *not* missing.'

'How do you know?'

'She went to her art class last night.'

Pearl frowned. 'But she hasn't been home.'

'She wouldn't. It's the end of a special module, they're always down at the studio for twenty-four hours. She won't be finished until tonight.'

'But Trevor was relying on her being back at the office.'

Maureen shrugged. 'Perhaps he didn't know.'

The freesias still bothered Pearl, their remembered scent on her hands as strong as garlic.

Finn was unconvinced. 'Where's this studio then?'

'It's run by the tutor down by Pineapple Wharf End. Part of an artist's co-operative thing. You'd have to go down there. They're not on the phone.' Maureen pointed at an address on a poster and watched Pearl peel if off the wall.

'How well do you know India?' Finn was still suspicious.

'She started me on the Open University – social anthropology.' Maureen's face glowed. 'She changed everything.' Her face went still. 'Go easy on her, she's really upset about Kevin Railton.'

Finn sniffed. 'If she shopped him it might make her feel a whole lot better.'

Maureen stared back at her. She went from pink to pale, thinking aloud. 'She could have landed him in it deliberately?'

Finn remembered India's tight face reading Railton's note.

'You mean the Paris auction? Would she, Maureen?' Pearl suddenly realised it was almost a certainty.

'I don't know,' she was thinking it through. 'But if Kevin thought she had . . .'

'Go on,' Pearl pushed her.

Maureen hesitated. 'I saw her with him once at a party. He got jealous and I saw how he looked at her.' She clenched her fist. 'I was terrified.'

Nigel Pearson smugly gained an hour when he came back from an emergency board meeting of the new consortium in Düsseldorf and landed early at the City airport. Docklands shimmered below the plane's flight path like a circuit board.

He drove through streets only just filling with traffic and arrived at Turnbull Motors' London offices with the sun already smoking through the car windows.

A scattering of vehicles in the car park betrayed the late nights and love affairs. Pearson nodded to the commissionaire and waited impatiently while the man went to the mail room to fetch the first post. Unsorted by his secretary and bundled in elastic bands, he carried it to the sixth floor as if it were shopping. He endured this indignity only for the letter he received without fail every Friday morning.

He extracted the familiar blue envelope. Impeccably typed and embossed with the logo of one of their suppliers, it was always marked for personal and private attention. It had gone completely unnoticed until last week when Judith, his lively, big-boned secretary with heavy silver jewellery like manacles, had flippantly joked about customers conspiring to slip through her net.

Judith saw herself as his protector and kept people distanced so efficiently that Nigel felt himself unwisely remote from everyday matters. He would listen to her dealing with the world and the clutter of calls and would occasionally reach for his private file and reread a letter from Gillian, his lover. This morning he placed it carefully within his desk diary and enjoyed the expectation of seeing his name adored in her precise looped handwriting.

The phones rang intermittently in other offices and began to be answered. Pearson angled his blinds against the sun and removed his jacket. In the outer office he could now hear Judith noisily slamming filing cabinet drawers, her bangles clashing. Coffee was being made; the smell made him recall the excellent German hotel and the most convivial evening spent with their new corporation partners. It appeared union problems were less volatile in Düsseldorf, and certainly he had dismissed their own casually as if they were already solved. On this occasion as a courtesy Mepham had translated his words, uncannily adopting his inflection. Pearson guessed that his German would be adequate although inevitably rather graceless.

Late last night over more coffee and brandy overlooking the grid of the city, Vincent Mepham, on the brink of promotion and a second office in Düsseldorf, had been cool and assured. The rising tide of emotive union support aroused by the left-wing press would serve them well. He had smiled as he had described the greater fall of Foxton with the tip of his cigar dropping sparks over the balcony. He had suggested that the moment was almost accomplished.

Judith appeared to be ill-humoured and slopped his coffee when she brought him the post, stacked in order of priority.

She placed two large folders on the side table. 'Express delivery from the architects.' She checked their covers. 'Extra information coming through now on the fax.' She rubbed her forehead, visibly suffering a headache.

'And here's another private and confidential.' She placed a small padded envelope on the desk.

Pearson shrugged, pleasurably free from guilt, and suggested that she open it for him. Judith dug scissors into the bound package resentfully and punctured the lining. Small drifts of grey padding shredded over the desk. Irritably she extracted a tape cassette and read the bold signature. 'Compliments of John Foxton,' she read the typescript underneath, 'General Secretary of NUAVE.'

Pearson stiffened and grabbed the note. 'I'm well aware of who Foxton is.'

Judith noticed he was still turning the tape over with his surgeon-like fingers several minutes after she was back in her office folding fax paper and subduing her hangover with coffee.

Pearson unlocked his car and rolled back the sunroof. The car park was thronged with office staff and already a bright white sun was melting tarmac under tyres. He dabbed his forehead with a handkerchief and testily felt his clean shirt already damp with sweat.

He punched in the tape and listened to a jumble of noise resolving itself into an afternoon on the golf course. Mepham was clearly and distinguishably plotting fraud and defamation.

'*The first rule of politics, Vincent,*' Railton's voice was a sneer and Pearson felt his mouth dry as he listened to the two men making the management plot into Foxton's private property.

The tape cut into silence and Pearson stabbed numbers into his mobile phone. The channel wavered then fixed. Mepham's voice was insolently sleepy.

'Get in to the office immediately.' Pearson snapped.

'But we've only just got back.'

Pearson watched his staff arriving for work. 'You're spending too much time on the golf course, Vincent.'

Judith looked up testily as he walked back to his office. 'Messages on your desk, sir, I didn't know where you'd gone.'

Hardly hearing her he sat down and made the problem into a diagram, itemising courses of action. Angrily he pushed his Düsseldorf report to one side and went through the messages.

John Foxton, timed ten minutes ago, requested a private meeting, that afternoon at two o'clock. He'd pick him up in a car.

Judith looked up as he placed the memo on her desk. 'He seemed sure you'd be agreeable,' she shrugged, 'but I think you're busy all afternoon with the architects.' She stared at the fax machine spooling out paper. 'Presumably this is just a tactical gambit?'

'Phone and confirm.' Pearson was glacial. 'And cancel the architects.'

Mepham was there within half an hour laden with files from their German partners. His face had a grey tinge and dark stubble already shaded his angular jaw. He faced Pearson's glare head-on.

'Problems?' He waited with some trepidation but refused to be terrorised by Pearson's court martial manner. Embarrassment turned to fear as he listened without poise to the tape on Judith's personal stereo. Privately replaying his own words he was appalled by how terrifying an old conversation could be. Sickened, he stopped the tape before it had finished.

Running his hand over his immaculate hair he became momentarily panicked. He took off his jacket and threw it over the back of the chair. He walked to the window.

'Foxton can't possibly go to the press with this.' Mepham struggled to contain his shock. 'He wouldn't want the publicity.'

Pearson turned on him angrily. 'Maybe not, but now he thinks he can lean on us.' Remembering this meeting, he opened the diary to check his day. The blue unopened letter fell out, throwing him for an instant. Vincent instinctively seized the chance to return to the offensive.

'You asked for a solution, sir. This is a temporary hitch. That's all.'

'I told you not to underestimate Foxton.' Pearson glared at the young man who had just closed down his career with so little finesse. 'You'd better get on the phone and tell your friend Railton that he's on his own.'

'*My* friend?' Mepham smiled and shook his head scornfully. 'He could implicate us both, sir, and were certain circumstances to arise, he'd be irrepressible.'

Pearson saw the threat and looked away dismissively.

Mepham leaned across his desk. 'If you ditch me with Railton I'll go to the press myself. Name a few names.' Pearson swallowed. 'We could finish off a ministerial career between the two of us, I would have thought?' He grabbed his jacket and walked towards the door. 'Don't even think about it.'

Pearson's eyes were unmoving and he smiled, levelling his voice. 'I appreciate your point entirely, Vincent. So we'd all better keep our heads, hadn't we?'

Mepham nodded, this moment of danger passing.

Pearson motioned him back to his seat and buzzed Judith for more coffee. 'Your position has become more central than ever, Vincent. And we need to regroup before I see Foxton this afternoon.' He tapped a cigarette on a silver case. 'As you'll appreciate, we need to devise a strategy. If we don't get these men back soon and on the prototype contract you can say goodbye to Düsseldorf.'

Mepham reached for his notebook and dialled Railton's number. As he waited for an answer, he glanced over to Pearson. 'I think you'll find there's only one route left open to us, sir.'

Twenty-four

Pineapple Wharf was a grey, desolate area beyond the redevelopment, dreary with mud flats and gutted buildings. Old barges lay on their sides like rotting fish. Finn stopped the car and looked over Pearl's shoulder. The map didn't include any real detail for the area, just white spaces representing warehouses and dry docks.

Hazy cloud covered the sun as they drove round the deserted flanks of buildings. Dust rose in clouds from wide makeshift roads narrowing back into high-sided alleys between warehouses and flagged quays. Fetid water, ladled from the river and beached in from the tide, rotted the sunlight in oily weals.

'What a poser,' Finn shivered with antagonism. 'She just gets off on being different.'

'And you don't?' Pearl tackled her gently. Finn usually made her mind up about people in a maximum of thirty seconds, then the bricks amassed in her defensive wall. You were either on one side or the other. There was something about her dislike of India which was strangely personal.

Finn grinned. 'Don't have to try, do I?'

The dock opened up into what had been a large loading bay. Huge metal pulleys were still suspended near loft doors. Moored by ropes and constructed from old parachute silk and chicken wire hung a six-foot angel with outstretched wings.

Finn looked unimpressed. 'This must be it.' She glanced at Pearl. 'Who else would have Christmas decorations up at this time of year?'

The doors beneath the angel's feet were locked so they began to walk round towards the edge of the building. A jeep bumped over the ground nearby and then juddered to a halt. A young man in jeans jumped out with binoculars and started to watch the seagulls.

They turned the corner and faced the side of the building. Pearl stared upwards. The entire gable end had been painted blue and silver. In the heat the effect was unnerving, the colours glittering like fragments of sky or water. Coiled animals with scales and horns writhed around the contours of the wall. A white pelican opened its beak in a perfect square. Within its gullet the wall had collapsed, and revealed the remaining three walls of a room. A streamer of the original wallpaper, flowered with roses, flapped silently.

Finn looked away, superstitious with the memory of a house she'd once needed to find. She had discovered the street demolished and singled out her auntie's house by the wallpaper, the coloured kites she had counted by a nightlight as a child. Mistaking her hesitation, Pearl took her arm firmly and walked her towards the open door.

The ground floor of the building had been knocked into a huge space supported by a series of beams and struts. Someone was working inside a vast hump of chicken wire. The sunlight sliced through the door throwing up shafts of spinning dust. The creature was netted with black gauze and was being built from the inside. There were notice boards on the walls with schedules of Open University courses and messages from tutors to students.

Finn crawled into the undercarriage of the black angel. 'Has anyone seen India?' she called out reluctantly, hating the way the name made people into explorers and continents.

A gawky boy in overalls and a hairnet crawled out and stared. He took off his protective goggles and blinked red-rimmed eyes. 'It's as hot as hell in there.'

'What is it?' Pearl was intrigued.

'Prince of darkness.' He sniffed. 'I'm doing the fall from grace, and India's tackling revelations.' He nodded. 'She made a start on the gable end. Think they've got an old gasometer lined up for heaven.' He moved his large hands up and down. 'Can't you just imagine . . ?'

Finn cut across him. 'Have you see her then?'

He shook his head. 'I've been in there for hours, but her car's still here.' He nodded towards a Ford Cortina parked just outside the far doors.

Finn glanced at Pearl. 'Where does she work?'

He fixed his goggles back over his eyes and pointed. 'Unit seven. And I'm Norman.'

The seven hung crookedly on a sturdy double door obviously leading down into a cellar. It was locked. Finn kicked it with frustration.

'She always seems to be one step ahead of us.'

Pearl pushed against the door; she was sure she could hear something. Finn tapped and pressed against the wood. Something seemed to scuffle, perhaps a rat or a draught. And then they heard a low, almost indistinguishable moan.

Finn ran back and dragged Norman out of his shroud. He beat on the door and shouted, 'Indy? You got your keys?'

There was silence as if whoever was inside had passed out. He hammered again; asked the same question. His voice was rising with panic. Someone groaned faintly.

He shook his head and ruffled his stringy hair, 'God knows, we've all got two keys, but it looks like someone's locked her in.'

Finn positioned herself where the two doors met and beat with her fists. 'Where's the other key, India?' There was no answer. She beat the door again. 'Tell us where?'

India was obviously getting nearer to the door; they heard a dragging noise.

'Has she got enough air?' Pearl whispered.

The young man nodded gloomily. 'Yeh. It can't be that.'

Finn called again hopelessly, hardly bothering to raise her voice, and heard India croak back the name of Railton. 'We'd better go for help.' Pearl pulled at Finn's arm. Finn followed her automatically and then stopped dead. 'Railton?' She went through her pockets and pulling out the bunch of keys, frantically went through them.

Pearl stared. 'Which one was it?'

Finn seized the long bevelled key, drove it into the lock and turned it smoothly.

The doors swung outwards and light poured into the cellar. India lay huddled on the cobbled floor amongst paint tins.

Pearl was first at her side and turned her over gently. Finn caught her breath. India's petite face was a terrible mass of bruises. One eye was completely closed and her nose and lips were swollen and patched with blood.

Pearl calmed India and looked back for help. Finn's face was paralysed with fear.

'Finn?'

Finn shuddered and bolted for the door.

Norman appeared with blankets and a miniature bottle of brandy. 'Found this.' He was trembling. 'I'll go for the police.'

'No.' India grabbed his shirt so fiercely he nearly toppled over her. 'Leave it, please.' He turned to Pearl anxiously. 'Tell him.' India's voice was thick with desperation.

Pearl nodded. 'Leave it to us, just for now.'

Finn eventually appeared in the doorway with a bowl of water and a first aid box.

India stopped shaking while Finn bathed her face and mopped away the dried blood. Her lip was split but she had no other cuts. She was adamant about the police, talking with difficulty, her whole face stretched with pain.

'It was Railton, just admit it.' Pearl saw Finn's hand trembling.

India shut her eyes and said nothing.

Pearl took her hand. 'You've *got* to help us now.' India looked away numbly. Pearl's voice was harder. 'Trevor's gone missing, and if anything happens to him . . .'

India limped to an arch at the back of the cellar where she had an old armchair and a kettle. Finn busied herself making tea. Huddled in the chair India moved her mouth slowly. She was calmer, almost dazed.

'I was so hurt I didn't know what I was doing. I tried to phone Trevor the day before the auction but he wasn't there.' She looked at Pearl. 'I tried to phone you. But I couldn't leave a message.'

'Why not, if it was so urgent?'

India held the warm mug against her cheek. 'I wanted revenge on him so much, I suppose I didn't really want anyone to stop me.'

Pearl touched her arm. 'You mean the auction?'

India nodded. 'A lot of them are rigged, it's part of the way the business works. Young rising painters don't get much at sales unless dealers hype them, nor would the dealers, you see?'

'I don't understand.' Pearl shook her slightly. India seemed to be falling asleep. 'What did you do?'

India sighed. 'A dealer buys a whole collection. The *Electric Shoal* for instance.' She smiled lop-sidedly.' Then another dealer, say American, buys the lot at an inflated price. *Then* sells them back. Under cover, several times, keeping the collection together.'

Finn looked lost. 'That means you both lose a fortune?'

'Wrong. Prices rocket because the artist is obviously so desirable, a name people are fighting to buy because of the soaring investment value.' She slopped the brandy into her tea. 'It just takes a brilliant stage manager. But it's not actually illegal.'

'But how could you blow it?'

India held her head. 'I burnt the authentication papers and put the word around they were forgeries.' She looked away. 'The auctioneer advised me to withdraw until the fuss had died down. But of course I insisted on carrying on, and bought off my bidding partner.'

'The guy we saw you with at the last auction?' She nodded.

'They were all sold at rock bottom prices and all Kevin's profit for the union went up in smoke. He had treated me so badly. I started with a few things to get him jumpy, and then I thought, with the right timing, Foxton would fire him on the spot.' She looked dazed. 'But it didn't work . . .'

Finn felt winded. India's beautifully constructed crime had just cleared her.

'And what about the union in all this, India?' Pearl was angry.

'I wanted to check. But I knew they wouldn't really lose, not when this is all sorted out. They'll be compensated by our insurance eventually, I saw to that.'

'But too bloody late!' Finn was at her side. 'Don't you realise?'

India seemed to nod and then looked like she might faint.

Pearl took her hand again. 'We'll get you home and call a doctor. But you've got to tell us where Railton's got the money. And tell us how to prove it.'

'I don't know.' India's eyes were contracted with fear. 'I really don't.'

'Why do you go on protecting that bastard?'

India stared at Finn. 'You've got it wrong. I *don't* know. He never trusted me. Only Trevor can tell you. He told me yesterday. He called me in a panic and I caught him at the office. He's got proof. He called it his life insurance.' Her head lolled forward.

Finn held her. 'Where is Trevor now, India?'

'I don't know.' She was slurring her speech. 'Isn't he handling the strike fund liquidation today? I went over to give him some advice. Took him some flowers. Poor old Trev.'

Pearl looked at Finn hopelessly and shook her head.

'She doesn't know.'

'And what she does, she'll never say.' Finn looked at India, asleep with exhaustion. 'He's made sure of that.'

Maureen hooted her horn twice outside the warehouse and then ran in. Pearl caught her before she saw India and tried to prepare her. A look of anger went across Maureen's face as she listened and then she straightened up briskly.

'I'll take her to Casualty,' she said. 'I'll take care of her now. You've got to go to Spain.'

'What?' Pearl sagged against the wall, tiredness and shock catching up with her.

Maureen nodded. 'I've worked out where Trev's gone. It was quite complicated. I checked this morning with our travel department and found out that the day he didn't come into the office he went and stayed in a hotel. Apparently he stayed in his room all day. Room service said he was working.' She looked anxiously towards Finn sitting with India. 'Anyway he posted a letter in their box and when I rang this morning they said would I collect it for him; he hadn't put a stamp on it. It was to his wife in Spain.' She looked triumphant.

'So he can't have gone.' Pearl shrugged. 'Why write a letter if you're going there?'

'Because letters take at least four days.' She looked upset. 'Poor man, I think he's just given up. It's made him desperate. After all that work trying to sort things out, he's gone off with most of the files. We haven't got all his records on disc, and a lot of it's in his head.'

Pearl made her concentrate. 'What was in the letter?'

Maureen looked a little sad. 'It was a sort of love letter. I got the feeling he was planning to do something stupid.'

'We'll have to get out there quickly then,' decided Pearl. 'I'd better phone Millie.'

Maureen handed her an envelope. 'I've done that. It's all sorted. Two returns to Malaga; you collect a hire car when you get there. Trevor's address is in there too, and the letter. It's only a short drive, he told me once. And you'll need this.' She handed Pearl a padded envelope. 'It's your float in pesetas; I cleared it with Millie.'

Finn sat in the traffic jam and frowned into the sun. 'I just can't believe it . . .'

'No.' Pearl was thoughtful.

'Flight *and* a float?'

Pearl frowned. 'You don't think . . ?'

'What?'

'That it's a trick, Maureen's getting rid of us for Railton?'

Pearl moistened her lips. 'And Millie doesn't even know?' Pushing the door open she jumped out of the car.

Finn watched her marching down the line of stationary cars. Finally she got into one and emerged a few minutes later. 'I persuaded a guy to let me use his carphone,' she said frowning. 'He wasn't too pleased when I paid him pesetas.'

'And?' Finn inched the car forwards.

'Millie told me to stop wasting time with phonecalls. She told us to get the hell on that plane and find Trevor.'

Finn grinned ruefully. Reaching into the glove box, she flipped a large 'Doctor on Call' card on to the dashboard and accelerated away up the hard shoulder.

Twenty-five

After Mepham left Pearson's office on his way to make another threatening phonecall to Railton, Judith stirred in her ornamental chains and watched her boss through the open doorway slitting open a thin blue envelope. Fabricating an excuse to enter and collect coffee cups, she quickly recognised the familiar blue loopy writing and was gratified to see him guiltily pushing the letter under the Düsseldorf papers. Judith knew that shortly, once read and committed to memory, Pearson would file it in chronological order, under G, in his confidential staff filing system. Vetting the file carefully on every occasion he was away on European travel, Judith was currently up to date and understood with growing interest that Nigel and Gillian were going through a difficult patch.

Pearson read his love letter quickly, sacrificing the usual savouring of the regulation double-sided sheet of longing and enforced separation. Their meetings never contained such unrestrained declarations, such explicit expression. Nigel explored the letters like some foreign territory and trusted that they would remain so.

Gillian's single side this week was depressing and unaccountably lacking in emotion. There were small hints of resentment and demand; her final lines were less fulsome and were restrained by semicolons and brackets.

He folded the letter back into the envelope and punched in the security code to open his desk files.

Judith, looking less belligerent, brought him another coffee and he spent the rest of the morning finishing his Düsseldorf report. Gillian's punctuation had given him a dull ache above the temples. He massaged his forehead; the memory of his recent meeting with the minister in his club started the pulse of a distant migraine. It had been made very clear that he was being given the personal opportunity to demonstrate model behaviour for future government-approved practice. James Cauldwell, MP and member of the Cabinet, had ordered whisky and counselled sanity. Large corporate deals ensured a streamlined strategy for future industrial policy and reduced the necessity for government subsidy. Cauldwell's message had been low and soothing like a story.

Pearson put his head in his hands and breathed slowly and deliberately. The Minister had made it sound perfectly acceptable, almost altruistic. But Pearson understood precisely what he was being instructed to do. The government wanted to take on the unions and set them against each other. Turnbull Motors, old, established and in trouble was a classic test case. He was fettered but not blinkered. Within five years he would accept a peerage and retire. Cauldwell was a shrewd man and had selected him with care.

Nigel Pearson pulled on his jacket. Company directors who cared more for honour than material reward were a rare breed these days. He recalled the undisguised violence in Mepham's face and cautioned himself to be vigilant. Pearson stepped into the glass lift and watched the cityscape sinking beneath his feet. He calmed himself formally like a duellist, and, fixing on a distant point on the horizon, contemplated his sense of posterity.

Foxton's driver was waiting at reception and escorted Nigel to the car. As they swept out of the car park Pearson leant forward. 'Where exactly are we going?'

The driver's face, partially framed by the driving mirror, remained impassive. 'Won't take long sir.'

Pearson was irritated. 'I asked where?'

The driver took a sharp left through narrow streets heading for the water. 'All Mr Foxton told me sir, was that it's such a nice day, it would be a shame to waste it.'

John Foxton watched the union car advance jerkily over the derelict factory yard. A clutch of seagulls took off noisily and swooped on a small patch of mud drying in the afternoon sun. The metal frames of the small complex of buildings were buckled and deserted. On the edge of the site against the skyline, the old power station was black like a cathedral.

Pearson peevishly got out of the car and assembled a smile.

'Some sort of a joke, Foxton?'

'A sick one, maybe.' He didn't smile but simply motioned that they should walk.

Pearson picked his way after him. 'Your sense of melodrama makes you an increasingly dangerous man to follow. Your men will see that soon enough.' He frowned. 'What is this place exactly?'

Shielding his face from the sun, John assessed his enemy. 'It's nothing, *Sir* Nigel.' Pearson caught the insinuation. 'That's what we'll be calling you soon enough presumably?' He stared at the wasteland thoughtfully. 'I started my first job here.'

Normally Pearson would have employed a way to diffuse what he clearly saw coming, but Foxton was insistent. 'Fresh to London, and joining a small successful firm; I would have stayed with it all my life perhaps – watched it grow.'

'A takeover presumably?' Pearson was disinterested. 'These things happen.'

'Dumping men for money's never been right, but at least it's understandable. What you're planning is downright immoral.'

Pearson frowned at the old factory. 'I fail to see how this is relevant?'

'It's just an image. A no-man's-land.' Foxton smiled grimly. 'It's as good a place to talk as any.'

They sat down amongst the bricks. Pearson was interested in Foxton, divining in him an integrity of leadership close to his own. He listened to him now coherently laying out the case for saving the plant, calculating a percentage of early retirement, but insisting on sharing the skilled workforce with their German partners.

'It's a viable solution. There's very little in it financially.' He summed up. 'Apart from the future of almost two thousand men in Nottingham.'

Pearson stood up and brushed a smudge of dust from his trousers. 'There's one other option you should discuss for the sake of your membership.'

Foxton waited angrily.

'You tell your men honestly that the writing's on the wall. The future is not debatable, while the quality of their departure *is*. Get them back without delay and we will guarantee full work for the next year and negotiable lump sum payments for redundancy.' Pearson inclined his head. 'Time to adjust; it's a fair offer.'

Foxton faced him. 'No thanks. I think I'd prefer to take the taped version of your alternative solution to the press.'

Pearson smiled. 'They'd have a field day with your finances.'

'And you'd be ruined.' Foxton glared and turned and started to walk away.

Following him briskly, Pearson raised his voice. 'You are obliged to put my offer to your men.'

Foxton swung round furiously. 'My men stay out. You'll lose your wretched contract, and your place in the consortium.'

Pearson felt him touch a nerve but showed no sign. 'They can't hold out for very long without strike pay.' He smiled. 'Do you really want them to see what a sham your union's become? You've got no choice, Foxton. I'll give you the weekend to think it over.' He stiffly declined the car and set off across the factory site towards the distant main road and a taxi. His silhouette trembled in the heat haze.

Foxton angrily buzzed stones at an old sign, each one on target and spinning off like shrapnel. It had been a final gamble to confront Pearson and negotiate a quick, swift, honourable solution. As he watched him walk away he glimpsed the bloody reality.

A thin voice of doubt cut through the silence like the man in the crowd, the breaking glass in the restaurant. Catching a shiver in the hot sunshine, Foxton stared at the deserted buildings rippling as if they were under water. He covered his eyes against the glare and allowed a new thought to develop. He experienced a wave of nausea and for the first time considered that he might be doing the wrong thing.

Fitz's record store used every available part of its ground plan to trap customers. Denzil had worked out a dazzling theory within the space available during one long and tedious recording session. Imports, exports, twelve inch, New Age, New World, cult genre and concept Indy albums ebbed and flowed amongst the more regular stock with rewarding results. Fitz's customers understood themselves as dealers in a rich and alternative art form.

Rufus looked through the shop frontage approvingly. He had read about places in the Bronx and Greenwich Village where musicians and artists met and shared ideas, listened to music and created a climate as real as sunshine. His reflection swayed to the latest rough cut from his posse, a new rap backing track with electronically sampled sounds. They had spent long hours one night working on the three-second acoustic of breaking glass. Slowed down and speeded up, stretched with sampling and echoing against itself into a rhythm, it now made a surreal harmony of its own. Rufus walked into the shop smiling, charisma like a sheen on his skin.

Denzil raised an eyebrow from behind the counter, crouching over the columns of a dubbing chart. 'Forget it, Ruf.' His smile dipped. 'It's not a good day.'

Rufus grinned and patted his black portfolio. 'I've made an appointment man, he knows I'm coming.'

'Oh yeh?' Denzil uncomfortably motioned him into the back room, but a customer arrived at the till with a pile of record sleeves, one slithering onto the floor. Rufus left Denzil on his hands and knees and loped up the stairs to Fitz's office.

It was empty and untidy. The smoked glass trestle desk overflowed with papers and posters and PR news releases. Two phones were on the floor in a tangle of wires, and coffee mugs lined the hi-tec metal bookshelves. Rufus stared at the golden disc in its steel frame, Fitz's big charity album success. He rubbed the dust on the glass with his finger and logged a dream.

The computer was on and sulked, abandoned with a screen of accounts figures in the corner. Sitting at Fitz's desk, Rufus opened his case and looked again at his presentation for his promotional video. He had recced the locations, drawn up a storyboard and worked on a draft shooting script. His heart surged for a moment as he flicked through its pages.

Fitz angrily moved boxes of stock into an alcove in the storeroom. Powdery whitewash crumbled from the walls and smudged his black trousers, falling like snow on his bare arms.

Staring round the haphazard clutter of boxes and equipment, Fitz considered his life gloomily.

Rufus appeared in the doorway with a flourish and hesitated as he observed his manager and record producer up to his waist in chaos.

'Stay away from me,' Fitz growled, wrestling with microphone stands. 'Don't even *think* the word "video".'

Rufus considered rescheduling his plea but knew that Fitz's mercurial moods were the key to his talent. Rapidly laying out large sheets on the packing cases, Rufus described the visual potential of the sketches and photographs with irrepressible enthusiasm. 'What do you think?' He noticed Fitz was still glaring, wiping his dirty hands on his white T-shirt. 'It's a conspiracy.' Fitz kicked a box furiously.

Rufus looked back to his title sheet and continued uncertainly. 'Main idea for shooting style comes from this guy Hockney,' he explained.

'What?'

'He's big in polaroids; uses them like jigsaws.' Rufus felt the temperature dropping rapidly, and suddenly remembering Denzil's look, guiltily swept up his papers. 'I'll rejig the whole concept, no problem.' He was heading for the door.

Fitz blocked his way, his arm across the entrance. 'You'll get your act together Rufus, and learn to respect my equipment, or you're out in the cold.'

Rufus looked doubtful. 'I can explain, honestly, we were really careful.' He shrugged. 'There was no other way to do it.'

Fitz seemed to lose interest; he dropped his arm and sat down wearily. 'Do you hear me complaining?'

Rufus shook his head and waited for the explosion. 'Pearl didn't turn up, so I stepped in to help, and to operate the rifle mike.' He smiled reassuringly.

Fitz stood up when he heard Pearl's name and stared emptily around the room. 'Ever since P stopped working here the system's gone to hell.'

'Maybe she'd come and do some freelance? Return the favour?' Rufus faltered and felt the blood rise to his face.

Fitz turned his back on him miserably. 'We'll have that rap

about the video later. Too much on my mind right now.'

Rufus nodded and backed out slowly. Fitz appeared to be talking to himself, making points on his fingers. 'Orell's broken his arm, and I feel like it's all my fault. They were all meant to be going away for the weekend and now they're not. Someone broke a window yesterday and the freezer's bust.' He looked over to Rufus vaguely. 'It's defrosting the whole time.'

Rufus shrugged sympathetically. 'Family life, huh?'

'Right.' Fitz closed his eyes and tried to remember when he last felt completely untroubled.

Kevin Railton watched the last secretaries leave the union building. He lounged across his chair behind *The Financial Times*. Occasionally his hand tightened on the paper when he recalled Mepham's fierce phonecalls. Still furious from his meeting with Foxton, he had spent the afternoon in his office running through every possible scenario. He had caught Trevor at home the day before and given him a brutal ultimatum over the phone. His threat was undisguised this time.

Shifting in his seat, Railton was still angry at Mepham's tone. He'd had no need of his advice and had automatically set another plan into motion, making a crucial call as soon as he'd left Foxton's office. It would be a costly precaution but he regarded it as a sound investment.

Foxton's detectives had really caused havoc. Railton confirmed his decision to effect a dignified exit as soon as possible, and sitting in his office smarting with the need for revenge, he grimly considered the loose ends he had not yet tidied. Clenching his fist round his car keys he worked out the chronology of his next moves.

The building was deserted when he finally spotted Foxton getting out of a taxi, wiping his shoes, and brushing dust from his clothes. He waved at the security guard in the lodge and came through the pass door using his security key.

Railton walked towards him briskly, extending a hand. 'Think I owe you an apology, John.'

Foxton barely nodded. 'Hardly necessary.'

Railton fingered his beard edgily. 'I need to run some figures by you.'

'Can't it wait?' Foxton sighed. He had decided to go back to Nottingham as soon as possible.

'Better not.' Railton raised an eyebrow. 'Unless your investigators have already found Mitchell?'

Foxton stared at him. 'What do you know about that?'

Railton looked thoughtful. 'Perhaps we might talk?'

They went upstairs. The office was as quiet as a weekend. Foxton threw his briefcase down and dropped into his armchair. 'Well?'

Railton loosened the knot of his tie. 'I've discovered a way to get round our immediate problem.'

Foxton watched him warily.

'One of your hidden bank accounts was left untouched. There's nearly enough there to cover the first strike payment.'

Foxton stared at him. 'That's not possible. We've been through those figures endlessly.'

'You didn't have *these* figures.' Railton was almost casual. 'And neither did I, until I received this from Mitchell.' He held out a postcard with a plane flying through a vividly blue sky. It simply had a bank account number and a name scrawled on the back. 'He banked the money in the name of his dad.' He whistled. 'Didn't even tell me about it.'

Foxton tensely turned the card over. 'How much?'

'Five hundred thousand, give or take a pfennig or two.' Foxton stared at the plane blankly. 'It's oddly appropriate, don't you think?' Railton grinned. 'Old Trev's final glorious gesture.'

'What's the catch?' Foxton was unsure, trying to get a fix on him.

Railton looked irritable. 'I know you can't stand me, Foxton. But strangely enough you can trust me. Honour amongst players?' He enjoyed Foxton's discomfort. 'Mitchell knew I'd get the money mobilised straightaway, and I have. Cash on the table, simple as that.'

Foxton ran his hands through his hair and stared at Railton's bony, blatant face. 'OK, when can we have it?'

'Tell me what to do and we'll be ready to distribute on Monday.' Foxton walked back to his desk, rang the lodge and cancelled his car.

Twenty-six

Krish finished blocking in the agenda for the following week and closed the practice diary. Millie was already clearing her desk and locking drawers.

Gathering his papers he collected up a series of mugs and watched her sombrely. 'Do you really think it's worth it?'

Millie grinned and passed him three telephone directories. 'Please, this late on a Friday?'

Krish drummed the desk with a pencil. 'I mean, flying them out to Spain?'

Millie sighed. 'It happens to be the destination of the man who's either a culprit or the key to the entire mystery. Our client is convinced that it will lead to the resolution of the case.'

'He can't be that sure.' Krish chewed his lip and paced towards the window. 'Our client's judgment has already proved to be less than consistent.'

Millie looked defensive. 'No case is orderly, Krish, until it is concluded; we just have to live with that.'

'But he's too personally involved.' Krish tapped the window frame with his pencil. 'And we should take that into account.'

Millie flushed and sat down slowly as Krish walked back to her desk. 'This Trevor thing, I mean,' he shrugged, 'how relevant is he now, really? He's washed up, run off with a few files. It's this Railton character we should be concentrating on.'

'Mitchell could tell us everything,' Millie replied firmly, her doubts reviving uncomfortably.

'He could go and hurt himself.' Krish sniffed. 'So Foxton sends our investigators off to hold his hand while . . .'

'While what?' Millie felt vulnerable.

'While nothing. Time is running out on the union thing and

Railton's still running wild.' He looked away awkwardly. 'I'm getting the feeling that people aren't being very objective.' He sat down and stubbornly traced the pattern on his waistcoat where a single thread of gold ran through black serge.

'I happen to trust his judgment,' Millie said directly. 'And we can only advise. In the end what's more important?' She remembered John's helpless face when he'd read Trevor's letter.

'Those poor sods at the factory I guess.' Krish stood up. 'That's where we came in, isn't it?'

'I'm glad you can find it all so simple.' Millie withdrew, no longer sure what she felt. 'But sometimes you just have to go on your instincts.'

Krish gave her a faint smile. 'Doesn't sound very business-like?'
'I've given them forty-eight hours to come up with a result.' Millie noted his expression. 'That includes travelling time. Don't worry Krish, I've got my own reservations.'

Krish withdrew discreetly to the far corner of the office where he swiftly changed into his hired stiff-fronted shirt and dinner jacket to go straight on to Covent Garden with Lavinia. He was nervously struggling with his white tie and experimenting with ways to tell her that their liaison had reached its natural conclusion, when Laura rushed past him.

She stood white-faced by the window and waited for her mother to ask the right questions. Millie was on the phone and busy dialling restaurants. The third, like the others, was fully booked. Millie replaced the receiver guiltily and without looking up thumbed through her address book.

'Won't be long. Where's Eric?'

'Paris.' Laura stared at buses. 'So we can cancel Joe Allen's and have fish and chips at home, just the two of us, OK?'

Millie felt wounded. 'Do you want to talk?'

Laura shook her head and moved away from her mother's tentative hand on her shoulder. 'Why should you understand?' She leant her forehead against the window. 'He didn't even talk to me about it. Just left a note.'

Millie felt an illogical sympathy for Eric, believing pragmatically that there was nothing courageous about inflicting pain and then staying around to witness it. She stroked Laura's hot cheek.

There was no help for this; no comfort to be derived from a departing lover. And no healing to tell her daughter.

The phone rang shrilly in the outer office and Millie watched with some astonishment while Krish answered in evening dress. He smiled a little sheepishly, pointed at the receiver and announced John Foxton like a butler, enjoying her amazement.

'*Traviata*,' he explained, slightly embarrassed, and pronouncing his destination like a takeaway.

Millie picked up the phone nervously and was relieved to see Krish talking to Laura. She absorbed John's question slowly.

'Do you think it sounds all right legally?'

Millie re-engaged. 'Of course. But I don't pretend to understand.'

'Maybe Railton's covering tracks, trying to sweeten me up?'

'Sounds like it, but I keep thinking, Maureen told me about . . .' Millie swallowed hard.

'India . . . I know. But you should have seen him; he was totally composed, almost subdued.'

'India hasn't actually said *who* it was yet.' Millie stopped their speculation briskly. 'John, if you've got the money, use it. Whatever his motive, it buys you time. Hold your position and hang on for some news about Trev.'

'It's going to be a difficult weekend.'

She tried to ignore his longing. 'What happened with Pearson, any progress?'

He cleared his throat and seemed to withdraw. 'No change. Deadlock.' His voice had tightened. 'Maybe I could come round Mil? Just for a drink?'

'I'll call you.' She hung up despite herself and walked back in to her office and her daughter.

Krish had his arm round Laura and she'd been crying, black streaks smudged round her eyes. Off-balance, he set Laura down and gently touched Millie's arm. 'I've got to go.'

Millie nodded gratefully and followed him out. Krish self-consciously examined himself in a mirror perched on the filing cabinet. She noticed he had a small tear stain of mascara on his perfect shirt front. Glancing at Millie in the reflection, he combed his dark hair into waves.

'Did she tell you anything?' Millie watched him anxiously.

'That burk Eric's two-timing her; she's well out.' He frowned and turned to face her questioningly. 'And something about finding a dead bird in your kitchen?' Checking his watch, he noticed she had gone very pale. 'You all right, Millie?'

'Fine. Enjoy the opera. It's got a rather sad ending.'

He seemed to consider this, then impulsively kissed her on the cheek.

Millie went back to where her daughter was stranded, slumped at her desk. She knelt down and kissed her forehead. Laura followed her towards the door and while she waited for Millie to set the alarms, she gave a sudden sob. She wept like a child, her lip pushed out, her face screwed up with pain. Millie realised with a lurch that she hadn't seen her cry for years, hadn't comforted her. She held Laura's hot face against her. 'Try not to let it mean too much.' She said the words silently, for them both.

The airport information board at Heathrow rippled with disappointment. The bland letters dropped into place and announced that the eighteen hundred flight to Malaga was indefinitely delayed, due to a baggage handlers' strike in Spain.

'Haven't even got any baggage,' said Finn, moodily consuming her fourth hot dog, and watching angry holiday-makers jostling around an airport official.

Pearl checked her watch impatiently. 'Perhaps we should phone Millie.'

'Have you seen the queue?' Finn nodded towards the booths and the crowds of fractious passengers stretching around the departure lounge. One elderly woman had erected a small deckchair and had fallen asleep, already wearing a man's straw hat against the promised sun.

The flight left after midnight, accelerating into blackness. Finn watched her breath steam up the window, her heart pounding. Below her, for a moment, she saw the brilliant golden mesh of the city and its dark scar of river, and then thick cloud. They arced away towards the sea, the plane dropping and rolling slightly in the turbulent air.

Finn leant back into her seat swallowing hard and holding her hands over her ears.

'You've gone yellow.' Pearl undid her seat belt. 'You don't get airsick as well, do you?'

'How should I know?' Finn nervously read through the instructions for baling out at sea. 'You flown before?'

Pearl shifted in her seat nervously. 'Not unless you count a simulator at the amusement arcade.'

A young man with salt-white hair and a weatherbeaten face opened up a newspaper in the seat opposite. He smiled as he reached up to switch on his reading light. Pearl adjusted the beam above Finn and examined her friend's face carefully. 'That's improved your colour anyway.'

Finn relaxed and picked up a magazine. 'Here comes the food. Perhaps I'll get my own back.' Pearl closed her eyes and tried to sleep, refusing the miniature shepherd's pie and queasily accepting mineral water.

Finn downed two individually wrapped quarter bottles of champagne and busily went through a large plastic wallet of paper using the surfaces of both their collapsible tables. She reduced one pile to a single sheet of paper and nudged Pearl awake. 'Any idea what this lot means?'

Pearl opened her eyes reluctantly and read through a computer script list of names. 'Prado, Alte Pinakothek.' She pulled a face. 'No idea. Where's this from anyway?'

'I borrowed it from India's studio.' Finn put the rest of the papers back and met Pearl's frown unrepentantly. 'She's holding stuff back. What she refuses to tell us, we'll just have to find for ourselves.'

Pearl nodded and unsteadily made her way down the aisle to a stewardess. Finn noticed that the young man with the suntanned face was watching her obsessively. When Pearl fell back into her seat she was breathing heavily; her walnut skin had paled. 'Art galleries.' She slapped the list back to Finn. 'A list of art galleries. You've just nicked her homework, congratulations.' Chastened, Finn stuffed the list back in her pocket and relaxed into a light and restless sleep.

It wasn't until their descent that Pearl began to feel better. She looked out into the darkness and saw small spreads of light making cities and villages and roads below. At her side Finn moaned slightly and moved unhappily in her dream. Her knuckles were still red and bruised from hammering on India's door. Pearl remembered Finn's desperate efforts to rouse the girl she so disliked and her rage against the attacker. Uncomfortably she recalled again Finn's frightened reaction when she looked at India's beaten face. And her sudden flight.

Finn slumped towards her and gently Pearl shook her awake. She gave a start, then pulled out of sleep with a shudder of relief.

'Dreaming,' she mumbled. 'Nightmare.'

'What was it?'

Finn rubbed her face, shivering, still on the edge of her fear.

'Tell what happened back there, when you saw India?'

She hunched into her seat and didn't answer. Pearl squeezed her arm. 'I want you to tell me, Finn.' Leaning against her and watching the runway splay out below them, Finn returned her touch, and then withdrew her hand.

There were several hours of darkness after their delayed plane landed, and no cars could be hired before what was vaguely described as morning. They fought for plastic chairs with a party of irritable schoolchildren in the airport lounge and slept fitfully against the incessant cajoling of the tannoy.

They finally signed for a car in a stifling portakabin after a portly man in a blazer had waddled towards them waving a sign with 'Maureen' printed on it.

'Obviously thinks her name's got more international credibility than ours,' observed Pearl stiffly, noticing the young man from their plane heading towards the makeshift office, his white hair oddly inaccurate in the fierce sunlight.

As they jolted the first few yards, searching for gears and tapping the petrol gauge, she saw him take the keys of an old land-rover and watch their progress as he knelt down to check the tyres.

Maureen's short journey to the villa turned out to be a complete fiction. The brown scrubby road blazed on hour after hour. They vigilantly stopped at garages to buy bottles of drink and stare from the map into the melted distance. A daze of travelling overtook them and left the events of the last few days like the column of dust rising behind them.

Pearl shut her eyes and through the open window let the hot wind whip her skin. Finn was smiling, strangely unburdened by their deadline in the sun. The elderly tape machine in the car played the odd collection of tapes bizarrely at a slow and sombre place. Three white windmills with crisp tiled roofs and black paddle blades were visible for miles and then receded: hardly moving, they rowed against an occasional cloud and in time to haunting slow-motion songs from Pavarotti.

It was late afternoon when they stopped at a café in Val d'Orado and asked for Villa Daphne. Pearl showed the picture of the cheerful Daphne outside the white-blocked villa. Excitedly, an old woman pointed them down the street, mimicked the mountainous climbing of a hill and waved them goodbye with brittle laughter.

'What's so funny?' said Finn peering ahead as they climbed a winding road. 'And where's the sea?'

Pearl licked her cracked lips. 'And what happens if Trevor's not there?'

Finn swung grimly round two corners and down the hill. Away in the distance the sea coloured the horizon beyond neat oblongs of maize and fruit trees. Below them a small estate of white villas curved in a semi-circle, each one with an identical square of land and a swimming pool, like a child's picture. One of these was undoubtedly Villa Daphne.

Finn climbed out of the car and walked unsteadily towards a fat pink man wearing a pair of shorts made from deckchair material, and brown socks.

Finn smiled and asked for the Mitchells. 'Whatd'yeknow, a Geordie. We're from Barnsley.' He mopped his face with surprise.

The melting man pointed to a replica villa opposite. 'They've got best site, truth be told,' he confided. 'No noise from road, and a sea view.' He took off his sunglasses and peered at Finn. 'Mind you, we get sun on't patio first thing.'

Finn squinted at the holiday settlement adrift in the sweltering plain of sweetcorn and sunflowers. Somewhere the cicadas were soothing and a generator throbbed. It seemed one of the quietest, sunniest places on earth.

Maureen had spent a long Saturday morning working in the office with John Foxton, checking through the records of workers at the Nottingham plant and making sure that all the paperwork was in order. During their mid-morning break she'd managed to phone India who had gone to stay with a friend, and was reassured to hear her steadier. She had just squeezed in her pre-arranged call to Judith, jotting a few relevant notes in shorthand before turning her attention to Kevin Railton.

By employing an ingenious repertoire of assumed names she had been building up an accurate picture of Railton's movements. This lunchtime for instance she knew he would be dining at the Savoy Grill with a client.

Now, as she waited to begin dictation notes for John's speech for Monday, she could only wish to hear from Pearl and Finn with some indication of their next move. Privately she was beginning to feel that behind every great detective team was a good personal assistant. Maureen filled the spare moments by getting up to date with her cuttings file. Three days behind with her records, she was scanning a tabloid from Wednesday when she saw the photograph of John Foxton leaning on the bonnet of a car with an angry expression on his face.

'LEADERS CLASH ON PICKET LINE,' the caption declared in bold black print.

When Foxton returned to the office she pushed the paper towards him. 'You didn't say you'd seen Freddie Jones?' her voice was peremptory.

He glanced at her moodily. 'The man's gone soft,' he muttered as he gathered his notes together.

'He's been in touch then?' She remembered laying out the post yesterday, noticing the ATE logo on an envelope.

Foxton looked impatient. 'Yes, Maureen. He was suggesting some half-baked partnership if you must know. Another of his devious deals. I turned it down flat.' She flushed, wounded by his irritation.

He sighed and sat down behind his desk. He broke their silence awkwardly. 'I'm sorry. All this waiting must be getting to me.' She accepted his apology and thoughtfully turned over a fresh page in her notebook.

Maureen regarded John Foxton as a leading exponent of the art of dictation. A natural speaker, he would fluently construct sentences from the air and punctuate them with her as she read his lines back, honing and refining as they progressed together. That afternoon he seemed to have no heart for it and read notes to her listlessly before scrapping them all and going out to pace the car park and clear his head. Maureen took the opportunity quickly to phone Millie.

'Any news from P and F?' Millie reminded her that it was unlikely that they'd report back before their deadline on Sunday evening.

'John's in bad shape.' Maureen's tone modulated to the strictly confidential.

'Sorry to hear that,' said Millie objectively, aware of Laura whipping eggs in the kitchen. 'What's the matter exactly?'

'Attitude. He's very touchy.' Maureen sounded depressed. 'My theory is that something happened between him and Pearson during their unofficial summit.' She assessed Millie's hesitation and added, 'Think he needs reassuring, legally.'

'It's Saturday, Maureen.' Millie calculated her reluctance carefully against Maureen's suggestion and relented gracefully. 'Tell him to call round when he's finished with you, if advice is what he needs.'

Gratefully Maureen replaced the receiver and waited to gauge the correct moment to confirm John Foxton's appointment with his lawyer.

Twenty-seven

The Wolsey drove through an archway towards a sweeping white staircase and a lavish villa gold in the early-evening sun. Finn stopped the engine in surprise and then with a grin edged forward, switching off their slow-motion opera singer.

The pool glinted ahead of them and they saw a woman reclining on a lounger under a huge yellow umbrella. She didn't seem to hear them. They left the car by a squat building with no windows.

'Even the garage's got air-conditioning.' Pearl nodded at the fan outlets and shook her head. Trevor's modest descriptions were collapsing around them.

The plot was laid out in the style of an English garden with flowerbeds of baked red mud and cracked around dying specimens of French marigolds and roses. The matted remains of a lawn dried like a skin all round the villa. A water spray turned vainly. The front door was framed with the kind of porch where wellingtons are left. Pearl ran her fingers over the pebbledash.

'Looks different out here, doesn't it?' She grinned. 'Almost exotic.'

Finn pointed at a package left half-unravelled by the door. It was the Daphne sign, still in its English newspaper.

Daphne looked up as the two young women materialised in the shimmering heat. 'You're early,' she observed, going back to her magazine, 'but wait for me inside and we'll start in a minute.'

'Where's Trevor, Daphne?' Pearl squatted so Daphne could see her.

'John Foxton's sent us to collect some paper work.'

Daphne struggled up in her chair and pulled her flowery dressing gown around her shoulders as if she might catch a chill.

She lowered her sun glasses and looked at the beautiful black girl in crumpled khaki shorts, and at her companion in jeans with short spiky hair and a strikingly pale complexion.

'English,' she said eventually, almost gratefully. 'Why don't you stay? We're having a party this evening.'

'Who did you think we were?' Pearl smiled curiously.

'My women's group.' Daphne was confidential. 'They have to come here because they disapprove in the village.' She smiled ruefully. 'Dead resistant, my age-group, but you can't blame them. Liberation is very disruptive and not always comfortable.'

Finn looked baffled and noticing she was swaying, knelt down to make talking easier. She was gentle, holding Daphne's hand and explaining carefully. 'We've got to speak to Trev as soon as possible. Where is he?'

'Don't ask me.' Daphne jerked her hand away, spilling her drink. I made it a rule not to know, and not to care.'

Pearl topped Daphne's glass up carefully with tonic and put it back in her hand. 'When was he last here?'

'This morning. Only stayed a few hours, then went off again at lunchtime.' Daphne sighed. 'Didn't say how long.' She shook her head, and putting her hand out tenderly she stroked Finn's hair as if it were a mirage. 'He always says goodbye as if it's forever.'

Slowly she took them into the shady villa and stopped in front of a large framed map over an ingle-nook fireplace. 'The only way half of them can leave this place is to go to England and be au pairs.' She rolled her eyes. 'The whole trend is blatantly sexist of course.'

Pearl watched Daphne angrily slapping the mantelpiece to make her point. 'So you teach them to speak English?'

'Yes.' But she shook her head as if Pearl had missed the point. 'But it only gets really useful when we can move on to consciousness-raising and assertiveness training. That's how I came into it in the first place.'

A high-pitched shrieking started from an adjacent room like a demon. Daphne smiled distractedly and looked through the bead curtain. A small wiry monkey with a hairless face scuttled up and down a wooden bar. It pointed and screamed wildly when it saw her.

'That's Amigo.' She watched him with no expression. 'He was

already called that when I bought him.' The monkey called out piteously as she turned away and then quietened into occasional yelps.

Daphne returned to the map dreamily and tapped her finger on a bite out of the coast. 'That's where he goes, La Bajia del Angel,' she confided in Finn. 'We used to go there together.' She moved away from them abruptly, turning only once on her way back to the pool. 'Not that adventurous, poor old Trev. While I've changed my whole life.'

The car was like a furnace by the time they climbed back in, the seats burning the backs of their legs. Finn rested her head against the wheel and closed her eyes.

'You were great with her,' Pearl touched her shoulder uncertainly. 'Her theory's fine, but she seems rather muddled.'

Finn smiled, started the engine and felt the ventilator blow back boiling air. 'My auntie used to drink like that. And get all weepy.' She screwed up her face and accelerated down the road taking them towards the coast.

It was getting dark by the time they reached the coast. They ran along small beach settlements and colonies of straw-roofed huts and bars and, infrequently, past ramshackle farms. Stopping where they saw a lantern in a yard they found a woman with her lap full of feathers plucking a turkey, its red neck hanging broken against her legs. She was singing a lullaby as she tweaked and stroked the grey stippled skin. Wiping down her bloody fingers, she gave them directions.

'Enough to turn you vegetarian.' Finn turned her face back to the road.

As they jolted back down the potholed track Pearl counted through the hours. 'Perhaps we should just turn back,' she said. 'If we've got to get back by tomorrow evening, we're running out of time already.' Finn pursed her lips and, setting her eyes on the dancing track, drove hard at the blackness. Leaning back, Pearl closed her eyes hopelessly to the sea breaking on the shoreline and the drumming of the car engine. Too much time to think. She looked down at her watch face, suddenly jumping the hour back to England, and to Fitz.

Finn splashed her face with water from a bottle as they lurched onwards. There were no houses or beach bars now, just the liquid dark and the sound of sea. In the mirror running with water she caught sight of her face. There were times when she felt herself slipping around the rim of a circle, covering distance with no sight of the middle. She glanced back to the mirror; somewhere behind them a set of headlights flared and disappeared. Straining at the darkness she tried to pick them out again but they seemed to have melted away.

Soon the road turned into drifting sand blown from a ridge of dunes. A light toasting wind whipped the marran grass until it rattled; invisible waves muffled the beach with shingle.

They got out and scrambled up to the top of the ridge and scanned the long dark sands below them. A few fishermen's lights dotted the waterline where they cast their lines and waded into the shallows. Finn slithered further towards the shore and swept the binoculars back towards a small inlet. Someone on the beach appeared to be having a barbecue and distinctly, by the erratic light of fire, she saw a Ford Sierra.

They ploughed on along the sandy track until they reached the head of a small estuary. Jumping out, Finn forged ahead, stumbling along the bed of a dried-up stream. Gasping for breath and rubbing her legs torn from brambles, Pearl caught her up on the beach.

Finn was watching through the binoculars again, breathing heavily, waiting for the figure to move nearer the firelight. The shadow drifted and the man threw on more armfuls of wood. Finn passed Pearl the binoculars.

She steadied her hands and focused. 'It's him. It's Mitchell.' Pearl was smiling, breathless with relief. She looked again, frowning, almost laughing. 'What the hell's he wearing?'

'A raincoat.' Finn looked wary. 'You go first, at least he knows you.'

Mitchell was singing softly to himself as he prodded the fire with a long branch, stirring the embers so they threw out sparks. He shuffled to avoid them, digging his bare feet into the warm sand. The wood glowed as he carefully banked on more fuel. The fire almost went out before it caught and leapt with flames again, suddenly high and spiked with greens and blues. Acrid smoke drifted in the breeze.

When Pearl walked into the light, he stepped back with surprise, and then stared back to the flames, warming his hands.

'You all right, Trevor?'

He blinked with surprise and pulled up his collar. 'Pearl? I used to think I could talk to you.' He sounded confused.

She nervously moved closer, keeping her voice casual. 'Expecting rain?'

He gave his light, nervous laugh and looked down at his bulky coat as if it were a dress. 'I didn't bother to pack.'

Trevor suddenly saw Finn at her side. He seemed to be visibly adding them together and the effort made him crumple. Sudden tears dribbled down his face, but he gave no sound, just wiped them away.

'You can't make me go back.' He had recovered quickly, his face tightening as he stared at them.

Pearl sat down close to him. 'We need all the union files, Trevor, and some information.' She was firm as a teacher. 'What you do after that is nothing to do with us.'

A sudden wave distracted him for a moment, and looking away from the fire he rested his eyes wistfully on the darkness. 'I didn't ever want John to know about this, not ever.'

'What were you going to do then? Pay it back in instalments?' Pearl heard herself mocking him.

He nodded. 'I thought I could.'

'Three million quid between you? Come off it Trev, what on earth did you spend it on?'

Mitchell drew lines in the sand. 'Didn't.' He corrected himself deliberately. 'Didn't realise it was that much until it was too late.'

'So how much of it went to Railton?' Pearl grabbed his lapel and made him look at her. He closed his eyes and pulled away.

'It's too late, I'd never prove a thing, it's not worth the risk.' Pearl noticed two deep scratches on his cheek as his hand went up defensively and he rocked miserably on his heels. The fire gave out little spurts and colours as if it were burning tar.

Near the car Finn saw something in the sand catching the firelight. Bending down she picked up a brown pebble, perfectly smooth, like an egg. She closed her fingers round it, remembering, and then stuffed it in her pocket.

A stack of empty cardboard boxes were stacked untidily near

the open boot of the car. Finn examined them curiously and dragged them towards the fire. Abandoning Trevor, Pearl watched her empty out two files on to the sand. Sheets of paper fell out and blew towards the fire. Pearl grabbed one and angled it towards the uncertain light of the flames. It was NUAVE headed notepaper.

Finn lunged back at the fire and grabbing a stick saw the powdered shapes of box files and piles of metal clips glowing white hot. Frantically she tried to rake at the embers but the shapes collapsed into soot.

'You must be mad.' Pearl stared at Mitchell.

'I just want it to finish.' It was all he could say, over and over again.

Pearl watched him huddle over the flames and wanted to hit him. 'You selfish bastard.' She grabbed his arm and pulled him away. 'Now it will always be your fault.'

He shrugged. 'The strike may fail. But John will sort it.'

'Freddie Jones, you mean.' Pearl dredged the name back from Mepham's golf course conversation. 'It's not just your union at stake any more, Trev. If that strike collapses it will be about a lot more than your men.'

Trevor walked towards her suddenly sobered.

'Freddie Jones? What's he got to do with it?' Pearl angrily explained what Maureen had pieced together, her personal theories with some additions gleaned from John. She'd done some phoning round and discovered an old college friend working in Nigel Pearson's office. Judith had confirmed that Freddie Jones had recently attended some high-level management meetings at Turnbull's.

Trevor stared at Pearl painfully as if dazzled by the fire.

'I'm going to help you.' He shook his head shamefully. 'It's my duty.'

'Railton?' Pearl didn't give him time to think.

He looked cowed and nodded. 'But *you'll* have to find the proof. I'll help you, show you how.'

Finn moved closer, skirting the fire. 'Don't play games Mitchell. India's already told us that you've got evidence of your own.'

'Where is it, Trevor?' Pearl made him concentrate. Hugging himself as though he were in pain, he shuffled nearer the light.

'I've been such a stupid man.' He stared into the flames still shimmering with the colours of plastic. He watched the way the metal centres of the melted discs buckled with the heat. 'I'll make sure you get your evidence.' He looked at Pearl gravely, his eyes moving, thinking ahead.

Suddenly fired with a new sense of purpose, Mitchell started to throw sand on the fire. 'You'll have to come to the villa. There's something you're going to need, and I have to make an urgent phone call.'

'Why should we trust you?' Finn was watching him suspiciously.

Trevor smiled at her foolishly, and opened out a clean handkerchief. He blew his nose and pathetically dabbed his face. 'No reason,' he said, as he fumbled his handkerchief back into his pocket and calmly drew out an old black revolver. He pulled the hammer slowly with a click, weighing it in his hand sentimentally. Pearl saw Finn freeze. The waves raking the shingle seemed very loud as she watched Trevor staring down at the gun. She saw him going back over his decision to be alone at all costs.

He turned to Pearl and threw the gun down on to the sand.

'I just wanted it all to be over,' he comforted himself as he nudged the gun with his foot. 'This was my father's. He was a man prepared to fight for what he believed in. A man of honour; made some difference to the world.'

Pearl nodded and Trevor straightened up. 'You reminded me.'

They followed his car back over the dunes and on to the road, Finn straining after Trevor's tail lights as the road curved back inland.

Pearl leant back wearily. 'Take it easy, Finn, he's on our side now.'

'You reckon?'

'What else?' Pearl watched the black fields slipping past. 'Let's hope he comes up with the goods.'

Finn drummed her fingers on the dashboard and saw a van following them at a steady pace some distance behind them. She watched it anxiously until the headlights swung away into a junction.

'What's bugging you?'

Finn shrugged. 'Where do you think Trevor got these marks on his face?' She took a deep breath. 'Looked like he'd been scratched by fingernails to me.'

Twenty-eight

Villa Daphne was blazing with light as they drew up an hour later behind Trevor's car. Music thumped from the floodlit pool area and a handful of guests were arranged in deckchairs near the water's edge.

Trevor leant against his car despairingly. The air was still hot and heavy with the scent of wild thyme growing in the scrub. Pearl noticed Finn was shivering.

'Come on.' Pearl braced herself and grabbed Trevor's arm. 'Let's get this over with.'

He walked them quickly towards the side of the villa, but when they approached the french windows he faltered. As if he had made a decision he broke away from Pearl and walked towards the light. In the centre of the room a large group of people were gathered around a long table; Daphne was vivacious. A female croupier span a roulette wheel, shouting instructions in Spanish and English and pulling coloured chips towards her with a rake. The silver ball span into a number and the players, colourful in Bermuda shorts and transparent dresses, rocked with excitement. Almost in slow motion, faces registered pleasure or anguish. Trevor stood silhouetted before them like a refugee. No one seemed to notice him.

A large leafy creeper spread like a canopy across the side entrance to the annexe. Trevor took out a key and clumsily fumbled with the lock, his distress exaggerating his movements. He motioned them into a small study and locked the door quickly behind him. His breathing was laboured with the effort.

'No need to lock us in Trev.' Pearl felt her mouth drying.

'Keeping them at bay more like.' Trevor threw the key on the table. 'Bloody savages.' His voice shook, and wiping his mouth with the back of his hand, he opened louvred doors into a larger room.

'Wait in there.' He pushed them through roughly, throwing them matches to light the lamp. But Pearl followed him back out and found him frantically searching through the drawers of his desk. 'What the hell are you playing at, Trevor?'

His forehead glistened with a sweat as he spilled a box of closely-typed index cards. He slammed his fist down hard on the table.

'I meant what I said back there.' Dismissing her, he dropped to his knees and started to scrabble through the cards on the floor, mumbling to himself.

Pearl hesitated. 'Maybe Finn was right about you.'

He lumbered at her and grabbed her wrists. The whites of his eyes gaped and she smelled whisky on his breath. 'You'll get your stuff on Railton, Pearl.' He nodded towards the noise from the casino. 'There's a wall-safe in there. They'll be gone soon.' His hand shook. 'I can't go in now.'

Letting her go apologetically, Trevor lit a cigarette, breaking the match, and pointing towards his desk. 'If I could just find this phone number and make the call, it might solve something.' He smiled his collapsing smile. 'You're going to help me make this better, Pearl.'

He brightened with this new idea and seized a key on his desk. Putting it in his pocket he bundled Pearl through into the other room. She struggled but his bulky weight propelled her forward. He locked the louvred door. As she squinted back through the slats she could see him on his knees again, muttering, picking up cards, apologising.

Pearl slumped next to Finn on a wicker sofa and drank tonic water from a bottle. In the corner of the room were boxes of soft drinks, all with English brand-names.

'We're trapped, then.' Finn stared angrily at the barred and shuttered window.

'Or waiting,' said Pearl, her hope receding. Through the adjacent wall Daphne's party grew louder and more reckless.

Trevor poured himself another whisky and copied the telephone number from an old notebook on to a scrap of paper. His hand shook as he punched the long international code and then the number into the phone. It rang out each time unanswered and he tried again and again, hoping each time he had misdialled, that someone might just walk through the door. Eventually he talked to the operator in halting fragments of Spanish, slurring the digits, begging pitifully for help.

The bottle had rolled off the desk and smashed on to the stone flags when he heard Pearl shouting his name above the music.

'He's not there you see.' He spoke vaguely to the doorway as if he had forgotten they were there. 'I'll have to try again in the morning.' He put his glass down carefully before staggering to his feet and unlocking the doors.

'Probably gone out. It's Saturday night.' He lost his balance and slumped to the floor. He was panting slightly, his breath reeking of whisky. He gave a feeble laugh.

Pearl bent down and tried to shake him awake. His eyes rolled and shut as his groaning subsided into a snore. 'I know what night it is, you old fool,' she said miserably, as she slapped his stupid, hopeless face, knowing he was out cold.

'They look like pre-stressed concrete.' Laura gloomily pulled a tray of slate-coloured meringues out of the oven. She toppled them noisily into the bin, gratefully abandoning the therapy of home cooking. She observed her mother carefully. They'd spent a day and an evening avoiding each other.

Millie was piling a stack of encrusted cake tins into the sink and remembering back to a barbecue, when Laura tugged at her sleeve and made her sit down. 'It *was* John, wasn't it?'

Her mother looked at her with a jolt.

'You've got to tell me sometime, haven't you?'

'What do you mean?' Millie felt like running away. It was too late in the evening to face this conversation. Too late anyway, perhaps.

Laura spoke in a rush. 'It was John who came between you and Dad and made you miserable for absolutely years. Wasn't it?'

'You were too young to know anything about it.' Millie laughed and gripped the edge of the worktop. Her daughter sat down on a stool and watched her seriously. Millie felt the thread between them tighten.

'Yes. It was John.' She heard herself say deliberately.

Laura nodded. 'It's probably more of a shock for you than it is for me.' She stated it simply, folding and refolding a paper doily.

'How did you know?' Millie felt vaguely out of control.

'Obvious,' Laura shrugged, 'like electricity between you, anyone could see.'

'"Yes?'

Laura smiled. 'Dead romantic. Gives me hope for Eric and me.' She scraped a tin thoughtfully. 'Quite odd really. Made me think of you as a person.'

Laura's cross examination had an alarming effect. Millie sat up late by herself, in front of the fire with windows open, in a state of shock. The sudden revelation of a secret suspended for years disturbed her profoundly. Laura's uncomplicated reaction was almost a disappointment, as if by admission something was suddenly concluded.

John finally appeared on the doorstep at midnight and she followed him into her own sitting room like a stranger.

He threw down his briefcase and smiled. 'Thanks, Mil. You're right as usual. No point going off at a tangent now.'

She poured them both a brandy, measuring each one pedantically, without noticing. He seemed to be talking hard to fill in the gaps, almost to establish that she wanted him there.

'What's shaken me is that until Railton came up with that money, I had almost decided to give in and accept Pearson's offer.' He explained uncertainly, slowly turning his glass round, not meeting her eyes. Millie drifted away from what he was saying, still remembering the excitement in her daughter's voice.

He was asking detailed questions about the legal pitfalls of redundancy buy-outs when she reached out and took his hand. He faltered.

'You don't mind, do you Mil, talking it through?' He leant forward, 'I've decided I have to put it to the stewards, at least. It's the only honourable thing to do.'

She smiled. 'I'll make sure you are properly briefed; there are lots of precedents you can refer to.' He met her eyes gratefully. The clock ticked steadily between them. 'And I'd like you to stay tonight, John.' She said it easily, suddenly realising what a relief it was to be honest.

Millie heard Laura moving round in the kitchen the next morning and savoured the absence of guilt. Lying up against the warm curve of his back, Millie gave in to the relief of his steady breathing, his head turned away from her in sleep. She suspended any thought beyond the exact moment. Pulling the sheet over them like a fragile tent against the light she fell back into a deep sleep.

Laura's knock on the door startled them both awake.

'It's the phone for John. It's urgent. Really sorry.' They heard her running away back down the stairs.

He lurched out of bed fumbling for his shirt and trousers.

'Who knows you're here?' Millie was dislocated.

He shrugged. 'Maureen's probably guessed.' He touched her foot under the sheet and ran down the stairs.

Millie's heart beat uncomfortably with a jolt of realisation. She got up slowly and followed him downstairs. He had just replaced the phone and was heading back with two coffees.

'There's a phone in the bedroom.' She wasn't even sure what she was saying. 'So what couldn't I hear?'

'It *was* Maureen.' He smiled ruefully. 'I'm sorry, awkward I know, but it was an emergency – work . . .'

Millie watched his face, watching her, full of concern. He turned, noticing the door closing quietly behind Laura as she escaped into the garden. Looking back he had that old distant look, a way of being already away from her. She took her coffee from him and went slowly back up to the bedroom. Eventually she picked up the phone and slowly dialled her best friend's number, imagining it ringing in Kate's lush conservatory full of orchids.

Twenty-nine

It was getting light through the half-opened shutters when Pearl realised the party had faded. A last car accelerated over the bumpy road and a door slammed. Trevor was still deeply asleep on the sofa, his mouth half open like a drowning fish. She turned stiffly in her chair and fell back into a light doze. The church bell started like a memory, a single tolling Sunday chime, and a blade of sunlight fell across Pearl's face.

Trevor sat bolt upright, staring into space, his hair jagged with salt and sleep. He blinked slowly, touching his head as if it was in pieces, and frowning at the piece of paper crumpled in his hand.

Pearl threw open the shutters and breathed in the morning air. Sunflowers scorched a white wall. The colours were blinding. A coloured umbrella rolled about in the breeze on the concrete drive. She closed her eyes and for a second nursed blackness and no sensation. Trevor looked towards her feebly and shielded his eyes.

'Sorry,' he said simply. 'Sorry.'

Finn had disappeared and Pearl bad-temperedly searched for her through windows and open doors as she led Trevor round the villa to the kitchen. It was ten o'clock and she started to make decisions. Trevor was getting an ultimatum and then they were getting out. Ahead of them stretched a journey like a desert. She opened a cupboard to a battery of patent medicines, cold cures, cough mixtures and corn plasters, all from England.

'Don't they have Boots in Spain, then?' She dropped soluble aspirin into a glass of water.

He shook his head soberly. 'You can't be too careful.'

Pearl held a bag of ice-cubes out to him moodily and looked at him slumped over the formica.

'Not really cut out for a life of crime, are you Trev?' She had to laugh.

Finn materialised, looking as white as paper, stubbornly wearing her leather jacket and gulping orange juice. Catching Pearl's urgency she pointed to the main sitting room.

'Come on Trevor, let's get that safe open.' He nodded obediently and they followed him through upturned chairs in a sea of glasses and bottles. The roulette table was still strewn with coloured chips. A column of plastic money teetered as they slammed the door and then slithered over the green baize board. Broken glass crunched under their feet and in the next room they heard the monkey scutter and sob for attention.

Trevor moistened his lips and pushed his hair flat. He went over to the fireplace where a garish picture of a flowergirl cried on the steps of a cathedral. It hung drunkenly, its gilt frame burning in the sunshine. Trevor straightened it and then took it off the wall apologetically.

'It's all rather predictable,' he said as he clicked his way through the wall-safe combination. His hand shook as he pulled on the unyielding door. His face flickered with panic. Finn touched his arm.

'Whatever it was, do it again, and finish each move to a definite click before you travel the other way.' He listened and nodded. 'You were rushing it, that's all.'

He repeated the sequence ponderously and the door swung open. Glancing nervously at Finn he took out a cigar box. 'Railton works his private deals from home; it'll all be there. All you've got to do is get it.' He wiped his face with his sleeve. 'I went there once to tell him I wanted out.'

'What happened?'

Trevor flinched, his eyes going vague. 'Cold place. He had this huge marble table.' He opened the box nervously. 'He had it done up like Fort Knox; calls it his HQ.'

Finn went through the box hopelessly and picked out a set of Railton's keys, three mortises and a yale. She glanced miserably at Pearl.

Trevor reached into the safe and took out an airmail envelope containing a small black wallet. 'My brother runs a top security outfit. He did the place, specifications were unbelievable.'

'Holograms?' Finn checked dully.

'Totally obsessed.' Trevor nodded, preoccupied with a plastic moulded card which he slid out like a jewel from the wallet.

'The front door key.' Finn took it eagerly.

'Thought it might be a sort of insurance policy.' But he looked doubtful.

Pearl turned the card blankly.

Finn pointed at the circuits. 'Like a central locking system on a car – computerised.'

Trevor was about to swing back the door when Finn turned and quickly put her hand out to stop him.

'Where do you keep your garage key, Trev?' He stared at her for a second and went on pushing, trapping her fingers. Pearl threw herself at him and knocked him away. The monkey screamed and clattered in the other room.

Trevor struggled to regain his balance. He took another, smaller wallet out of the safe and handed it over to Finn bleakly. 'You might as well know it all now.'

Trevor looked resigned as he led the way out to the drive. They stood in the broiling sunshine while he inserted the plastic circuit card into a concealed flap within the doorframe and pressed it into place. Using a flimsy yale in an ordinary-looking lock, he completed the sequence and a small red dot glowed above the card as the door opened.

The air-conditioning whirred as he led them into a cool and darkened building and switched on the light. The refrigerated storeroom was crowded with marble statues and paintings in racks.

'Some garage,' Pearl gasped, and ran her hand along the cool stone limbs of a young god. She walked along rows of small angels and madonnas in bronze and stone.

Trevor sat down in a wicker chair, apparently revived by the cool, and watched them placidly like a curator.

'It's all Railton's.' He surveyed the room dismally. 'They crate it and bring it out from London in removal vans, like it's our own furniture. And then take stuff away.' He lifted his face towards the cool draught. 'He's been using the union's investment fund as a legitimate cover to fence for dealers in London. It's stuff stolen from churches all over Europe. They disappear into private collections. And he pays us rent – storage.'

He plucked at his watch. 'And now I just want it finished.'

Pearl tried to dial Millie's but she couldn't get the number to connect. Clicking the handrest she tried to raise the operator and realised the phone was dead. Exasperated she stared out of the window and watched a landrover disappear down the road, throwing up a red stain of dust.

Suddenly alarmed, Pearl ran out into the garden, shading her eyes from the glaring sun.

Daphne, strangely transformed by jeans and a T-shirt, was sitting on the steps talking to Finn. Occasionally they threw pieces of fruit to the monkey who begged by sitting up with his small paws clenched to his eyes.

'It's his party piece,' Daphne explained. 'He pretends he's crying.'

Pearl looked back at Trevor, still crumpled in his London suit. He touched his cheek gingerly.

'When I left yesterday the bloody animal went for me.' He watched it take a grape from Daphne. 'Instinct I suppose.'

Finn glanced ruefully at Pearl and smiled.

'Who were you trying to phone last night, Trev?' Pearl was still thinking about the speeding land rover.

'Freddie Jones.' He straightened up hopefully. 'We know each other from way back. I thought there might be something I could do. It was just an idea.' He tailed off, aware his wife was watching him.

'You need to do more than pay Daphne's gambling bills,' Pearl said quietly.

He nodded solemnly. '*I* made this happen – working too hard, never there. Don't suppose John will ever know what I gave to that union.' He shook his head. 'Daphne should have walked out on me.'

He lowered his voice. 'All this independence business is her way of doing without me, I suppose.'

'Can't she have both?' asked Pearl carefully.

Trevor looked. 'A second chance she called it when we got this place. Don't think I listened too carefully.' His voice was full of regret.

They left them sitting on the step together.

'Daphne read that letter Trevor never posted,' Finn told her. 'I think it helped. She seemed really surprised he needed her.'

Pearl took Finn's arm and walked her towards the car. The monkey scittered around them playfully darting in zigzags over the burnt turf. Laughing, Daphne waved it back, calling its name in separate syllables.

Amigo scrabbled onto the roof of their car, and clutching the aerial swung itself through the window into the driver's seat.

Finn only vaguely remembered throwing herself across Pearl, and the dull sensation of earth falling down on them in a delayed avalanche. An explosion like a long drawn out eruption of gunfire tore through the silence and the car was engulfed in flame. When she looked back the metal trembled with fire and a pall of black smoke covered the rising red dust. Over the road the couple from Barnsley watched in horror from their patio.

Trevor gave them his car and it was only after she had been driving for an hour that Finn began to come out of her shock. Together they started to collect the pieces: the Land Rover that morning; the headlights following them over the dunes; the white-haired young man trailing them off the plane.

Pearl nodded shakily and closed her eyes to steady herself. She was seeing India's hand raised to cover her battered face, and Trevor, letting Daphne comfort him as they left, cornered and panicked like an animal.

She had no doubt that this was Railton's doing.

John Foxton swung away from Millie's street and drove hard for twenty minutes without registering a single street name. Glancing in his car mirror he rubbed his stubbled chin and saw himself accused.

A couple with a dog ran across the road to get the Sunday papers and as he waited behind a milk float it started to rain. Drops fell on the windscreen and blotted the pavement. He left the window open and let it blow on him. The Embankment slipped past in a blur. He stopped again behind a bus and watched a pavement artist frantically covering his chalked squares: 'Sunflowers' ran with water.

Maureen's words echoed in his head until his thoughts came round full circle. Suddenly he pulled on the wheel and, crossing the traffic abruptly, turned back the way he'd come. He clipped a kerbstone clumsily and as he turned to look, saw an ice-blue Jaguar completing the same manoeuvre. He turned sharply down a side street and then speeded through changing traffic lights. He checked his mirror again and confirmed that he was being followed.

Foxton automatically accelerated and dangerously overtook two cars before he suddenly slowed down, pulled over and switched off the ignition. The rain hammered on the roof of the car and splashed through the window. He leant across calmly, unlocked the passenger door and waited for Railton to join him.

'Your car's too distinctive, Kevin. Spotted you straightaway.'

Railton laughed, his lips unnaturally red against his beard. 'I wasn't following you John, I was merely hoping to deliver this, as soon as possible.'

Foxton cautiously took the document case. It occurred to him that he had never seen Railton without the hard edges of a suit. Sitting there in a Hawaiian shirt and jeans he smiled as if he were a friend. Foxton opened the case and looked bleakly at a grainy black and white photo of himself kissing Millie. It had been taken with a telephoto lens through her sitting room window. It was the first of a sequence. A printed report documented his movements over the last few days, meticulously logged with dates and times.

'You bastard, Railton.' Foxton stared straight ahead at the rain on the windscreen. 'You've run your errand. Now get the hell out.'

Railton rubbed steam off the window. 'When I have someone followed, John, I have it done professionally. I don't hire women and kids who end up getting hurt.' Railton wound the window down angrily on the rain.

'What do you mean, hurt?' Foxton turned on him with alarm.

Railton looked at him contemptuously. 'Second rule of politics John . . .' He left his sentence unfinished with a sneer.

John numbly started up the engine. Railton stepped out of the car, and poked his head back through the window.

'Our proposal is what you might call an out of court settlement. The deal's still on offer with Pearson. And as far as I'm concerned, I can help put your books back into some sort of reasonable order, without too many casualties, naturally.'

Foxton released the handbrake and put his foot down on the accelerator. The comfort of seeing Railton reeling in the gutter was only temporary.

Maureen wasn't in the office when John arrived, breathing hard from running up the stairs. The lifts were undergoing a Sunday maintenance check and the men's shouts echoed through the building.

He noticed a sleeping bag rolled tidily in the corner next to a small suitcase, washed-up crockery from what appeared to be breakfast and a jar of marmalade on the shelf. Maureen hurried in, wiping her hands on a towel and carrying a washbag.

'Looks like you've moved in.' He looked exhausted.

'I have.' She looked at him anxiously. 'Only temporarily of course.'

Foxton sat down uncomfortably. 'Anything I can do?'

'Hardly.' Maureen laughed, almost bitterly. She glanced through the venetian blinds, talking quickly and quietly. 'I spent yesterday keeping tabs on Railton.'

'Why?' He was confused.

Maureen wandered why he looked so alarmed. 'Because it might well be crucial when Pearl and Finn get back from Spain. Besides he's as guilty as hell and we don't want him disappearing.'

She poured him coffee and sat down with her note pad.

'I tailed him in a taxi last night.' She ignored his startled look.' He was at Nigel Pearson's house with that Vincent Mepham.'

'They're out to get me.' He told her without expression.

Maureen nodded and got up swiftly, and as if presenting an exhibit in court, placed a letter on the table between them.

'This is why I had to call you. Delivered by hand, left at the security gate.' He paled and picked up the envelope. 'They obviously thought you wouldn't get it until tomorrow.'

'You've read it, I suppose?' He unfolded the sheet of handwritten paper.

Maureen frowned. 'Railton regrets to inform you that to his concern he's found out that the money you've primed for the strike fund is dirty.' She produced the postcard of the plane from her handbag. 'This wasn't from Trevor. Railton must have forged it. It must have been his own money; he was using it as bait.'

'Dirty money?' Foxton felt sick.

'Read the second page.' She tapped the paper. 'The money's come from stocks from a firm recently exposed for insider dealing.'

'And union funds must always be above public reproach.' Foxton repeated their ethical code like a catetchism and saw the delicately poised trap. 'I was meant to receive this when it was too late to call it back, and then they'd expose me?'

Maureen's face wavered. 'They win either way. My guess is they'd have been happier if you'd panicked and pulled the money out. The strike would collapse and Railton's in the clear because he warned you.'

Foxton grimly put the letter in his wallet and was on his feet. 'You've done really well, Maureen.'

'What are you going to do?' She looked alarmed.

'I think he's bluffing; he's trying to hussle me into hanging myself.' He placed the document case in his desk drawer. 'My instinct now is to use the bloody money. I'll need some advice on this but I'm not giving in now.'

Maureen had a shrewd idea where he was going next. She stood up awkwardly. 'About this morning, John . . .'

He shrugged. 'You did absolutely the right thing.'

She accepted his faint smile and watched from the window until he had driven away from the car park. She started to dial Millie's number to give her some warning and then decided against it.

Maureen opened a psychology textbook and watched the print swim.

'*You've done really well.*' She replayed his words and thought about what she hadn't told him. That she was sure that Railton had spotted her as he left Pearson's home in Kensington, that she'd come back to the office late last night because she was too frightened to go home. 'But I'm safe enough here,' she reassured herself. 'With our own guard on the gate.'

By eight that Sunday evening the subway leading from the airport to the car park was awash with rain water. Finn pulled Pearl through the dark tunnel and hurried her out into the open air.

'Don't see why we can't pick Rufus up and go straight to Railton's,' she argued.

'And breeze in and find him with his feet up watching TV, I suppose?' Pearl muttered irritably.

She walked off through the puddles to the pay phones and Finn made her way slowly towards the Wolsey. She lifted her face up to black sky zigzagged with aeroplanes, and let the rain wash down over her face.

A parking ticket in a plastic bag flapped on the windscreen. Finn swore and was just about to unhitch it from the wiper when Pearl shouted and ran towards her. Finn jumped backwards, fear coming easily now, her heart pounding against her ribs, her back breaking into a sickly sweat.

'What if he's nobbled ours too?' Pearl was shaking.

'Too late. I've just kicked it twice. Must be all right.' Finn grinned. 'You know how I hate parking tickets.'

The car park at the flats was deserted. As they walked over the wet tarmac Pearl realised there was a light on in her flat. It glowed softly through her yellow blind. Feeling light-headed and shivery she hesitated before she put her key in the lock. Testing her head against the door, she listened for the sound of the television, or someone walking across the room, any sign. Finn pulled her jacket around her, wet hair sticking up at angles, and watched her anxiously.

'What's up now?' Pearl shrugged and opened the door. There was a small light on downstairs but the flat was exactly as they had left it. Pearl stared at the lamp next to the window.

'Must have left it on,' she said dully.

Finn pulled off her wet T-shirt. 'No, I did. In case we had burglars.'

The answerphone had one message from Maureen saying she could be reached in the office, any time.

'Can't be now,' said Pearl. 'It's nearly ten. Even Maureen.' She spooled on uselessly, it was the only message.

Finn saw her bending over it, touching the buttons. 'Come on P. Maybe we should phone Railton's number; see if he answers?'

Pearl swung round, her face crumpling. 'Just don't call me that, OK?' She hunched her shoulders, raking with silent sobs.

It frightened Finn to see Pearl cry. She felt her own heart pounding again. She watched Pearl crouched into herself, sobbing without hope of comfort. Finn moved closer and watched helplessly. She had let this happen with a single word, and everything about it felt like a kind of violence.

Pearl looked up and saw Finn's white face. She shuddered for breath like a child, and held out her arms. 'For Christ's sake, Finn?' Finn walked towards her and Pearl hung on to her, holding her as she knelt down, leaning into her shoulder. Her tears were scalding hot on Finn's neck.

Pearl stopped crying gradually and sat shivering on the sofa. 'Not a message, not a note.' She sniffed into her sleeve. 'It was meant to be last night.'

'Maybe he came?'

Pearl shook her head. 'I gave him a key.' She took a deep breath and rubbed away the tears as if they might stain her face forever. 'I'm not going to do this any more.'

Finn collapsed against her and Pearl touched her arm apologetically. 'The last thing you need now, right?'

'I'm not much help, that's all.' Finn almost backed away.

Pearl watched her curiously, and took her hand, it was freezing cold as if she'd fallen overboard.

'You're OK.'

Finn shook her head. 'Somebody let me down really badly once. I told myself I wouldn't ever let anyone get close to me again,' she said in a rush, as if it were something she'd just realised.

Pearl sniffed. 'You'll get over it, Finn. No need to run away forever.'

Thirty

Maureen had fallen asleep, stretched out on the chairs in the waiting area, when the phone rang. She lurched awake and, swaying slightly with the shock of opening her eyes to the dazzle of office wallpaper, stumbled to the phone. It was not until she placed it to her ear that she realised how dangerous it might be to say her name.

'Maureen?' It was Pearl, surprised. 'Don't you ever go home?'

The phonebox demanded money and Maureen gripped the receiver. 'It's Railton, isn't it?'

She heard Pearl struggle with the coin. 'You sound like you could kill him.'

'Long story.' Maureen felt the adrenalin returning again. She felt excited, almost reckless. 'What do you want me to do?'

Pearl wiped rain off the window and watched Rufus hobbling into the car and greeting Finn with a hug. Her eyes ached. 'Can you help us get Railton out? All we need is a clear run.'

The phone went very quiet. 'Maureen?'

'Just thinking.' Maureen's voice wavered.

'You've got the perfect story.' Pearl felt the wholeness of the case return, her mind concentrating on making the pieces fall into place.

'You call him from the office and tell him he has to come in for an urgent meeting with Foxton. Would that work?'

'Probably.' The reply came slowly.

'When he gets there you tell him how annoyed you are to be brought in etcetera and now you find he's changed his mind, can't imagine what's got into him, sorry Mr Railton and goodnight.' She heard Maureen take a deep breath. 'It would be just long enough for us to get out with the evidence to nail him.' Pearl's voice started to sound desperate. 'I don't think he'll buy anything else and we've got to be sure he's out.'

'I'll do it.' Maureen sounded as if she were standing to attention, her voice had gone slightly faint. 'I'll give you quarter of an hour to get into position and then I'll phone. 'I'll keep him as long as I can.'

Pearl got back in the car and nodded to Finn. As they pulled away she turned to Rufus and he kissed her on the cheek solemnly.

'You OK, sis?'

Pearl hugged him. 'Course. Who's been telling you I'm not?'

He stretched over the back of her seat. 'I've been talking to your friend India.' His face was dazed with the memory.

'How come?' Pearl turned back, surprised.

'She came round looking for you, wouldn't say why. Apparently you put our address on your temping form.' He brightened. 'She's really into rap.'

Pearl gave him a withering look.

'I got worried about you.' He put his arm around her. 'About you both.' He touched Finn's shoulder. 'Fitz was frantic.'

Pearl gave no reaction, just stared straight ahead until they pulled into a side street close to Railton's house. She glanced at Finn nervously and pulled on a pair of thin cotton gloves.

A light dimmed on the first floor within five minutes and white curtains were drawn smoothly in the living room. Railton appeared at the front door in jeans and a colourful shirt. It was getting dark early and the air was hot and close. Cumulus clouds flickered with a distant storm.

Pearl felt her hand tighten on the edge of her seat as she watched him calmly open the sunroof and start his car. She swallowed hard, her throat still raw from the smoke and flames.

The front door was brightly lit and they huddled against a cedar hedge while Finn prepared the sequence of keys. Pearl looked back to where her brother waited and dubiously checked the pager on her jacket. Rufus had bought the device from a friend and was keen to try it out. Working at short range he could bleep them if he thought there was any immediate danger.

'Looks like it fell out of a cracker,' sniffed Finn, refusing to trust it.

Pearl watched her lay out the keys on a handkerchief and carefully feel over the surface of the door for the electronic panel. There was nothing visible in the frame and the mouldings were solid wood. Pearl knelt down and gingerly touched the brass letterbox. The thick frame to the flap lifted up by prising the side, and revealed a rectangular opening, rather like a tape deck.

Finn sighed and went swiftly through the unlocking routine, each key turning softly. Then taking the circuit card from Pearl, she slotted it into the panel, hearing it click firmly into position. She pushed on the door but it held firmly; there was a small glass button immediately above the card, but no red light glowed.

Pearl edged to the front windows and thought she heard a voice. Through the creamy curtains the silhouette of a man of Railton's build paced up and down the front room and answered the phone. She stilled Finn's arm and they froze.

Pearl watched the shadow. 'What do you reckon?'

Finn listened again close to the window. 'It's the burglar alarm again, different programme this time. Must be. We saw him leave. Besides, listen, no footsteps.' Pearl sighed with relief and looked back at the door hopelessly.

'Let's split. He must have changed it.' Finn caught her fear like a wave of a nausea and tried to think logically. She closed her eyes and saw Trevor inserting the card, smiling feebly in the sun, turning the flimsy yale. She grabbed Pearl's arm.

'Wrong order. Card first.' Methodically she locked up again, re-inserted the card, and went carefully back through the routine. The red dot glowed and the door pushed open.

Shutting the front door behind them Pearl started to shiver violently. Finn turned back anxiously, and put a hand to her forehead. Pearl was freezing, her skin clammy, her hands shaking with cold. Taking off her jacket, Finn put it round her. 'What's up?' she asked, warming her hands between her own.

'Too much sun, I think.' Pearl ruefully pulled on the jacket and gradually stopped shaking.

Railton's taped voice in the other room was answering the phone again. Pearl grimaced. 'Listen to it. Even when he's talking to himself he's a bastard.'

Her anger seemed to revive her. An ornamental spiral staircase led up into Railton's study, lit by panels in the roof. Switching on two squares they started their search. Steel racks were neatly stacked with books and files. In one corner a photocopier, fax and answerphone were grouped like instruments of torture in plastic dustcovers. Surrounded by leather hide chairs was a long marble table, white-veined and silent as a slab.

Working their way carefully up and down the room and pulling aside tables and screens, they arrived back at Railton's wide, empty desk.

Pearl rubbed her eyes and frowned. 'I give up, where else would you keep a computer?'

In the corner the video clock placidly flipped through the minutes. It was ten thirty. Already half an hour since Railton had driven away.

Pearl collapsed into the desk chair, pulse racing. Drained of energy she put her head down on the cool leather of the desktop. Staring sideways into the shadows, she noticed a small red dot of light.

Kneeling down they squinted at the electronic keyhole in a concealed door set into the wall.

'Must be in there.' Pearl shivered. 'But where's the key?'

'He's left it in the lock.' Finn stretched her hand towards the light and pushed the card. The door opened with a sigh into a smaller room.

Maureen had waited fifteen minutes exactly after she had finished speaking to Pearl, then phoned Railton. He listened to her request impassively before readily agreeing to come to the office. He mentioned that he had been expecting her to call.

Unnerved, Maureen rang down to Security to authorise his entry to the building. She carefully instructed the guard to wait ten minutes, and then, if Railton did not rapidly reappear, to report to her office immediately. The man on duty in the lodge was watching snooker and took her number without enthusiasm.

Maureen wandered out into the corridor and noticed the lift maintenance crew finishing their shift. They shouted to her cheerfully and, with a small wave, she gloomily watched her anticipated second line of defence disappear noisily down the stairs.

The lift numbers lit up one by one and settled on five. The doors opened and Maureen watched Kevin Railton step out. The vivid colours of his shirt hade him look vaguely anaemic, like a patient on a ward. She smiled confidentially and escorted him to the office.

'John's not here yet,' she apologised. 'I've just rung down.'

Railton marched into the office and sat down at Foxton's desk, blatantly glancing through papers and memos. 'I don't mind waiting,' he said, flicking open a diary. 'It will give us the chance for a little talk,' he watched her lazily, 'about last night.'

Maureen froze, her plans in a jumble. She walked shakily towards the phone. 'I'll just see if John's arrived.' She punched the security number. It was engaged.

Looking up, she saw Railton smiling at her. 'He's not coming, Maureen.' He stretched suddenly, got up and walked towards her, cutting off her route to the door. 'What are you up to exactly, you little bitch?'

'I've got something you ought to see.' Maureen sounded faintly indignant as she pushed her hair behind her ears and put on her glasses. Railton paused with a slow smile.

Lowering her voice, Maureen pushed her way behind John's desk. 'I didn't dare talk to you before.'

Railton lolled over the desk and watched a flush redden Maureen's neck. He was mildly intrigued to hear her lies before he terrified her into silence. She deserved a warning for meddling.

Maureen opened John's desk drawer briskly. Inside was a zipped document case, and John's keys on top of it. She took out the case, nudging the keys back into the drawer.

'You know about *that* do you?' Railton raised his eyebrow. Perhaps he had misjudged her. She would probably know a great deal about her boss's private life.

Maureen nodded blindly and groped for the keys. Railton suddenly lunged at her. Instinctively she grabbed at the keys, and noticing they had become hooked up in the zip tab, swung the case, catching Railton a violent blow across the face.

He staggered backwards, swearing and clutching the red line burning across his cheek. Maureen scuttled towards the adjacent office, untangling the keys and slamming the door against him.

He stormed after her and found her levelling a glue aerosol directly at his face. She pressed it, spraying wildly. Railton staggered backwards clutching his eyes.

Maureen saw him reeling against the wall and, throwing herself into the stationery cupboard, swiftly locked the door behind her. Splashing water on his face from a vase, Railton recovered and blundered after her, beating his fists madly on the door.

Maureen sat on the floor and clutched her knees, adopting the position recommended by health and safety regulations in the event of a nuclear blast. She closed her eyes and, breathing hard, she heard herself shouting angrily, manically, to drown his blows.

'You've had it, Railton. They'll have got what they need on you by now.' She regretted it immediately.

The hammering stopped and she heard the outer office door slam.

Maureen huddled on the floor, paralysed with fear. She stared uncomprehendingly at the document case which she had been clutching, the pattern of the zip printed on her palm. Opening it, she examined the contents, her mind numbly registering that Railton must be racing home.

Flicking on the light, Finn stepped into the white cubed room. Stacked like bricks on a work station were a small monitor and miniaturised units of computer equipment. The walls were completely sound-proofed and swallowed any noise. A modem crouched in the corner next to another fax and a phone.

'Bet he thinks he runs the whole world when he locks himself in here,' muttered Pearl, as she sat down at the desk. Finn watched her feeling her way round the system, checking for switches and looking through drawers for boxes of discs.

The monitor responded immediately with an empty screen of light. Pearl anxiously flicked the main computer switch and checked all the connections. The machine was dead.

Looking at her watch frantically, Finn started to pull out all the drawers. 'We'll just grab the discs and get out.'

'That's the point.' Pearl dispairingly tapped the large grey base to the monitor.' This is a hard disc and the keyboard's locked. Finn looked blank.

'They're heavy-duty with a massive memory.' She stared at it gloomily. 'And they can weigh a ton.'

'Could we get through this lock thing if we had more time?'

Pearl nodded, 'I think so.'

'Right then.' Finn was pulling out plugs and coiling flex. 'We'll have to take the whole thing.'

'Be careful,' Pearl held out her hand warily, 'if we drop it, we'll wipe the lot.'

Retracing their steps. Finn clutched the keyboard and the cables while Pearl struggled with the monitor and disc. They carried them in short stages, gently resting the equipment on the floor or a table. As they reached the stairs the hard edges were cutting painfully into Pearl's hands. Her blood pounded with the effort.

She stared down at the spiral steps steadying herself, balancing the disc precariously on the banister. Suddenly the bleeper screamed on her lapel. Terrified, she clutched herself as if she had been shot, and tore the alarm button from the cloth. The computer rocked in her arms, and losing her balance she toppled sideways, missing her footing on the stair.

She lurched forward and, trapping her foot between the steps, she fell sideways, wrenching her shoulder as she cushioned the computer.

Finn watched her falling like a nightmare. She ground the howling pager under her foot and slithered down after her. Still embracing the machine, Pearl's face was contorted with pain.

'Do you reckon it's OK?' Finn supported her, as she clung to the banister.

'Bloody better be,' said Pearl, feeling the jag of pain in her shoulder.

Finn heard a car engine as she pulled the front door open.

For a moment her eyes were dazzled as she stared out into the dark, and she saw a man's shape lunge at her from the hedge.

She lashed out, smashing her arm against his chest.

'Finn.' Rufus staggered and hung on to her shoulder. 'Railton's back.' He turned to Pearl hunched behind her. 'I've delayed him, blocked the road with our car.'

Finn ran a few steps down the drive and saw Railton fuming at the Wolsey straddling the road, his own car stranded with its engine running. He hit the bonnet with the flat of his hand and looked up and saw Finn in his front garden.

Dropping beneath the line of the hedge, Finn waved Rufus back. 'Just get Pearl out with the gear,' she hissed, scrabbling along the foot of the hedge. Then she sprinted towards the road. Railton ran into his drive, his shoes skidding on the wet gravel, and nearly collided with her. Finn veered to one side and he slipped, crashing to his knees. For the briefest moment he saw the terrified white blur of her face and understood everything. 'You stole my car,' he screamed, his face contorted with rage.

Finn was back on her feet and running frantically down the drive, her boyish figure flickering like a shadow. Railton looked back furiously at his closed front door, and staggering to his feet, he sprinted after her.

Hanging back in the hedge until he was sure Railton had gone, Rufus ran to the car and squealed it backwards into the drive. He cradled the computer on to the back seat while Pearl huddled beside him holding her arm, almost passing out with the pain.

Throwing the car into gear, he lurched forwards.

'What about Finn?' With her good arm Pearl grabbed at the wheel.

Rufus glanced at her wildly and slammed on the brakes. 'She's doing this so we can get away.' He shrugged Pearl off and put his foot down on the accelerator.

As they moved off into the road, Pearl threw her arm across the steering wheel. Ignoring Rufus and the throbbing pain she painfully held her hand hard down on the horn.

Thirty-one

It was nearly midnight when Laura took John's call and suggested he should come round. He seemed cautious; it was very late. Laura let him stumble on before saying her piece.

'You owe it to her, don't you? After all she's done?'

He agreed but suggested that her mother might not wish to see him.

'I think you're wrong.' She said it with such passion he swallowed further words and put the phone down gently.

Laura felt dislocated. Their day had been unending and grey. Millie had stayed in her room until lunchtime and when she did emerge she was speechless and blank. She suggested that Laura might prefer to go home to her father.

Laura had no intention of leaving while Millie was behaving like a stranger. She made cups of coffee watchfully, fired with the thought that she was needed and could make a difference. Whatever had happened had finally taken away her mother's ability to pretend. Laura instinctively felt a moment of reckoning shaping like a curve.

She worried now that inviting John was a mistaken impulse, too clumsy, mistimed, not to do with the clear sense of destiny she had felt earlier in the day.

She decided to ring him back and rifled through Millie's bulging old address book. Foxton's name was written at the top of a page in faded ink at an address in Brixton. Pages of years later Laura found a more recent entry, again at the top of a page and underlined, with the union building details. But no home number.

Laura had just built herself up to confess to Millie when John arrived with a bunch of flowers enveloped in a cone of white paper. Filling all the spaces with her talk, Laura grabbed the

Sunday papers and left them together, her mother opening a bottle of wine and John laying the flowers carefully on the table.

He walked round the room restlessly and took his wine, relieved to meet her smile.

'It's good news I think, Mil, and I wanted you to know straightaway.' He pushed his hand through his hair and it flopped away from his face. His coat was damp, as if he'd been walking in the rain.

'I had a phone call when I got home.' She sat down and watched him gesturing in the way he did when he was speaking to hundreds of people. 'From Freddie Jones.'

Millie nodded; the volatile, rather elderly leader of the rival union was a well-known figure. She remembered John had mentioned him late the other night, his voice harsh with contempt.

'We had a long talk.' John shook his head. 'He was very generous, listened a lot. It hadn't occurred to me how little he really knew about what was happening to us.'

'But he'd refused to meet you.' Millie remembered him telling her.

Foxton clenched and unclenched his fingers. '*I* refused to meet him, Mil. It's a long story but I was convinced we couldn't trust him. Different styles of leadership, I suppose.'

Or clash of egos, thought Millie cynically, but without malice.

'Anyway, he made the move and we've agreed to thrash out a joint strategy. Basically he's on our side, Mil, there's no way he'll let Pearson use them against us.'

'Are you sure you can trust him?' Millie instinctively stepped back from his excitement, weighing it up.

'It's better than that.' He clenched his fist, smiling with relief. 'Trade unionism's international in more than spirit these days. Freddie's flying to Düsseldorf tonight. If we get support across the board, the management will have no choice. They'll have to find a compromise we can all live with.' He considered the contents of his glass. 'The merger with Freddie's lot is not ideal, but as prices go . . .' He faltered and seemed to lose his point.

Millie smiled. 'Not quite how you imagined it, John, but it sounds like you're nearly there.'

He put his glass down deliberately and tugged the paper open on a bunch of blue cornflowers. 'You always said red roses were a bit of a cliché.' He teased her tentatively with their past.

She didn't look at them, steeling herself for the question. 'Tell me the truth, John?'

He smiled nervously. 'You can ask Maureen.'

Her look stopped him. 'It's complicated.' He glanced away miserably. 'I've been beside myself. I wanted to find the right moment . . .'

'To tell me you and your wife had got back together?'

He gravely watched her face, his hands still. 'Mil, I didn't want to tell you anything before . . .' He abandoned his explanation and reached for her hand.

She pulled away. 'Before you were sure it was worth the trouble? Maybe I was too useful to upset?'

He sat down and stared hopelessly at the perfect blue of the flowers. He had imagined it differently. Telling her the whole story quietly, maybe talking in bed, Millie listening and understanding, an impossibility pulling them together again. Like it had before. Instead he blundered forwards, holding only wreckage in his hands.

'It doesn't change anything we've said or done. Linda and I, well, it was sensible. We don't see that much of each other, I'm away a lot, in my position I needed . . .'

'. . . a wife to take care of you. Yes, I can see that.'

He stared at her wordlessly until she got up and walked to the window. When he went after her and put his arms around her, she didn't move.

'Millie, I was so in love with you. When you left me, I thought I'd never recover.'

'But we always do, don't we?' she said miserably.

'No, we don't.' He made her turn to face him. 'We just adapt.'

She pulled away, refusing to listen. 'You must think I don't understand.' He looked up hopefully, held out his hands to touch her. She stood beyond his reach, explaining. 'I mean that's what I could do with, someone to take care of me. I mean I'm a busy person; I work hard.' Her voice was firm. 'Maybe I should do the sensible thing and get myself a wife too.'

Laura heard the front door close behind him. It seemed a long while before the car started and moved slowly off down the road. Millie was standing in the garden. The grass was still fresh with rain and the scent of the honeysuckle ran like a colour. With no hesitation Laura walked over to her mother and put her arms around her. Millie allowed herself to be held.

Thirty-two

Finn could hear their car horn wailing, and still running hard down the pavement, she quickly glanced over her shoulder. Railton had stopped, breathing hard, his hands on his hips, trying to place the noise. Looking back he saw her disappear around a corner and sprinted on again, shouting wildly.

The road spread out into wide-fronted gardens, and spotting a couple getting out of a car, Finn charged past them into their back garden. The lawn was floodlit, with a forgotten sprinkler spraying water in a drunken arc. Finn ran across the sodden grass and through the puddles, recklessly heading for the dark and gambling on a way out.

Behind her the woman screamed and she heard Railton's voice shouting at them as his footsteps crunched on the gravel. Gasping for breath Finn crouched amongst spiky fruit bushes and watched him suddenly stop on the lawn. In the artificial white light he was black, like a gash in paper. Trembling in the shadows, Finn saw him spot her footprints in the wet grass. He ran straight towards her, kicking over the sprinkler and plunging through the bushes. She took off sideways and throwing herself at an old wall just higher than herself, tried to scramble over it. The brick crumbled and she fell back, tearing her hands as she fell.

Railton spotted her and swerved, forcing his way through the thorny bushes and crashing into a cold frame. Finn heard the sound of splintering glass as she threw herself against the wall and, slithering over frantically, started to run across a wide piece of waste land.

There was nothing but the nightmare of running. Railton had lost ground, but was over the wall and catching up again. Finn slipped sideways as she looked back to see him flailing through a

208

patch of water. Ahead of her a marooned row of derelict houses offered the only possible place to hide. Finn had seen Railton's face maimed with hatred and now she sprinted, her legs giving way over the uneven ground. She could hear his footsteps behind her, his only obsession to hunt her down.

The houses had the remains of a street in front of them and Finn's feet echoed on the broken tarmac. Sobbing for breath she ran round the back where a door swung open. Without thinking, Finn hurled herself through it. The only light was the neon glow from outside and broken windows threw shadows up the wall. As she ran up the rotten stairs they gave way like cardboard. Finn heard Railton lurch through the front door and call out roughly. She froze, grabbing back her breath, waiting for him to climb the stairs. Lighting a match, he caught sight of her crouched above him. Finn felt the old sickness wave across her.

Railton lit a cigarette as he paused, lolling halfway up the broken stairs. His dark beard made his face collapse into shadow, his lips uncannily thin and red as he exhaled slowly. Finn closed her eyes and saw her uncle's wheedling smile as he reached out his hand towards her.

Railton looked her up and down. 'Who are you, you little bitch?'

Come on, Finn. She glared at him as he inched further up the stairs. Railton grinned, she was quite attractive. He was going to teach her a lesson.

Finn was back with the memory of a man who had cared for her. Back with the way he stared at her, his stupid smile making her trust him. Her uncle had reached out his hand. She backed away. *What's the matter with you?*

Railton was shouting now, and her uncle had been softly spoken, but it was all the same thing. He was getting angry. They were alone in the house.

Railton threw down his cigarette and crushed it with his shoe. Hauling himself up the splintering stairs and stumbling on the top step, he lunged towards her.

Finn attacked with every memory she held within herself. The large-framed man not hugging now, but falling to the floor, pulling her down with him. Finn finally lashed out. This time she would hurt him back.

Railton pinned her arms and tried to kiss her, his hot breath on her face. She bit his lip. He felt her nails against his face gouging and clawing. He pushed his body against her, tearing at her clothes. She bit into his hand and brought her knee up sharply into his groin. He gasped with pain and felt her launch herself at him, her weight knocking him backwards from the steps. They fell together, tumbling against the staircase. Railton groaned as she struggled off him and pushed her foot hard into his face.

Finn gulped at the fresh air and crying hot scalding tears she ran from the house, untidily flailing the air with her arms, staggering away from the nightmare and on towards the river.

The old quay was a pile of a rubble and jumbled wire fences knitted in great barricades. Finn looked back and saw no one following her. She stopped and checked again. She had broken free.

Across the water the lights framed the unreal constructions of riverside flats, and marinas decked with flags shimmered in neon colours.

The only way back to the road was across a shallow creek. Finn waded across slowly, one step after the other. On the other side was an old boat pulled up on its side and draped with tarpaulins. Finn crawled inside, tugged the canvas over her, shut her eyes to a perfect black and fell asleep.

The beginning of the rush hour throbbed outside the practice window as Millie went to set up the coffee machine for the second time that morning. She waited for the jug to fill with the early sun on her face. She ached with the weariness of a sleepless night.

They had cleared her desk and set up Railton's equipment. Krish unscrewed the keyboard fascia, and as delicately as if he were dismantling a bomb, he shorted two wires and overrode the security lock.

Hunched towards the screen he had accessed his way through the vast network of files, making cross references and searching his way around the logic of the system.

Her right arm in a sling, Pearl watched the figures scrolling through the screen, and dictated notes of key words and headings to Millie. They worked laboriously through the data; it was uniformly mundane.

Krish stood up stiffly, stretching and smoothing his shirt. He went to pour them coffee. 'We'll get there, Pearl.' He touched her hand gently and smiled. She nodded, staring in a daze at the figures arrested on the screen.

The previous night was a vague series of disparate events, dissolved and faded by her pain. Waiting in Casualty, she had let Rufus hold her, slipping in and out of consciousness.

'What about Finn?'

She had been talking in her sleep through the night. Rufus had sat beside her with blankets for hours while they both waited for the phone to ring, or for the familiar tattoo on the front door. It had been getting light, the sun scattered on the blinds, when she had pulled herself out of disturbed sleep and away from the flickering of the burning car.

'What about Finn?' she asked again.

Rufus' face was pitted with exhaustion. 'Nothing. Not yet.' Pearl was still wearing Finn's jacket and hugged it around her as she headed for the phone.

Millie had appeared to be wide-awake, almost waiting for Pearl's call. She organised them briskly, her voicing catching with anxiety when Pearl told her about Finn. Rufus drove her to the office where Krish, dishevelled without a waistcoat, was already clearing space for the equipment. Rufus, holding out little hope, took a taxi back to Railton's neighbourhood to retrace every possible route. Without the confusion of the fever, Pearl knew, like a physical ache, that Finn was in trouble.

She dug her left hand into Finn's jacket and took out the security key card, a brown pebble, and the crumpled list of India's art galleries.

She opened the list out again, remembering back to the plane, and suddenly looked at the screen. The names of the galleries had appeared in all the accounts where they had detected missing information or minute, inexplicable discrepancies.

'Hidden files, Krish.' She sat down at the keyboard. 'There must be another layer. We've got to find our way in.'

India's list was headed, 'But is it Art?' in bold script. Pearl counted the ten letters, standard for a file heading on a computer menu. She typed the letters with her left hand and tried to access the file.

'Butisitart?' Krish breathed the steam off his coffee. 'Hidden files,' he frowned. The disc whirred and surged, searching for the heading.

'Whatever it is, it wasn't on any of the menus.' He was leaning on the chair watching the screen intently.

'You can operate a conceal command on this software.' Pearl willed the screen. The whirring suddenly clicked off and the file heading quietly presented itself. Pearl moved her finger to open it. 'Very handy if you've got something to hide.'

They scrolled through what appeared to be a completely normal account of insurance payments made by the union pension fund to the listed art galleries.

'I don't get it.' Krish tapped his pen on the screen. 'If they've bought the pictures, why are they putting them in galleries and paying for the risk? Be simpler to lock them up wouldn't it?'

Pearl looked at him. 'That's it; you've cracked it.' She sat on Millie's desk and dialled India's number.

'I've only just got there myself.' India sounded relieved to hear her. 'As soon as I got suspicious, I started digging. That was another reason why he got so vicious.' Her voice wavered, then recovered. 'It's invisible crime. If you buy a painting you have to insure it, and that's expensive even if you keep it in a darkened room. But if you lend it to a gallery they pay your insurance for you. So effectively you store your picture free.' Krish's face was close to Pearl's, trying to listen. 'Railton was doing this but still charging the union for the insurance. Faking the paperwork's the easy bit.'

Pearl looked down at India's homework sheet. 'But it sounds so ordinary.'

'That's its beauty. The union holds hundreds of pictures every year, insuring at several thousand each, minimum, the money mounts up amazingly. If you're not used to the art world you'd never spot it.'

Krish was back to another balance sheet and excitedly underlining figures, putting the final pieces of the jigsaw into place. Triumphantly he matched a six-month insurance fee for a Goya with a Railton deposit in an offshore investment fund. After that, he went down every deposit, tracing its illegal source.

Millie watched Krish swiftly uncovering Railton's elaborate sequence of paper robberies. Yet another account emerged, cruelly coded TREVSCAM, and containing two and a half million pounds, the lion's share of the stolen funds. Krish obsessively worked on through the menu, but one final file mysteriously resisted his explanations. It detailed accounts with a firm of international furniture removers and a series of fees to customs and excise for artefacts which the union had no record of purchasing or selling. Krish was completely baffled.

'Trevor's garage and Railton's removal vans,' muttered Pearl.

'We've got more than enough to nail him.' Millie patted Krish's shoulder. 'It's time to hand this over to the fraud squad.'

'But won't they expect you to know how your investigators got hold of all this gear?' asked Krish.

'Certainly not.' Millie looked at him reprovingly.

Pearl suddenly smelt something like rotting vegetables or possibly drains.

Krish pulled a face. 'The river, this summer . . . when the wind changes, we should sue.' He got up and shut the window, and sunk into his shirt and his own aftershave.

The bell rang on the outer office door and Millie reluctantly went to unlock it for the start of another working day.

Rufus was standing at the top of the stairs with Finn wrapped in a black dustbin liner. She reeked of the river.

John Foxton arrived at the office early Monday morning to find Maureen already hard at work typing, ears clamped by the dictaphone. He had to bend over her desk before she acknowledged he was there. She started, white-faced, eyes shadowed with lack of sleep.

'You should take a holiday,' Foxton suggested, 'when all this is over.'

She nodded briskly. 'I've booked leave, starting tomorrow. I was just getting everything in order.'

John looked startled and asked her to reserve him a seat on an afternoon flight to Düsseldorf.

'You can stop worrying about the strike pay anyway.' He sat on her desk and spoke confidentially. 'I made the crucial decision to negotiate with Freddie Jones for the good of the men. The strike was finally called off an hour ago.' He sighed. 'It's been a nerve-racking business, I don't mind admitting it.'

Maureen looked unmoved. 'So Pearson caved in, did he?'

'And sacked Mepham. They were totally outmanoeuvred.' John smiled. 'The takeover deal's in ruins. A united front from our two unions was strong enough to say no to the consortium's wretched plans for the plant.'

Still holding patiently for the airport booking desk, his secretary showed no reaction, almost as if she were hearing the story for the second time.

Taking an envelope from his pocket, John somberly ran his fingers over the Spanish stamps, and pulled out several sheets of typed paper. 'Poor old Trev's confession got delayed in the post. Communication never was his strong point.'

'But he managed to make that call.' Maureen looked up angrily, and flushed, before returning to the phone and confirming that she would continue to hold.

Her boss looked puzzled, and sliding off her desk, stood in front of her, awkwardly waiting for the call to finish. Putting her hand over the receiver, she glanced back fleetingly, 'What's going to happen to him then?'

'We'll have to press charges but I'll get Millie to keep them to the bare minimum. It's Railton who's the real villain. He caught Trevor nicking peanuts to buy his hacienda, blackmailed him and started on the big stuff.' Maureen listened to him thoughtfully. 'Let's hope we come up with the proof soon and nail him for good.'

'*They*,' she corrected him bitterly, 'they, not we, have been risking their necks to get your proof.'

Foxton looked chastened as she gave his name to the airport booking service, and poured himself a cup of coffee.

'Black for me please,' she said. 'By the way John, Nigel Pearson phoned first thing about leaking that material to the press . . .'

John's cup rocked on its saucer.

214

She shrugged. 'He didn't tell me directly, naturally.' She consulted her pad. 'His message is cryptic. But basically he has no intention of proceeding with the blackmail.'

'How on earth do you know about that?' John looked dazed and sat down.

'The point is,' replied Maureen, too tired to embark on long explanations, 'I mentioned the problem to Judith.'

'Judith?'

'Nigel Pearson's personal assistant.' Maureen emphasised the title deliberately. 'She happened to be in possession of material of a reciprocal nature.' Maureen paused censoriously. 'The negotiations were very straightforward, with minimal loss of dignity.'

It was lunchtime when Millie finished seeing clients and tentatively dialled the union number.

'Sorry, Mrs Millington.' Maureen's voice was full of concern. 'He boarded an early flight to Düsseldorf. Looks like the German workers are going to support us, so management will have to negotiate.'

'That's good news.' Millie realised she was consciously echoing his words from the previous evening. 'Just to let you know that the fraud squad have all the evidence and they're hard on the heels of Kevin Railton.' Maureen's reaction was grateful but unusually subdued. Millie faltered, 'Tell John, I'll see him some time.'

Maureen put the phone down and placed a cup down on John Foxton's desk. 'More coffee, sir?'

'Please, don't.' He put his head in his hands. 'When does that flight leave?'

'Four o'clock.' Maureen was stony. 'I'll order a cab for three.'

He looked up and watched her dialling. 'Could you do me a small favour, Maureen?' He straightened his tie uncomfortably. 'Just ring my wife with a message?'

Maureen held her hand over the receiver while she waited for the switchboard. 'No,' she said, 'I'm sorry, John, I'm not willing to do that.'

Still hearing the tone in Maureen's voice, Millie immediately phoned Heathrow and waited while a booking clerk courteously checked through first the morning and then the afternoon passenger lists for flights to Düsseldorf. Thanking him for his persistence she replaced the receiver and redialled, reading her credit card number briskly and arranging for Mr John Foxton at the Union Building, Red Lion Wharf to receive a modest bunch of red roses, no later than three o'clock, message: goodbye, no signature.

Relaxing in her chair, she absently watched Krish vacuuming river mud off the carpet. She stretched forward suddenly and rapped on the glass partition. He switched the machine off impatiently and appeared archly at her door with a pad and pen.

'What will it be madam, tea or coffee?'

She sighed and stood up. 'Take me out and buy me a drink, Krish? I think I need it.'

Thirty-three

'Can you imagine Millie's face when you submit your expenses?' Rufus gleefully lounged on the sofa sketching on a pad. 'One car destroyed by fire, one roving secretary and her taxi bill, air flights to Spain, a sprained shoulder and a bottle of painkillers.'

'I'm not claiming for my shoulder,' said Pearl reasonably, pulling him off the sofa.' Please go Rufus, I want some peace.'

He nodded. 'Can I borrow the car?'

Pearl handed him the keys. 'Don't leave the country.

He grinned, 'I'm going to India actually.' He showed her his pad and she saw he'd drawn an exact ground floor plan of India's apartment. The parrot perch was marked with a cross. 'Haven't you heard the good news?' He grinned jubilantly.

Pearl shook her head.

'Fitz has agreed to go ahead with the video. And India's lending me her place for filming. You should see it, it's really incredible.'

'Yeh, I know.' Pearl closed the front door and heard him hum and rap his way down the corridor.

Finn nursed a slight temperature in a cloud of steam waiting for the bath to fill.

'You should have undressed in the car park.' Pearl walked round the bathroom spraying air freshener. 'I've had to chuck all your clothes away.' She handed Finn a hot drink. 'And I should wash your hair before it disintegrates, or takes the enamel off the bath.'

Finn tasted the drink and pulled a face. 'It's disgusting. What is it?'

'Nettles, Maureen's homeopathic. It'll help your chill.' Pearl nursed her arm and sat down on the floor with her back against the bath.

'Wouldn't have a chill if I hadn't spent the night without my jacket.' Finn quietly poured the brown liquid into the bathwater. Pearl stared at the bathroom wall.

'I was really worried about you, you know.'

'Yeh?' Finn was pleased.

'Where did you go, when you got away from him?'

Finn took a deep breath. She pulled at the towel and shivered. 'It's a long story.'

Pearl turned off the bath and slowly poured in a whole bag of bath salts. 'So, tell me the long story. No more running away.'

Pearl left Finn to soak and lay on the sofa in front of the television. She pieced together Finn's words again, carefully sorting through the fragments: Finn adopted by her aunt and uncle and living with their kids; how they had made her special; her auntie talking with her late at night after she'd finished work at the pub and showing her small things she treasured. Finn's face had softened as she talked about her, and then shadowed.

Her uncle taking her on jobs and making it exciting at first; her trips to Smithy's and the fire and melting metal and new keys glowing in the darkness. Her uncle teaching her how to make a lock tumble; listening to the keys' whisper and the tiny mechanisms with their own sounds waiting to be stifled into submission. Only one step further to real houses.

And the old sick feeling.

The man who was there to look after her had begun to stare at her, a stupid smile which made her doubt her trust in him. Reaching out his hand towards her, wheedling. Her uncle, a large-framed man, not hugging now, but falling, pulling her down with him.

Finn had lashed out and run away. The police had brought her back, asked questions, had given her uncle a bad time. There were social workers and her auntie had cried all night. Then Finn ran away again, this time for good, but not forever.

'What about your auntie?' Pearl had asked her eventually.

And Finn shrugged. 'Couldn't have her without him. But she

sent me her new address, when I got into trouble. Whenever I send her postcards I say "See you soon".'

Pearl hugged the cushion and tried to doze.

Fitz turned the key in the lock and pushed the door open gently. Hearing the television in the sitting room below, he crept down the stairs and saw Pearl huddled up on the sofa, her face turned against the kelim.

He touched her shoulder. 'You asleep, P?'

'No.' She didn't move, didn't respond to his touch.

'I'm sorry.' Pointless to explain, he could imagine her face as he listed how events had conspired against him. Orell's broken arm – family life.

'You didn't make it then?'

He kissed her cheek but didn't answer.

Pearl sat up. 'I was away anyway.'

'I heard. Congratulations, Princess. The dynamic duo solves another case.' He held her face towards him. 'Let's go out and celebrate.'

'No thanks.' Pearl stood up and looked at him. He was dressed in black, mourning us she thought, and his red cummerbund – daring but never quite real.

'I've made a decision.' She got up, pulling the kelim round her. 'Well, faced up to something.'

Fitz watched her. 'Don't, P, I don't want to hear this.'

Pearl saw him leaving again. She had heard him say this before.

'What matters is what we feel about each other. The rest we can work out.'

'That used to sound so convincing.'

Fitz tried to hold her. 'What about the other night?'

'One-night stands can be great . . . now and again.' She said it casually to hurt him, to make him leave her.

Fitz took the blow and looked confused. He wandered towards the kitchen aimlessly and bumped into Finn wrapped in a towel, shaking water from her hair.

Finn glanced at Pearl awkwardly, and accepted Fitz's hug and ducked back to the kitchen.

'It's time I went,' Fitz said softly to himself, not looking at

Pearl and putting her key down on the table. He closed the door quietly and she heard him running down the corridor.

The bath had a thick rim of sludge where the water had been, and a stench like rotting vegetation still wafted through the flat. Pearl tracked it down to Finn's trainers, hidden undisturbed, still oozing mud and water. She opened the window and threw them out.

She followed a trail of wet towels to the kitchen where she found Finn thoughtfully licking the icing from a cake. She looked up apologetically. 'Bad timing, I know. I'm sorry.'

'Doesn't matter.'

Finn hungrily broke the end of a French loaf and dunked it in a tin of syrup.

'So what happens now?'

'An evening in with a support bandage and a couple of soluble aspirin,' said Pearl, noticing that the tissue box had been dropped in the bath.

Finn looked guilty. 'I know, don't say it, I'm a lousy lodger.'

'I'll tell you something, Finn.' Pearl looked at her seriously. 'Apart from one or two gross little habits, you're easier to live with than any man.'

Finn smiled doubtfully.